Terror Tales #5 (January 1935)

Starting in 1934, editor (and publisher) Harry Steeger unveiled *Terror Tales*: perhaps the flagship magazine in Popular Publications' so-called "Weird Menace" lineup of titles. Running for almost 50 issues, *Terror Tales* showcased some of the best suspense, mystery and terror stories to see print in the pulps. This facsimile of the January 1935 issue contains stories by Arthur Leo Zagat, G.T. Fleming-Roberts, Wyatt Blassingame, Nat Schachner, and Franklin H. Martin, among others.

Authors:

Arthur Leo Zagat, Henry Treat Sperry, Ben Judson, G.T. Fleming-Roberts, Wyatt Blassingame, Franklin H. Martin, Nat Schachner

Illustrators:

John Newton Howitt, Amos Sewell

NOTE: We have attempted to restore the original page scans in this facsimile in order to provide an enjoyable reading experience. However, in some cases there can be text loss due to damage to the original pulp, tight bindings, or other reasons.

Volume Two | January, 1935 | Number One

Cover Painting by John Howitt

Story Illustrations by Amos Sewell

Published every month by Popular Publications, Inc., 2256 Grove Street, Chicago, Illinois. Editorial and executive offices, 205 East Forty-second Street, New York City. Harry Steeger, President and Secretary, Harold S. Goldsmith, Vice President and Treasurer. Entry as second-class matter pending at the post office at Chicago, Ill., under the Act of March 3, 1879. Title registration pending at U. S. Patent Office. Single copy price 15c. Yearly subscriptions in U. S. A. $1.50. For advertising rates address Sam J. Perry, 205 E. 42nd St., New York, N. Y. When submitting manuscripts kindly enclose stamped self-addressed envelope for their return if found unavailable. The publishers cannot accept responsibility for return of unsolicited manuscripts, although care will be exercised in handling them.

I'LL SEND MY FIRST LESSON FREE

Here's Proof

It shows how EASY *it is to learn at home to fill a*

GOOD JOB IN RADIO

Clip the coupon and mail it. I'm so sure that I can train you at home in your spare time for a good job in Radio that I'll send you my first lesson free. Examine it, read it, see how clear and easy it is to understand. Then you will know why many men with less than a grammar school education and no technical experience have become Radio Experts and are earning two to three times their former pay as a result of my training.

MANY RADIO EXPERTS MAKE $40, $60, $75 A WEEK

In less than 15 years, the Radio Industry has grown from a few million to hundreds of millions of dollars. Over 300,000 jobs have been created by this growth, and thousands more will be created by its continued development. Many men and young men with the right training—the kind of training I give you in the N. R. I. Course—have stepped into Radio at two and three times their former salaries.

GET READY NOW FOR JOBS LIKE THESE

Broadcasting stations use engineers, operators, station managers and pay up to $5,000 a year. Manufacturers continually employ testers, inspectors, foremen, engineers, servicemen, buyers, for jobs paying up to $7,500 a year. Radio operators on ships enjoy life, see the world, with board and lodging free, and get good pay besides. Dealers and jobbers employ servicemen, salesmen, buyers, managers, and pay up to $100 a week. My book tells you about these and many other interesting Radio jobs.

MANY MAKE $5, $10, $15 A WEEK EXTRA IN SPARE TIME WHILE LEARNING

The day you enroll with me, I send you instructions which you should master quickly for doing 28 Radio jobs common in most every neighborhood, for spare time money. Throughout your training, I send you information for servicing popular makes of sets! I give you the plans and ideas that have made $200 to $1,000 a year for N. R. I. men in their spare time. My Course is famous as the Course that pays for itself!

TELEVISION, SHORT WAVE, LOUD SPEAKER SYSTEMS INCLUDED

There's opportunity for you in Radio. Its future is certain. Television, short wave, loud speaker systems, police Radio, automobile Radio, aviation Radio—in every branch, developments and improvements are taking place. Here is a real future for thousands and thousands of men who really know Radio—men with N. R. I. training. Get the training that opens the road to good pay and success.

YOU GET A MONEY BACK AGREEMENT

I am so sure that N. R. I. can train you satisfactorily that I will agree in writing to refund every penny of your tuition if you are *not* satisfied with my Lesson and Instruction Service upon completion.

FREE 64-PAGE BOOK OF FACTS

Mail the coupon now. In addition to the sample lesson, I send my book, "Rich Rewards in Radio." It tells you about the opportunities in Radio, tells you about my Course, what others who have taken it are doing and making. This offer is free to any ambitious fellow over 15 years old. Find out what Radio offers you without the slightest obligation. ACT NOW! Mail coupon in an envelope or paste on a 1c postcard.

J. E. SMITH, President
National Radio Institute, Dept. 5AS9
Washington, D. C.

You Get PRACTICAL EXPERIENCE with Radio Equipment I GIVE YOU

I'll show you how to use my special Radio Equipment for conducting experiments and building circuits which illustrate important principles used in such well-known sets as Westinghouse, General Electric, Philco, R. C. A., Victor, Majestic and others. You work out with your own hands many of the things you read in my lesson books. This 50-50 method of training makes learning at home easy, interesting, fascinating, intensely practical. You learn how sets work, why they work, how to make them work when they are out of order. Training like this shows up in your pay envelope—when you graduate you have had training and experience—you're not simply looking for a job where you can get experience.

I have doubled and tripled the salaries of many

CLEARS $4,500 IN 18 MONTHS

"Before taking your Radio Course I was making $18 a week. I came here three years ago and in 18 months I made about $4,500 in Radio. I cannot say too much for the wonderful help I have received from N. R. I."
NOEL W. RAY,
619 Broad St.,
Gadsden, Alabama.

SPARE TIME WORK PAYS $18 A WEEK

"I only do spare time Radio work and average $18 a week. People who in good times would buy a new Radio, now have the old one fixed."
STEPHEN J. DRAPCHATY,
407 Wunderlich Ave.,
Barberton, Ohio.

RADIO ENGINEER AT WSUI

"Upon graduating I accepted a job as serviceman, and within three weeks was made Service Manager. This job paid $40 to $50 a week. Eight months later I obtained a position as operator with Station KWCR through your Employment Department. Now I am Radio Engineer of WSUI."
SYLVANUS J. EBERT,
University of Iowa,
Iowa City, Iowa.

The Tested Way to BETTER PAY

MAIL THIS NOW!

J. E. SMITH, President
National Radio Institute, Dept. 5AS9
Washington, D. C.

I want to take advantage of your offer. Without obligating me, send me your Free Sample Lesson and your book, "Rich Rewards in Radio."
(Please Print Plainly.)

NAME.............................. AGE.........

ADDRESS..

CITY..................... State............. "R"

WHAT *will you be doing* ONE YEAR *from today?*

THREE hundred and sixty-five days from now — what?

Will you still be struggling along in the same old job at the same old salary — worried about the future — never quite able to make both ends meet?

One year from today will you still be putting off your start toward success — thrilled with ambition one moment and then cold the next — delaying, waiting, fiddling away the precious hours that will never come again?

Don't do it, man — don't do it.

There is no greater tragedy in the world than that of a man who stays in the rut all his life, when with just a little effort he could advance.

Make up your mind today that you're going to train yourself to do some one thing well. Choose the work you like best in the list below, mark an X beside it, and without cost or obligation, at least get the full story of what the I. C. S. can do for you.

INTERNATIONAL CORRESPONDENCE SCHOOLS

"The Universal University"

Box 3253, Scranton, Penna.

Without cost or obligation, please send me a copy of your booklet, "Who Wins and Why," and full particulars about the subject *before* which I have marked X:

TECHNICAL AND INDUSTRIAL COURSES

- ☐ Architect
- ☐ Architectural Draftsman
- ☐ Building Estimating
- ☐ Wood Millworking
- ☐ Concrete Builder
- ☐ Contractor and Builder
- ☐ Structural Draftsman
- ☐ Structural Engineer
- ☐ Electrical Engineer
- ☐ Electric Wiring
- ☐ Electric Lighting
- ☐ Welding, Electric and Gas
- ☐ Telegraph Engineer
- ☐ Telephone Work
- ☐ Mechanical Engineer
- ☐ Mechanical Draftsman
- ☐ Patternmaker
- ☐ Machinist
- ☐ Reading Shop Blueprints
- ☐ Civil Engineer
- ☐ Highway Engineering
- ☐ Surveying and Mapping
- ☐ Gas Engines
- ☐ Toolmaker
- ☐ Diesel Engines
- ☐ Aviation Engines
- ☐ Bridge Engineer
- ☐ Automobile Work
- ☐ Plumbing
- ☐ Steam Fitting
- ☐ Heating
- ☐ Ventilation
- ☐ Sanitary Engineer
- ☐ Sheet Metal Worker
- ☐ Steam Engineer
- ☐ Marine Engineer
- ☐ Refrigeration
- ☐ R. R. Locomotives
- ☐ Air Brakes
- ☐ Train Operation
- ☐ R. R. Section Foreman
- ☐ R. R. Bridge and Building Foreman
- ☐ Chemistry ☐ Pharmacy
- ☐ Coal Mining Engineer
- ☐ Navigation
- ☐ Agriculture
- ☐ Textile Overseer or Superintendent
- ☐ Cotton Manufacturing
- ☐ Woolen Manufacturing
- ☐ Fruit Growing
- ☐ Radio
- ☐ Poultry Farming

BUSINESS TRAINING COURSES

- ☐ Business Management
- ☐ Industrial Management
- ☐ Personnel Management
- ☐ Traffic Management
- ☐ Accountancy
- ☐ Cost Accountant
- ☐ C. P. Accountant
- ☐ Bookkeeping
- ☐ Secretarial Work
- ☐ Spanish ☐ French
- ☐ Salesmanship
- ☐ Advertising
- ☐ Business Correspondence
- ☐ Lettering Show Cards
- ☐ Stenography and Typing
- ☐ Complete Commercial
- ☐ English
- ☐ Signs
- ☐ Civil Service
- ☐ Railway Mail Clerk
- ☐ Mail Carrier
- ☐ Grade School Subjects
- ☐ High School Subjects
- ☐ Illustrating
- ☐ Cartooning
- ☐ Lumber Dealer

Name...Age.................

Street Address...

City...State.................

Occupation...

If you reside in Canada, send this coupon to the International Correspondence Schools Canadian, Limited, Montreal, Canada

By
Arthur Leo Zagat
(Author of "The Man Who Would Not Die!" etc.)

WHEN LOVE

Within the dank parlor of that empty, country house lay a corpse that had come up from the grave itself. While Emma Wayne watched helpless from the dirt-smeared windows of that darkened, tragic dwelling, fleshless grey Things crept relentlessly upon the man she loved, waylaid by horror on the night-shrouded slope of Big Tom Mountain. . . .

EMMA WAYNE'S small hand shook a little as she fumbled her key into the grey door of the ancient Sprool house, and she was shivering inside her thin suit-coat. But it was not only the sharp chill of dusk that had set her quivering. The old dread lay like a leaden lump in her breast, the dread that, as far back as memory went, inevitably had come when the sun's last red rim vanished behind the jagged ridge of Big Tom and night began to fill the valley's bowl.

As in the old days, the circumscribing mountains were tightening the ominous loom of their ring with the withdrawing light, were becoming formless, vast bulks

WENT MAD!

Complete Mystery-Terror Novel

of blue-grey menace; and, beneath the haze blurring their slopes, crawling, eerie things of the night stirred to unholy being—or so whispered the legends of the countryside. To Emma the very hills were endowed with uncanny, motionless life as they thrust gigantic shoulders against the darkling sky like quiescent monsters waiting in silent, age-long patience; waiting till at last their appointed time should come to crush, with contemptuous gesture, the puny human lives scuttering in the valley.

The girl's mouth twisted bitterly. Here she was, just as Kurt Tradin had predicted two years ago, returned to the mountains and their gloomy forebodings. . . . The borrowed horse she had tied to the gate down there whinnied, the sound edged with shrill fear. Startled, Emma whirled to it, peered fearfully into the gathering shadows. What on earth was the animal afraid of? Why had it cried out as if it sensed some threat in the unkempt, overgrown garden? Why was Emma herself afraid, not knowing of what? Perhaps because the place was so uncared-for, so desolate. Gram shouldn't have —

But of course, grandmother was dead. That was why Emma had come back, why Milton, the husband she had found in the city that had been otherwise so cruel, was joining her here. The little old lady whose bleared and rheumy eyes had pleaded with her not to go, was dead—and buried. Kurt's letter had brought the tidings when it finally had reached her, its painfully addressed envelope scrawled with the postman's notations that explained its week's lateness. Gram was in the little cemetery above, where the village was hidden by Big Tom's jutting spur, and the old house was empty. . . .

Something slithered along the door, thumped softly. Emma's breath caught in her throat. Tensely, she listened to the thud of her own blood in her ears and—silence. Silence that lay on the hills like a grey shroud, that was a living, tangible thing within the house. Silence that in itself was fear.

The girl bit her lip. "It's nothing," she assured herself. "Nothing at all." She did not realize that she was speaking aloud. "Just—just my imagination." And indeed there was now no sound, inside or out, save for the *pud, pud* of the restive horse still straining to break free the rein that held him. "I'm a fool to be scared." But why did the brute whinny again, then snort at something *she* could not see?

This was silly, unutterably silly! Milton would laugh at her when he got here and she told him how afraid she had been to enter the house where she was born. The lock grated protestingly, clicked over. Lucky she had kept that key all these months.

The door opened under the push of her icy hand. Except for a filming of dust the hall was just as she remembered it, with its antlered hatrack and the slender, graceful curve of the banisters where the stairs lifted to obscurity above. Light still filtered in dimly through the arched opening from the parlor, spreading ebony shadows on worn Brussels carpeting. Queer shadows! That one for instance, long and anguiar as if it were thrown by a horizontal box resting on trestles. . . .

Grisly fingers squeezed Emma's heart. Three years ago just such a shadow lay here, and in the parlor Granddad Sprool had been stiff in the coffin by which it was cast. *This was the shadow of a coffin*—and the sickeningly sweet odor of funeral flowers was heavy in her nostrils!

No! Gram was buried, *buried!* They wouldn't have kept her here, untended, for the two weeks since she had died! It was just a trick of light and her own taut nerves. . . .

That dark silhouette tapered slightly, just as Granddad's casket had, but it was smaller. Gram had always been shorter than Granddad and the years had shrunk her. Emma licked dry lips, and knew that she must get to the parlor door, that she must look to see what made that shadow. But her legs wouldn't move. . . .

She got them going at last. . . . It was as if the dusty air had suddenly grown thick, viscous, so that she had to push through it with all her strength. She reached the threshold at last, held onto the lintel and pulled herself into the musty parlor. The windows were grey rectangles in the faded wall; under her feet the floor seemed to heave, like the swelling sea. Emma whimpered, far back in her throat. The coffin *was* there—an ominous bulk in the gloom. . . .

ONCE started toward it she could not stop. She was close to the thing. She was looking down into it, where the half-lid had been removed—looking down at Gram's closed eyes and the almost transparent hands crossed on a bosom of black silk that was terribly still. The old woman's skin was drawn tight over her fleshless bones, so tight that a skull seemed to answer Emma's gaze. . . . They had edged the corpse-dress with a white neck-ruching. And that brown streak across its starched stiffness was the trail of a slimy, crawling thing. . . .

The girl swayed, grabbed at the casket-edge to keep herself from falling. Something gritty crumbled under her hand—earth! Mud had caked the sides and top of the black box, had dried there. And here were the gouged places where the ropes had rubbed that had let the coffin down into a grave where it had not stayed. . . .

A scream sliced through the walls of the house! Another, compact with ineffable terror. Outside, wood splintered, crashed. Across a window's oblong reared the head and shoulders of Emma's horse. A gate-picket dangled from its bridle and banged crazily against flailing forelegs. The brute screamed once more, plunged down and out of view. Galloping hoofs pounded away.

Not knowing she had moved, the girl was across the room, was staring out. A dust cloud thundered down the road, stopped suddenly. The horse reared out of it, whirled in a strange dervish dance. In the eerie half-light a grey, shapeless something clung to the beast's belly, reached grey tendrils for its foam-flecked, outstraining throat. Then the frantic animal was gone around a bend. Only the diminuendo of its *pudding* hoofs and the shrill panic of its almost human screams were left, coming back to Emma through quivering, affrighted dusk. . . .

Moments later, as night welled up the towering slopes, the girl still stood motionless, flattened against the window as that last awful glimpse had left her. She was poignantly conscious of the preternatually disinterred corpse behind her, but nightmare paralysis held her rigid and her larynx was sore, rasped by unuttered screams. The faceless Things of the hills had come down into the valley at last, into the precincts of her ancestral home. The drear dread of the mountains was a living, tangible presence in this house where she and the man she loved had hoped to find refuge from a world that had denied them. It was here, *here* in this room. She felt its chill fingers stroking her spine, its icy breath on her neck. *Something* was here, something that had brought Gram back from the grave, something that itself had come from that mountainside burial ground!

The vague clatter of hoofbeats impinged on her consciousness. Emma lifted burning eyes to Big Tom's rocky summit across the valley, to the pale ribbon glimmering along his darkening flank. That was the new highway, she remembered, the recently opened macadam trail Milt had pointed out on the map as the way he would come when he had finished the business that delayed him. And on it, miles away, the failing light picked out a tiny moving horse—her horse. Somehow, even across the space between, the girl sensed the incarnate terror flogging that anguished beast, flogging him to insane flight from the horror that clung beneath his belly and fled with him.

The distance-dwarfed steed staggered, fell. A final shrill neigh split the awed hush of the mountain-encompassed hollow. Horrible movement animated the prostrate beast; greyness flowed over it, merged it with the grey road. The pallid mound heaved, sickeningly, for long moments. Then the ash-tinted destroyer ebbed slowly from its victim, slithered into bordering trees. A tawny shape was very still as the up-surge of night's sightlessness engulfed it, and the highway, and the trees into which horror had seethed.

It was as if Satan had set a vaulted black lid over the valley to hide it from God's sight. There was no light in the sky, utterly no light in the broad sweep of the dale. No sound except a faint rustle of wind in the forest cloaking the mountain-sides.

Or *was* it the wind in the leaves? Grisly

fingers plucked Emma's quivering nerves to new apprehension. Was it not rather the slithering advance of the wan hosts that so long had danced as pale, mistlike wraiths on the twilight slopes, unleashed at last to their long-deferred invasion of the lowlands? Loosed by Gram's passing, perhaps; by the death of the pioneer's spouse who first had intruded into this valley and driven them back into the hills. . . . Was that why Faith Sprool had been brought back here from the sanctuary of consecrated ground, that in death they might wreak on her a weird vengeance for the thralldom to which her life had condemned them? . . .

Oh God! Oh good God! Emma's fingers twisted, interlacing, and her slender frame was a shell brimful with terror. The advancing sound was no longer a dim, just hearable rustle. It was a thrum pulsing toward her, a swift-coming burr momentarily louder. They were coming fast now. Faster. *They were coming for her!*

Of course for her! She was a Sprool, the last of the Sprools, and she did not know the secret Granddad and Gram had had that held Them back. She had always suspected there was a secret Granddad knew, the haughty patrician in whose leathery visage steely eyes brooded and who held himself and his family so high above the valley-folk. But she had never dreamed that this was it. Why hadn't they told her how to drive back the eerie company sweeping down on her?

A green light-beam scythed the darkness out there, struck the road into livid relief. Vague forms seemed to dart for concealment in the thick bushes of the garden. . . . A gigantic grey shape roared around the road-bend, skidded to a halt. The menacing thrum throttled down to the familiar throb of a motor, and a remembered profile was limned by dim dashlights.

"Kurt," Emma called, "Kurt!" The name was a sob in her throat as she shot into the hall. She was across the verandah, and running through the garden. "Kurt Tradin!" Briars snatched at her, murky foliage; a low-hanging tendril whipped stingingly across her cheek and some furtive thing scuttered out of her path. "Don't go away, Kurt. Don't."

SHE had reached the car, was clutching its sill with both hands. Gaunt-visaged, somehow older than when he had laid suit to her in the shy manner of a country swain, Kurt Tradin peered at her. His slow smile was tinged with some strange apprehension. "Em. Emma Sprool! Be you all right?"

"Yes—Kurt, why isn't Gram buried?"

"Why *what?*" He half-rose from his seat, shoving toward her. "She was! I see her laid to rest myself, in the graveyard."

Emma's last faint hope vanished. Her nails dug into the auto's steel, her throat worked. Then— "But she isn't. She's in there, in the parlor."

Kurt's lips were ashen. From above the lumping of his high cheekbones worm-like lights crawled in the depths of his shy eyes. "In—the parlor," he husked. "Almighty Godfrey! They knew ye was a-comin', then! Christopher, I'm glad I come out to see if you was here, like I done every dusk the past week."

"In God's name! Kurt! What is going on here?" Kurt's stalwart frame, his big-boned, handsome countenance, wavered in Emma's vision as though a heat-haze screened them. "Who—what knew I was coming?"

The young farmer seemed to have difficulty in forming words; his gnarled hand was trembling. "We—don't know. Whutever it is thet's been prowlin' the nights since yer gran-maw was buried. Grey things in the hills thet ain't shaped like man nor beast."

"Grey things!" Emma thought of the anguished horse and the thing that, hanging beneath its belly, had reached gruesome tentacles for its throat. "I saw one! It killed my horse, out here. . . ."

"Yer hoss!" He rapped the syllables out, and a little muscle twitched, once, in his cheek. "They've killed more nor hosses—Gaffer Wilson, an' Ely Trenholm's Iry an' Alice, an' Spad Perkins' hull family when they tried ter get out along Big Tom Highway. Thet's why I bin watchin' fer you to warn you not to stir out o' the house after sundown."

Emma did not hear that last sentence. "Big-Tom Highway— Kurt! Are they—is there any danger on that road?"

He laughed shortly, without humor. "Danger! Thet's whar they was first seen—an' thar ain't ary one got through thar by night fer three days. Spad's outfit was the last ter try. Jed Harker an' me found what was left o' them." Horror flaring in his eyes spoke volumes. "The car wasn't hurt aytall 'cept'n the gas tank was ripped open. . . . We buried 'em quick, an'—" Once more a hesitant, quivering pause. "An' found their graves open the next mornin', open an' empty."

The girl swayed. Her lips parted, but no word came from them. Kurt's smoldering gaze was fixed on her, and his voice was a hoarse croak. "No one's come in or out of Ekwanok by night, since then. Not by night. . . . Though by day thar's been plenty agoin' till thar ain't but a half-dozen families left in the valley. . . . Whoa up, Emmy!" He seemed to notice the girl's state for the first time, grabbed for her wrist just in time to keep her from sliding to the ground as her knees gave way. "What . . . ?"

Emma squeezed speech through her tight throat. "That's the way Milton is coming—maybe tonight."

"Milton?"

"My husband." She recalled that his letter had been addressed to Emma Sprool. "I'm married, Kurt. We had given up our room, had the car packed and ready to start for here, when someone sent for him to audit an account. It meant twenty dollars, the first in months; he couldn't turn it down. It was cheaper than a hotel for me to come by rail to Kingville. No one would drive me here, but I borrowed a horse. Milt said he would leave as soon as he finished—perhaps tonight. Tonight! *And he is coming by Big Tom Highway!*"

"Your—husband. . . ." The syllables dripped from Tradin's twisting mouth; evidently he had heard nothing else. "Husband." Life drained from his broad-sculptured visage; his eyes were dead things, and his upper lip trembled like a hurt child's. His shoulders slumped. There was something abject about his big frame. Emma had seen him thus once before, when old Jeremiah, her grandfather, had flayed with cutting words the yokel who had aspired to mate with a daughter of the Sprools. "I—*Great Jumpin' Godfrey!*"

Someone had screamed, far down the road. Some *thing*—for there had been nothing human about that high-pitched wail of agony. The girl twisted to it, her heart pounding to the anguish, the utter terror in that cry—and it came again. Tradin's hand was on her shoulder, was shoving her away. "Git in th' house, Emmy. Git inside an' keep the door locked."

She jerked away. "But you, Kurt. You. . . ." His face was set, his sleepless eyes ablaze. "Come with me and—"

"Can't," he snapped through tight, white lips. "I—maybe I'll get 'em this time. All week I've been too late. But thet warn't fur away. . . ." Motor roar drowned his voice—faded to let him shout, "Quick, Em. Git inside an' let me go. . . ."

His urgency got her started; panic spurred her, and she was hurtling through tangled brush that ripped and fought to hold her back. Her feet thumped on the creaking porch. As the door pushed open before her frantic rush she heard the farmer's car dart away. She slammed the portal. Musty dark swallowed her as she fumbled for, and found, the great bolt and shot it rattling into its socket.

CHAPTER TWO

The Terror in the Woods

THE mutter of the speeding car died in the distance. Emma moaned. A pulse throbbed in her temple and a steel band constricted her chest. She was alone in the blackness. Outside an unnameable doom prowled, and here within was the cadaver that earth and the worms had rejected. She was *not* alone! Livid, marrow-melting fear companioned her, breathed on her its icy breath. To stay in this house were to face a hell of terror, to flee into that outer dark peopled by the grey menace a prospect unthinkable. A spasm twisted her slender body and her small fists beat against the door-panel in frantic protest. Why had he let her come here alone? Why had Milton. . . .

New terror clamped grisly fingers at her throat. Milton might even now be climbing the pass, might be entering unwarned the macadam snaking along Big Tom's flank where the grey Things waited. "No! He's still working. Oh, God! Please make him still be working. Please let me phone him not to come." Phone! The telephone was in the parlor; she would have to brush close by the gaunt, terrible casket to get to it!

The girl whimpered as she pushed herself away from the wall. To save her own life she could not have entered that sepulchral chamber, but for Milton—for the man she loved! . . .

Straight through sightless blackness Emma strode, across the hall, into that fearsome chamber so strangely a sepulcher. Unseen, unseeable entities slid soundlessly from her advance, gathered behind in watching balefulness. The coffin-edge scraped her side to ripple her flesh with crawling revulsion. She sensed the wall before her, groped for the box of the rural phone, the tiny handle of the magneto. Gasped as the wire-whine in her ear told her the line had not yet been disconnected.

A startled man's voice grated in the receiver. "Almighty Godfrey, Mariar. Et's the Sprool house—" The Ekwanok exchange was in Elmer Barmes' kitchen. Then, "Who is—" A click snapped short Elmer's question, clogged the line-sound in Emma's ear. . . .

"Hello," she panted. "Hello. . ." And knew that she was not heard. In that moment, in that very moment the wire had snapped, somewhere—*or malevolently been broken!* "Elmer!" the girl screamed, despairingly. "Elmer! . . ."

The receiver dropped from Emma's flaccid hand. She heard it thump against the wall, dully, heard the tiny rattle of dislodged plaster behind the laths. Her lips formed words they did not utter. "God—help me." God had turned his face from the valley, from her. But—but perhaps Milton would not come tonight. Perhaps his work would keep him so late that he would wait till morning.

She grasped at the faint hope, even knowing that his longing to rejoin her would drive him to complete with all possible speed the task that held him from her. This was their first separation since they had become man and wife—sometimes the fierceness of their love frightened her—and he would be eager to end it. . . . No, at whatever hour he was free he would start out.

Maybe he had started, maybe he was there now, high up on Big Tom. *Why had the phone connection been broken except to stop her very warning?* But they wouldn't know about telephones, the pallid killers prowling the highway. Of course not. She laughed, but the short sound of her laugh was not pleasant. How silly she was. How silly. The rural wires often went out of commission. . . .

A dim vibration crept to her ears through the darkness, a far-off thrum, the infinitely distant sound of a coming car. Help was coming—Kurt was coming back to help her! He would take her to the village, to another telephone. Without seeming volition she was again at the window from which she had first glimpsed horror. She peered out, up the road toward Kingville whither Tradin's car had catapulted on its wild chase. Nothing save impenetrable dark.

But that vague burr of a speeding motor still sounded. It pulled her eyes up, up along what she could not see but knew was the slope of Big Tom, up to where the road must be where the horse had screamed and died. A star showed—but that tiny light was too low to be a star—and it was moving! It must be an auto headlight then, the light of an auto coming along Big Tom Highway. . . .

THE staring girl's hands closed on the window-sash at either side, while thought stopped and her skull was a void seared by the query she dared not think. Whose car? Oh dear Lord! Who drove that car?

The light split to two tiny specks. Some curve in that far-flung, high road sliced their beams to double dashes of yellow against the dark billow of foliage, one luminant streak canted upward and distinct from the other. Emma's hands clawed, raked down old wood, paint flaking and stabbing into the quick of nails that scraped it. She was answered. Oh merciless God, she was answered!

Those were the lights of Milton's roadster. Unmistakably. He had tugged at that up-bent lamp, trying to straighten it, only this morning. . . .

"Milt!" she screamed. "Go back, Milt! Go back! If you love me, Milt, go back!" He could not hear, of course he could not hear. *"Milt!"* Why could he not hear? Why could he not sense her anguished soul shrieking its warning to him across the miles? "MILTON!"

Steadily the twin beams moved across the vast screen of blackness. They seemed to be drifting infinitely slow, but Emma knew the speed at which they moved. A flash of inner vision showed her Milt's ascetic, dear face bent slightly forward over the wheel, the wind of his passage sweeping his hair back from his high, clear forehead, his brown eyes eager. He would be calculating the minutes still between them. His arms would be aching for the feel of her in their embrace. Her own breasts ached in answer. . . . Dear Mother of Mercy, protect him!

His love was hurtling him on to doom!

Across the vast night that had engulfed the world those tiny lights floated with even pace. Hours seemed to pass and some dim hope stirred in Emma's aching bosom. Kurt was wrong. Perhaps Kurt was wrong. Perhaps the Things in their descent on the valley had relaxed their watch of the highway. Milton was getting through. He *must* get through. He would.

In minutes now he would reach the place where the horse had died—right there—he would reach and pass it. Of course he would pass it. That would be the test. If Milt passed that spot he would be all right. He would surge down the hill, down into this connecting road that ribboned before the house, would honk his horn for her and she would be at the gate, on his running-board, in his embrace. In seconds now she would know. In seconds. He was almost there. He *was* there. He would pass—

His lights were gone! In that instant, in that very instant when he had reached the spot where instinct had told her the greatest danger lurked, his motor had sputtered, stopped—and his headlights had blinked out as if a black shroud had dropped over them! As if a shroud—his shroud. . . . The Things had him! The grey Things had swarmed over her husband, her lover. . . .

It was then that madness first probed gruesome fingers into the girl's brain. Glass crashed as she smashed the window before her with flailing, frantic fists. Keen, jagged shards gashed her jacket, her arm, as she clambered through. She was out in the garden, was smashing through tangled, wild shrubbery she felt but could not see. She was across the road, had plunged into thick woods that lifted under her feet, lifted and became the high slope of Big Tom.

She was climbing that slope, blindly, climbing to the highway above. Climbing to Milton, to help him against the grey death. To die with him if he were dead. To die whatever horrible death he suffered. Or save him. That was it, she would save him. She would drive the grey Things away from her lover with the very fury of her love.

The sound of her wild passage was a tumult in the silent forest. She caromed off a black tree trunk, plunged on. A trailing vine coiled around her ankle, tripped her. She slammed down. In the moment she lay gasping something rustled the carpeting of dead leaves, close by. She pulled herself erect, staggered on. The woods tore at her, would not let her pass. Snarling, like some creature of the wild, she fought it, fought through.

The way grew steeper, sapped her strength. She was moving more slowly now, but would not stop. Rock-face rose sheer above her; she found hand-holds, niches for straining toes, inched upward. Her labored breathing, the scrape of her toes against the stone, were the only sounds she made.

But there was another sound in the woods, though she did not hear it. The stealthy sound of a furtive something that slithered through the underbrush. . . .

HER reaching hand found dank earth at the brow of the cliff she climbed. She was up and over, lay panting on its very brink, face down over its edge where the air her laboring lungs needed was unimpeded. She pulled dampness into her aching thorax, fungus-smell, odor of rotting leaves. And another stench—alien, shuddersome—like nothing she had ever smelled. Infinitely menacing.

A patch in the blackness below was queerly lighter, somehow—a patch that moved to the base of the rock she had climbed. It was a pallid, formless shape that moved oddly, flowing like—like the greyness that had ebbed from a tawny still heap that had been a horse, like the grey horror-thing that had seeped into the woods—to wait for Milton. It was climbing now, climbing to reach her, grey-black tendrils reaching for her. . . . Her breathing stopped and an abortive scream retched her throat, was a soundless gust. . . .

She surged to her feet, and was blundering again through tight-laced undergrowth, through ripping brambles and whipping thin branches that lashed at her. Moist mold was slick under her feet; stones rolled, twisting her ankles. The forest was on the side of the noisomeness it had borne, was striving to hold her for that which pursued. God was against her—no, God had forgotten her, had forgotten Milton. God had abandoned them to Satan's spawn.

Emma crashed against an invisible tree-trunk, clung to it, momentarily stunned, saw the weird evil that followed her closer now. It seemed to move so slowly, yet it was closer. Terribly close. She was running again, fleeing the terror. Her clothing was in tatters, her white skin ripped and bleeding. Her body was an intolerable ache, her veins an icy network. But she climbed, climbed endlessly toward where the highway cut through primeval, lush timber, toward where Milton needed her. *Milton!* Good God! She was leading another of the creatures to him, she was bringing him not help but sure destruction!

The thought halted her, jerked her around to face that which she fled. If it took her, if she gave herself to it, would it be sated? Feeding on her would it be kept from joining the attack on Milt? There it was, an inexorable billow of menace, eddying effortlessly through the tangle that it had cost her so much to penetrate—coming for her with a strange quietude, certain of overtaking her, certain of its prey. . . .

The darkness here was absolute, yet she could see it, see its vague greyness, like a faintly luminous small whirl of mist emanating from the very ground. Against its vague light gaunt boles were silhouetted, trunks springing straight to the sky or twisted by some injury to a frail seedling. By all that was holy, she recognized the grotesque knotting of one gnarled oak! She remembered wandering here in the woods as a child, finding an abandoned loggers' cabin near that U-shaped trunk. . . . A cabin! Was it still there?

Emma twisted, sped away. Ten, a dozen steps and she saw it, a dark, welcome bulk, slab-sided. Saw it and felt a clammy cold touch on her back where jacket and blouse had been stripped away! Her body exploded into a long, terror-winged leap into the musty closeness of the long deserted shelter. Miraculously she found a door and slammed it shut against a soft, squashy bulk.

She heard the soft slither of groping tendrils against the wood, dug heels into the earthen floor and shoved aching, bare shoulders against the barrier to hold it against the sleezy surge of that which sought entrance. She felt the dig of a bar into her back, fumbled behind her and shoved it into a stout, angle iron riveted through the jamb. Then she slid, utterly spent, down along the splintered panel—lay, limp and gasping, at its base.

The fetor of the Thing threaded through still space, a putrescence of something rotting that initially was foul. The sound of its groping was doughy, horribly without stiffness. Clammy-cold as the slimy touch she still felt on her back where momentarily it had contacted her. Somehow blind—as though the sense by which it had trailed her had been not sight but an uncanny attribute of an entity from beyond the Pale. Sliding sound whispering of evil incarnate; livid, quivering evil.

What was that?

DULLY, almost beneath the level of hearing, another sound had come out of the forest night, like the shout of a human voice, far off. The Thing must have heard it too, for now it was quiescent, suddenly unmoving. Utter stillness fell—to be shredded by a high, shrill wail that clawed Emma's quivering nerves with gelid talons of new and supernal terror.

The fearsome ululation rose, and died away. And then—realization pulled the girl up to a sitting posture, her icy hand at her frozen lips—that which had groped for entrance against the saving door of her refuge was gliding away. She could hear it—the rustle of its ungainly weight out there—then it was gone.

It was gone and she was safe. But who was it that had shouted, briefly? Who could it be but Milton? No other human was near enough to be heard. He was alive, still alive, crying for help! And the Thing had abandoned its efforts to get at her in response to the weird call of its mate! It was hastening, even now, to join in the attack on Milton.

Awful certainty pulled the staggering,

half-naked girl to her feet. . . .Somewhere out there in the gruesome night, her husband was in deadly peril. Somewhere out there—but where? Oh God! *Where?* The answer flashed on her. She had *seen* the cabin, where all else had been darkness, had seen it silhouetted against a narrow paling of the blackness. That lighter strip against the gloom could be only Big Tom Highway, the turnpike along which she had seen Milton's lights drift and blink out, the road from which his cry for help had come. He was near—very near. . . .

It was not Emma Wayne whose slow hand sought the great bar that locked that door against terror and shoved it back. It was the frenetic errantry of a woman whose loved one was in peril, the incomprehensible devotion of the female who would defy Lucifer himself for her mate. . . .

Cold air was about her as the portal creaked open, the dank chill of the night still tainted by the fetor of corruption. She was out in the open, in an oppressive silence that held in its jetty womb muted sounds of a struggle: the heavy breathing of a strangling man; the thumping of tossed, heavy bodies, boneless and horrible.

Emma turned her head against neck-muscles that were taut, resistant bands, saw the pale glimmer of the road, yards away through the trees. Saw the familiar outlines of a cheap roadster against the wan light—and beside it, an amorphous mass that heaved sickeningly, heaved up, settled again!

"Milton!" she shrieked. "Milton!"

The formless, grey-luminant mound seemed to swirl, to break apart. A shape flicked into being at its center, an upsurging figure of a man. Emma glimpsed the pale oval of a face, heard the guttural mutter of a cry in what might have been Milton's voice. Then he was down again under the upheaval of the attackers. . . .

Briars tore at her, unseen branches lashed at her. She was on the road, was leaping toward the struggling mass. She had reached it, was tearing at it with desperate hands, was tearing away handfuls of viscid, doughy stuff that stunk to high heaven. The stuff clung to her fingers, clogged them. Beneath the mound Milton choked and struggled.

A thick, gluey tentacle rose toward her, coiled around her waist. It was dragging her down, irresistibly down into that corruption. She beat at it and her fists smacked into wet, cold softness that gave like wet and sticky clay. She sank into the noisome mound. Its foulness was in her mouth, was clammy against her nostrils. She could not breathe. . . .

Within the maelstrom that was her ego she whispered, "Milton. With you. In death as in life. . . ."

Something screamed through the darkness that swept into her brain. . . .

CHAPTER THREE

Madmen's Dance

IT ISN'T right, Emma thought petulantly. When you're dead you ought to stop hurting. It was as if she were still in that body of hers that glass and the forest brambles had sliced. Pain seared her everywhere, and her chest was an aching hollow.

"Emma! Darling!" Milton's voice cried from out the depths. "Emma!"

It was all right then; he was in the same place to which she had gone. They would be together through eternity. Something stroked her forehead—it was his trembling hands. Even here they thrilled her. Would the sight of him thrill her too? Emma dared to look.

A green light bathed him, and his face was contorted, anxious. "Milt, dear," she said weakly. "Don't look so worried. Nothing can happen any more."

"Oh God! Oh thank God! You're alive! I thought. . . ."

The girl's lips moved weakly. "Alive? Oh Milt. . . ."

His kisses were cold on her mouth, icy cold. The grey stuff streaking his cheeks was clammy against her.

Another voice said gruffly, from somewhere in the eerie light, "Come on. Let's get out of here 'fore them Things come back."

Past Milton's shoulder she saw Kurt Tradin standing over them, ashen-visaged, gun in hand, looking fearfully into tall shadows enclosing his headlight beam. And Milt had a gun. Matters became real again. She was alive. She was lying in the dust of Big Tom Highway, and her husband was kneeling beside her, holding her in his arms, kissing her.

She pulled away from him. "What—what happened?"

"God, Em, I'm not sure I know. I was pounding along, saw a dead horse right across the road. Braked and got out to pull it out of the way—then my car lights went out and something jumped me from the trees." He pulled an arm across his sweat-wet, white brow, and shuddered. "Something out of a nightmare. It had me down, was smothering me, but I got my senses back in time to fight it off. To *try* to fight it off. I couldn't get away from it. But it couldn't quite down me either. I think I fought it for hours.

"Suddenly it yelled and another like it lumbered out of the woods. The two ganged up on me and had me down. I was all through when I heard you scream. That was like a jab from a red-hot iron. I pulled away from them for a second, saw you coming, and then they flooded over me again. But I knew I had to lick them then.

"For some reason one of them let go. I pounded at the other. I must have found some vital spot, for the Thing screamed, squirmed away from me. I got to my car, grabbed a gun from the side-pocket, and turned to see both of them vanishing into the woods. You were lying here, more dead than alive. I started for you when there was the screech of a horn, and this gentleman came ripping around the curve."

"This is Kurt Tradin, Milt," Emma said then, dazedly. "I've told you about him. This is my husband, Kurt."

Tradin was strangely expressionless as he turned to her. "Reckoned so. You two agoin' to stay here till the critters come back? Ain't you had enough?" His tone was flat, dead, but little lights crawled in his eyes. Was it fear?

"Right you are." Milt lifted Emma, carrying her up with him in his strong arms. "Let's get going, friend."

He started with her toward the battered flivver.

"Better if we stick together," Kurt rumbled, not looking at them. "Take mine, it's faster. We'll come back an' get your'n in the mornin'—if we live to see the sun again."

Milt hesitated. "What do you mean?" he said sharply. "Why shouldn't we live? . . ."

The farmer whirled to him, his face livid. "Jumpin' Jehoshaphat, ain't you seen enough to know the hand of Beelzebub is heavy on the valley? We're marked for damnation, all of us." His voice broke to shrillness. "An' only the Lord's miracle kin save us. Get her in my car, if you love her. Quick!" His arm jerked so that his revolver was pointblank at Milt's midriff. "Quick! I ain't agoin' to risk my neck for your foolishness."

Wayne shrugged and slid his wife into the back of Tradin's grey limousine, came in alongside her. Kurt leaped for the front, was under the steering wheel. His motor roared, gears clashed, and the forest's dark loom whizzed by.

A vast weariness gripped Emma. She snuggled close against her husband, immersed herself in his strength, the comforting aura of his protection. She had him back. That was all that mattered. She had him safe and with tomorrow's light they would leave here, leave Ekwanok and its valley of dread. . . .

BUT there was still the night to get through. The dreadful night. "Where are we going, Kurt? Where are you taking us?"

"To yer own house, quick's we kin get there."

Emma pushed up. "No, Kurt," she groaned. "No!" She was quivering once more with the fear that first had found her there. "That's where the Things. . . ."

"Safest place in the valley," he growled, cutting her short. "Worse in the village."

"But—"

"But nothin'. You'll see." Grimly. "We go through the village."

"What's the matter with the Sprool house, Emma?" Milton interrupted, curiously. "I thought—"

"It's horrible, Milt. Gram's—"

"God! Look at that! The place is on fire!"

The road had dipped, suddenly, and debouched between dark, shuttered houses that were gaunt against a lurid glow from which dancing sparks flew straight upward.

"No," Kurt grunted. "Not th' place." And they were darting through the green Emma remembered as bordered by the staid facades of churches, the white columns of the town hall. But the open space was staid no longer. Great leaping red tongues of a huge bonfire soared avidly from its very center, and, limned grotesquely against it, a ring of prancing, black figures hopped, and gibbered, and howled in wild antics. She quivered in revulsion at what a tall, bearded man was doing. Distracted momentarily by their passing, he turned—and wild eyes glared at them from a face she knew. The incredible scene whipped behind them. . . .

"Kurt," she gulped. "Kurt. That wasn't Dr. Potter. He couldn't—"

"Yep," laconically. "Preacher o' th' First Presbyterian. That's Ekwanok, Em, all that's left. Want to stay there tonight?"

She shuddered. "No. Mother of mercy, no!"

They curved around the jut of Big Tom; the village of the mad was behind. A bridge rattled under their pounding wheels. The car swayed, jounced as the macadam ended. Kurt's green headlight stabbed through darkness again, darkness that blanketed grey terror, but Emma welcomed it. Even the horror of the skulking Things were better than that which she had just glimpsed.

"All them that's sane has went, a week ago," he said.

"All but you, Kurt. Why did you stay?"

"I was waitin' for you," he answered simply. "For you." There was bitter despair in his tone. "You forgot what I promised, but I didn't."

"Oh Kurt!" Emma remembered now the one stolen moment she had given him, to say good-bye, their one brief talk after grandfather had forbidden them to see one another. "You'll come back, Emmy," he had said. "Sure's shootin'. An' I'll be awaitin' for you." How could she have forgotten the dreary hopelessness with which he had thrown out his hands, and the dogged determination in his hurt eyes.

"I'm sorry, Kurt," she said. She had really thought herself in love with him, till she had met Milton and learned what love was.

"You shouldn't have risked it," she added.

"Risked!" Still that dulled bitterness. "I belong with them."

"Isn't that the place?" Milton broke in. "There to the left?"

Breath popped from Tradin's tight lips.

"Yes." He braked, swerved. His radiator crashed through the broken fence, the car skidded through the garden, nosed the porch and stopped. "Git out an' into the house. Hurry!"

Kurt's urgency lifted them out of their seats, out of the car, and to the door. Milt shoved it open, but Emma turned.

"Kurt," she called. "Kurt! Aren't you coming in?"

"No." He was already in reverse, was surging backward. "Git inside, for God's sake."

He was in the road—was gone. Milton's grip was on her wrist, pulling her inside. The door banged shut, and a flashlight beam sprayed the gloom. But for an instant, the girl's mind was tangled with a strange gesture the farmer had just made, a gesture as of final farewell.

"Creepy old place—no wonder you left it." Her husband's voice was unaccustomedly loud and harsh. She jerked to him, reproach on her lips. "Remember where there's a lamp? We've got to have light."

She saw his face dimly. It was infinitely weary, haggard. There were black rings under his eyes. She choked back what she had been about to say, realizing the tension he was under. He was as afraid as she, was dissembling, trying to be natural, in order to quiet her. His hand, behind him, had already slipped the doorbolt into its socket, and the long whiteness of his flashbeam flickered everywhere, probing the shadows. "There should be one on a table behind the stairs." The light darted there. "Yes—and it's filled."

"Here's some matches. I don't know how to work the thing." He poked the paper folder at her, fumbled it into her hand. But he kept close beside her as blue flame ran around the lampwick, guttered, lifted to a steady glow within the replaced chimney. Yellow luminance shoved back the shadows, Milt clicked off his flashlight, managed a wan grin. "That's better. So this is the Sprool mansion!"

Looking with his eyes Emma saw the curious old-fashionedness of the house, even here in the hall, its threadbare assumption of a dignity it had long lost. In Ekwanok they had always called it The Mansion, had kowtowed to its inmates, even when the patriarch had gone. Kurt had been no exception. His lovemaking had been a shy, timorous, hopeless yearning for something above him.

"This is the Sprool homestead," Emma assented gravely, while her glance slid to the parlor archway, tried to penetrate its blackness, "where your wife was born and bred."

"What is it?" His exclamation was like ripping silk. "What are you scared of, in there?" He had seen her look, had interpreted it with the sureness of their intimacy. *"What's in there?"*

"Nothing. Nothing that I'm afraid of." Two could play at that game. "Gram's in there, in her coffin. They—they didn't bury her."

"Good Lord! What were they waiting for? I never heard of—" He started toward the doorway. Emma got her hand on his arm, stopped him.

"Wait," she said. "Time enough in the morning. She—I—don't go in there. Don't!"

He gripped her shoulder, turned her to him, gently, but she winced as pain stabbed down her arm. "Em. You're trembling all over. You *are* afraid of something in there."

She made her eyes meet his, forced false frankness into them. "There's nothing in the parlor except Gram's Coffin, with her in it. I—I don't want you to go in there because I couldn't go with you. I couldn't bear it, and I am afraid to be alone. Hasn't there been enough to make me tremble, tonight?"

"Poor kid! I'll say there has." The harshness of his tone mellowed, she was close against him and his mouth had found hers. The rasp of his tightening arms on her lacerated, bare shoulders was somehow sweet and she felt his fear-cold lips grow warm, then burn, as the tight embrace fanned the spark of their love to consuming flame. Terror was forgotten in that long moment, fear ceased to brood. There was only the ecstasy of their oneness. . . .

A soft thud behind froze her, the drag of a jell-like mass across wood! Milt pushed her away, crouched, his eyes on the murky entrance into the parlor, his automatic tight-gripped, snouting. Syllables slid from his mouth that was suddenly a straight gash across a humid mask. "Watch it, Em! There's someone in there and I'm going in after him."

CHAPTER FOUR

The Coffin's Message

THE slow slither within the parlor that was a cavern of dread stopped, but Emma's spine prickled to the sensation of a baleful glare from the room's mystery, of fearful eyes glaring as the new menace crouched to match Milt's taut crouch and waited in ambush for his coming.

"No," she squeezed through the invisible fingers of fear clamping her throat. "No. There can't be. There can't. . . ."

Then she remembered the window she had smashed, the gap in their defenses! "Don't Milt. Don't go in there. Please, Milt, don't!"

His eyes flicked to her, flicked back to stare ahead, but she had seen into their lurid depths and was aghast. Milt! No! It couldn't be *her* Milt's eyes into which she had looked in that revealing instant! His upper lip lifted in a vulpine snarl. He shrugged closer to the ground, lunged into the blackness, leaving behind a low growl, the growl of an enraged dog. Leaving behind a woman whose world had smashed about her bloody head, a woman shaken to the very foundations of her being, utterly alone.

Shot-crash pounded dully to Emma's clogged ears; her dizzy sight was aware only of an orange-red flash that illumined nothing. Muted sounds of a terrific struggle were suddenly cut short, were succeeded by an awesome silence, a silence pregnant with queasy dread. There were furtive noises, sluggish movement, a whispering frou-frou of satin. And again the slow dragging of something that was neither human nor beast. Then stillness again, a stillness as ebony dark as the blackness veiling whatever horror had come to pass in there.

The girl came gradually to awareness that she was clinging to the banisters, waist-high just there, that grave-chill stiffened her limbs and corpse-smell was foul in her nostrils.

"No," she whispered. "Dear God. No."

There was no sound, sepulchrally no sound from the murk ahead. She was mistaken in what she had read in Milton's final flickering glace. She must have been mistaken. Of course she had been. The hands she unclasped from the slender round of the banister-rods seemed to creak, their joints paining. She must go in there. She must go in there to see what had happened to him. What had the Thing done to Milton, to her lover.

Her lover! She recalled the look in his eyes, and shuddered. Was *she* going mad or. . . ? But she must stop thinking. She had stopped thinking, except just enough to pick up the lamp and make her legs take her toward that parlor door.

The lamplight seemed tangibly to push back a wall of darkness that resisted it. To push back *something* hidden by the darkness, hidden by and eerily part of it. She was through the archway and the lamp's luminance filled the room, thrusting the darkness out through the gaping, jagged-edge window into the night from which it came. Thrusting the Thing the darkness hid—*not thrusting all of it!* In mid-air a shadow floated, unmoving. . . .

IT WAS no shadow, it was the coffin, the black casket so weirdly exhumed. The macaber object pulled Emma's look to it, pulled with a shuddersome fascination she could not resist. It seemed to have a message for her, a message of doom.

She fought the gruesome drag, drove searching eyes about the musty chamber, over age-patinaed furnishings long-familiar yet uncannily strange, into far corners, along the scrub-whitened floor islanded by the faded rag rugs Gram's fragile hands had worked. Stiff and decorous the parlor was as ever—empty, stark, staringly empty. Glass splinters still in the broken window were edged with grey stuff. But where was Milton? Oh God! Oh merciless God! *Where was Milton?*

Was that the message Gram had for her? Would she tell, her old grandmother, stiff and dead in the casket They had not let rest? Gram would help her in her agony. Gram, always so fluttering-kind despite her tight-lipped grimness. She would go and ask Gram where Milton was.

Emma's feet whispered across the floor, and her light grew stronger on the casket, grew stronger and yet somehow was swallowed by the dull black of its grave-smeared sides. Emma was at the coffin side, but her eyes had jerked themselves closed as she reached it. Why did she fear to look into the box where lay all that was mortal of Faith Sprool? Why did she fear to look, save for dread of the message she was strangely aware it held for her?

She—must—know! Still with shut eyes the girl lifted the lamp, so that its rays would strike down, would strike surely down into the uncovered coffin. So. Now she could take one swift look and turn away. Now!

The face that stared sightlessly up at her from the coffin pillow was not Gram's face. *Not Gram's!* Emma was a statue of stone, gazing down at a drawn, thin visage, well-conned but somehow utterly strange. It was Milton, *Milton* whose corpse-hued countenance lay on the white satin. MILTON!

Numbed, unbelieving minutes passed. Then the full horror reached her brain, and a scream ripped from her inmost being, shuddered out of that ghastly room, shrieked across the valley and was lost among the night-shrouded trees. Another.

The echoes of those screams were mangled by the mountain-side, were metamorphosed into a shrill laugh. The mountains were laughing at her, the mountains whose lifelong threat had come at length to full fruition. Big Tom was laughing at her. . . .

Emma was laughing too. Shrilly, unendingly. Laughing from a wide-open mouth that drooled, from a body contorted into a backward, spasm-twisted arc. Laughing while icy tears rolled down her face that was a network of tiny, quivering muscles, splashed from a little chin blurred by its tremors, wet a blood-wealed bosom racked by awful sobbing.

Even the stars might have pitied her, in that moment, had they not been shut out from the valley by the lid Lucifer had clamped over it. Even the madmen who danced about the red bonfire in the hidden village, had they heard her.

But there was none here to pity her. None in the desolate house save he who lay so ghastly still, cramped in a box for the dead that was too small for him, and could not hear her laughter or her sobbing for him, for her lover. . . .

SUDDENLY Emma's crazed laughter shut off, and her sobbing. Quite suddenly as if some grisly hand had twisted a streaming faucet shut. A crafty light crept into her eyes, and the tense rigidity that gripped her body relaxed. The glance she shot around that room was furtive; her free hand came up to her mouth and her forefinger pressed against her lips with sly cunning. She tiptoed out of the parlor, reached the hall, turned to the left where the light of her lamp fell on another door. She was through that door. It closed soundlessly and she was slinking with grotesque noiselessness through a huge room walled with dark oak. A massive table gleamed dully. Round plates were parti-colored circles on Dutch shelving high up. The slinking girl mumbled something inaudible, crossed to the gloomy loom of a carved buffet. The slide of drawer was a barely audible hiss as she pulled it out and fumbled within. . . .

She was returning now, and there was a knife in her hand—a long carving knife whose steel flashed brightly, whose edge was razor-keen. She reached the door, paused irresolutely, looked helplessly from her hand that held the lamp to that which gripped the knife, mumbled again. How turn the doorknob? She nodded as the solution came to her, set the lamp down on the floor.

They built well in the old days, and Jeremiah Sprool was exacting. No gleam came through the door Emma had closed behind her to shut off light from the forgotten lamp, no gleam at all. Utter darkness was around her as she moved with the silent sure-footedness of long usage. Utter darkness—in the hall, in the parlor—and in her mind.

After a while there was no sound, no slightest movement in the ancient structure that once was so proud to house the Sprools.

ON THE porch running across the front of the Sproól Mansion a board creaked to the pressure of a cautious foot. A figure, silhouetted against the one bright window, froze to immobility. Nothing but that oblong of light indicated that the house was anything but a shell enclosing only death. The prowler moved again. Faint clink of metal against metal was quickly hushed, well-oiled hinges made no sound, and the porch was once more vacant.

In the foyer of the years-worn dwelling the tomb-like odor of rotted flowers lay heavily, brooding its conquest. But another scent trailed across that corruption, the warm, charnel taint of fresh blood. The intruder sighed, and infinite weariness was in the brief, quivering exhalation.

"Em," he called in a hushed tone. "Emmy. Whar are ye?" A pause, broken by no answering voice. Then, more sharply, "Emmy Sprool. Don't be afraid. Et's Kurt. Kurt Tradin."

Still no response. Breath hissed from between tightened teeth. Groping feet shuffled, the knob of the dining-room door rattled sharply to the touch of a seeking hand, rattled again as it turned. A vertical bar of light leaped into being, blotted by the farmer's stalwart form. Alarm was in his voice now. "Em—*Jehoshaphat!*"

The exclamation was wrenched from him as movement thudded, from behind him, from the vaulted dark of the parlor. He whirled—to see a white figure leaping at him, to see a face distorted, glaring eyes, gleaming blade of a knife arcing at him. His arm jerked up before his face, took the slash of the blow, spurted blood. The girl avoided the clutch of his other hand, slashed again. Missed. Laughed shrilly, so that Kurt's flesh crawled. Bored in again.

His teeth gritted. God! He struck at her. She was a wraith, flitting away, out of the beam slitting through the dining-room door. She was somewhere in the dark; the sound of her mad laughter came from everywhere, from nowhere. She leaped at him from the dark, her knife sliced his cheek. He flailed at her, his fist found mark of soft flesh. And she laughed again. Horribly.

She was gone again in blackness. He

followed, reaching out for her, trying to find her. "Emmy. Girl. Whar are ye?"

Cold wind swept in, chilling him. And the great door slammed. Tradin was at it, was wrenching it open. Somewhere out there she crashed through brush, laughing.

"Emmy! Et's out thar! Come back. *For God's sake, come back!*"

EMMA WAYNE was crashing through underbrush that ripped her, tore her almost nude body. There was something in her hand—a knife it felt like— a knife whose hilt was slippery with—Oh God!—with viscid, warm blood. An instant ago she had been standing over Gram's coffin, looking down into it, seeing Milt's dead and ghastly face where Gram's should have been.

How had she come here? Why was she running? From what? Why was she laughing—*merciful Heavens*— why was she laughing so shrilly? Her hand went to her throat, pressed. Pressed the laughter to an end. But she was still running, blindly. There! Now she was standing still, in the dark that was so black it oppressed her, standing still in the frightening night.

Fear was back on her like a flood. Fear of herself, of the creature that dimly she knew she had been—for how long? Fear of the dark. Fear of the madness that stalked the dark. *Fear of the Things, the grey and grisly Things to whom the night belonged!*

They were here, out here somewhere, and she was out with them! In the house, at least, they could not get at her. Could they not? What was it then that Milton had fought in the lightless parlor? What was it that had killed him, had crammed him into the casket? That had been her fault. Hers. Because she had forgotten the smashed window. But she had waited for It to come back, had— Now what made her think that? The bloody knife? *Whose blood was it?*

"Emmy." A far-off voice was calling her. "Come back. Emmy."

She turned to the call. She was high up on the mountain-side. Down there, where the voice came from, a dimly yellow rectangle must be the door of the house. It framed a dark, familiar figure. Kurt's. Kurt—dear Kurt had come back to help her, was looking for her. She must go back to him. Quickly.

But she *couldn't* go quickly. The brambles were thick here, would not let her pass. She was sheathed in pain, every flick of a leaf against her torn flesh was agony. The scrape of rough bark, the tearing of thorns were sheer, exquisite torture. She whimpered with pain, with grief, with the fear that was growing on her again after the momentary relief that had come to her with her glimpse of Kurt Tradin's stalwart form. Every lumping of shadow in the blackness about her was a new threat, every minuscule rustle a new terror. She was on the hillside sloping down from Big Tom's mighty flank, in the thicket where the Things roamed. The grey and grisly Things whose touch was fearful death.

Why didn't Kurt come for her? Why did he stand there, motionless, peering into the night?— But he didn't know she was there, she hadn't answered his call. Her larynx swelled to cry out, her throat rasped with the coming sound.

And clamped on it, choking it back, as there arose before her, right before her, the same shrill, unearthly wail that had summoned the Thing from her cabin refuge to join in the lethal attack on Milt. High, and higher; knife-edged with appalling menace; glutinous somehow despite its shrillness, as though the ululation were being forced through some awful viscidness; it soared—and checked. Checked as earth pounded, as underbrush surged away and monstrous greyness lunged at her out of the night.

CHAPTER FIVE

"Yes, I Killed It."

EMMA screamed, slashed at the Thing with her knife. Instinctively. The blade felt something, something that took its stroke with a queasy softness like no animal, no human flesh; only barely resisting the plunge of the steel. The girl's arm jerked back for another blow, the knife soughed as it came out of its unreal billet. She slashed again. The Thing towered above her. It was falling on her reckless of her desperate stabs, was overwhelming her with its doughy, putrid mass. She went down under its nauseating bulk. Its noisome lump flowed shudderingly over her, pressing clammy, wet coldness into her nostrils, her mouth, into the hollow between her breasts.

This foulness wasn't real, couldn't be real. She couldn't breathe, couldn't see, but primal instinct for life, primal clinging to existence, sparked her muscles with a furious supernatural energy. She heaved herself up against the noisomeness, drove her fists and her knees into it. It gave. Horribly it gave and as her back arched in a spasmodic attempt to throw it off it flowed underneath, so that its damp and gruesome chill slimed every inch of her frantic body. Even in that moment, even in the red fury of her hopeless battle, her skin crawled with revulsion and her stomach retched.

The boneless, formless Thing held her clamped in its foul embrace, investing her with its corruption, making her a part of its putrescence. Her lungs pulled, pulled, and could get no air. Searing pain racked her chest. The clayey mass that had swallowed her tightened, tightened an inexorable, crushing band about her threshing body. Anguish burst in her darkened brain, exploded into a blaze of coruscating flame. Yellow pinwheels whirled against velvety black, green meteors darted across their swirl, purple rockets burst and blazed. Burst. . . .

The Thing shrieked, and suddenly let go its hold, so that she slid down, down, into swirling oblivion. Somewhere in vast blackness a tiny glow was an infinitely distant pinpoint. It grew, and as it grew its hard glow faded till it was the phantasmal, pallid, sleeping face of her lost mate. Of Milton! Its eyes opened, and Emma shrieked soundlessly as she saw in those eyes that look, that darting, awful look with which he had left her, to die. Her scream changed the bodiless head so that it wore Kurt's face, drawn, haggard, with bloodshot, sleepless eyes deep-sunk in chasms of weariness. She could not see his body, but she could feel his toil-roughened hand on her shoulder, dragging her out of the fathomless pit into which she had fallen. She could hear his voice too, his muffled voice, calling her.

"Emmy. Emmy. Come back."

Why—didn't he leave her alone—in death? She had been safe then. She had been rid of horror, of nameless terror, of pain. Of PAIN. Of the agony that now scraped her skin with fire; clawed her chest, her entrails. Of anguished knowledge that Milton was jammed, waxen-visaged, into a coffin too small for him. Of the memory of what she had seen in her lover's eyes. Now it was all back. All! God! Why wasn't she dead? Why didn't he let her die?

"Emmy. Wake up."

Her eyes opened. Milton—no, Kurt. Kurt Tradin said, "Thank God!" His bleak face was grey, but not as the Thing had been grey, somehow not. His eyes were tired, so tired, and a muscle twitched at the base of his broad nose. His sleeve was gashed, soaked with clotted blood, and his gun was again in his hand. He was already bending to her, he stooped nearer and his arms slid under her. His strong arms closed about her, lifted her, and as she swung effortlessly up she saw a grey, foul mass, motionless on the ground.

"You killed it," she mumbled.

"Yes," he responded, and his accents were oddly thick. "Yes, I killed it."

SHE understood now. Kurt had killed the Thing and saved her. Kurt had saved Milton and her before, up there on the Highway. All night, many nights, Kurt had been patrolling the roads, fighting the grey horror, fighting the madness that the Things had brought to the valley, to the village, to Milton. Fighting alone, always alone. Why had not Kurt run away? Why had he stayed here to fight his lonely battle?

He was climbing down, holding her, pushing through the brambles, but he answered her, as though he had read her thoughts. "I love you, Emmy." His tired voice was thick, broken. "I have waited for you so long. So long."

"Hush," Emma said. "You—mustn't." She closed her eyes to shut out the dreariness that made his lined face even more bleak. "Not—yet."

The memory of Milton was too warm, too dear as yet. Even with what she had read in his eyes between them. But later. . . Kurt's arm cradled her so powerfully, so gently. She was so safe . . . so . . . Emma sighed, slid into exhausted sleep.

Kurt drifted through her dreams, padding barefoot along the dusty road from school, carrying her books. Kurt, standing, a dark and somehow lonesome figure at the gate, watching her window whose curtain he could not know veiled her responsive watching. Speaking his love, haltingly, in a quiet dusk that for once was not gloomy with dread. Kurt, in that last scene, that last but one, his ungainly figure bowed, cringing beneath the awful blast of Jeremiah Sprool's wrath. "Marry Emma," the old man roared. "Marry my granddaughter! Put the taint of your blood into the veins o' the Sprools! We're clean, Tradin. We're clean. By Jehovah, you're as mad as the rest o' the valley. Mad as. . . ."

The look on the young man's face had stopped grandfather there. The lifeless look and the blaze in his dark eyes, the lurid, flaming blaze whose agony had stilled even the ancient's unruly tongue. But Kurt turned, blundered blindly out of the house. And the dream ended with grandfather's gigantic figure in the doorway, his voice recovered, shouting out into the night. "Mad, damn you. Crazy. Crazy as a bat."

Emma had not been much frightened by Jeremiah's apoplectic rage; his fits of uncontrolled temper were all too frequent. She had waited for Kurt to return, had sent him messages despite the old man's prohibition. But she had never spoken to Tradin again till he had appeared, unexpectedly, at the station in Kingville, had husked his promise to wait for her, and vanished before she could respond. That incident too, was repeated in her dreams, and then her sleep deepened to a dreamless torpor.

And she woke with a start. Bemused by her dreams and her sleep she could not for a moment tell the source of the welling tide of fear that seemed to sweep up and over her in that instant of waking. But fear lay on her breast like a leaden, oppressive hand, and the shadows on the papered ceiling at which she stared were dark shapes of brooding menace. She was on the old sofa in the parlor, Gram would scold. . . .

Memory seeped back, distorted, but full-panoplied with horror. Gram was dead. Milton was dead, they were in the same coffin and that coffin was in this room. Kurt. . . .

Kurt was bending over her, it was his hand that was heavy on her breast. Yellow lamplight, glancing at some odd angle across his face, made of it a shadowy *chiaroscuro* that was somehow demoniac. His lips were too full, creepingly sensuous; his nostrils pinched, quivering; tiny lights crawled wormlike in the abysmal depths of his eyes. Emma fought down fright that plugged speech, husked something. "Don't," she meant it to be. "Don't."

Tradin moved, and the girl came fully awake. It *must* have been a trick of light and shade, the appalling mask his face had been, for it was not like that any more. Contorted by emotion, though—that it was, and ashen with fatigue. But his hand *was* on her uncovered breast. "Don't," Emma repeated and pushed at it feebly. It fell away. Released, she sat up, became aware that he was kneeling beside her, that he was quivering. That his lips were moving, were dripping passion-slowed words.

"Em. Em darling. I couldn't help it. I love you so."

Weakly, she swayed toward him, toward his reaching arms, though deep within her a warning bell rang shrilly. With Milton so newly dead! She was mad, *mad*. Her eyes slid over Kurt's shoulder, across the room, appealing to the coffin where Milton lay for help against this madness that ran riot in her veins. Queerly it seemed to rock, to sway on its trestles.

Pale fingers came up out of the grim casket and gripped its edge. A torso jerked upright, rising grotesquely from its ebon depths and Milton's pallid, reproachful face turned toward her. His arm lifted—the arm of a dead man—and his long, bloodless hand clenched, opened, pointed at her in ghastly accusation!

"MILTON," she heard herself gasp, "Milton! I. . . ."

Kurt exploded to his feet, blotting the grisly sight from her. "You!" he screamed. "You!" and lunged toward the awakened dead, his great fist lifting, knotting in the lamplight. "Damn you!" That rocklike fist swept down. . . .

Some power outside herself hurled Emma from the sofa, catapulted her from its springs in a catlike leap to the enraged farmer's back. Her shriek was a feline mewl as she raked Tradin's face with the nails of her one hand and swiped at his descending arm with the other—swiped aside that crushing blow to make it land on wood instead of Milton's skull that it would have crushed.

Tradin was thrown against the coffin under the fury of her onslaught, toppled it. It crashed thunderously, wood split. Emma ripped nails again through flesh, gouged for eyes like the wild thing she had become. Kurt ducked forward, suddenly. She flew over his head, crashed among the splintered fragments of the casket. The jagged wood of the smashed coffin ripped her, but its cushions of funereal satin pillowed her fall. Her leg signaled excruciating pain, and she could not move it. She squirmed over to the stamping of feet, to the snarl of battling beasts.

A heaving mass reeled about the room, the two men locked in tearing, primeval combat. Two men—oh God! Kurt was a man, but the other—Milton. *What was he?*

His slender form was so frail, so weak, against the other's bulk. Ordinarily Tradin could split him in two, tear him apart with those great paws of his that had wrestled so long with the soil. Not now. Not that vibrant, terrible being who had returned from death. Now that creature who bit, and tore, and kicked, was an overpowering, black whirlwind that drove Kurt back. drove him back, across the floor. No human being could stand against that snarling, growling, squealing fury come back from the grave.

The whirlwind of combat struck the wall. Milton—whatever it was that Milton had become—swarmed all over Tradin. But the farmer, at bay, crouched and lashed out with his giant fists. Lashed and landed. Milton was thrown back, was staggered. Suddenly his figure was red with the tint of hell-fire, was wreathed in black smoke, and he hurtled in again, hurtled at the embattled rustic. Resistlessly the *revenant* drove Kurt along the wall as the long, fluttering shadows of battle were lurid-edged. Emma watching, was rigid with awed horror, with a fear that came from beyond earth. The jagged void of the broken window gaped behind Tradin; in the instant the girl realized that it had been his goal he hurled himself backward through it, was gone.

Milton screeched blasphemy, vanished. Emma was not sure, not quite sure, that he had gone through the window after his victim. But gruesome thumpings came from outside, were succeeded by sudden silence.

By silence that was broken by a strange crackling, here within, by an ominous hiss. Milton had vanished, but a red glare still danced in this parlor where horror had flared to unbelievable life, and edged billows of greasy, black smoke. The stench of burning was acrid in her nose, stung her throat. Good Lord! The place was ablaze! Sometime in the whirlwind, eerie battle the table had been overturned on which Kurt had set the lamp, and spilled oil on dried old wood fed flames like kindling.

Emma sprang to her feet, toppled as agony stabbed her thigh, crashed down to the floor. God! Oh God! Her leg was broken. She could not stand. Could not run to escape the flames!

The fire spread rapidly now, having gained strength while she watched the gruesome fight. The floor was a sea of wavering, leaping orange, and red, and curling, spitting blue. The door was cut off, by which she might have crawled to the foyer and out to safety. Rivulets of flame ran between her and the window. A curtain caught and flared.

Pungent smoke tore at her lungs with its black knives. Heat beat at her, stinging. Long fingers of flame reached out across the floor for her. She beat at them, beat them out with scorched, blistering hands.

But the forefront of the main blaze roared closer, ever closer. And she could not beat that back.

CHAPTER SIX

Descent into Hell

ALL across the side and the front of the room, the flames soared, incandescent, their glare blinding. The roar of the fire was a vast surf, the surge of heat from its blaze was a great wave overwhelming the helpless girl. A black pall of smoke eddied along the ceiling, billowed, billowed lower and lower to engulf her, to throttle her. Emma smelled burning hair —a viscous insect stung her scalp—she snatched at the ember—tore it from her head with a handful of her hair. She rolled away from the flames, agonizing to the grating of fractured bone surfaces one on the other—rolled against the furthest wall. Groveled there, mewling, as inescapable destruction crept nearer with cruel tongues.

Emma's skin crisped to the furnace blast beating on her doomed body. She writhed in the searing heat, as a worm will writhe in flame, and her arm flung over, thumped on the hot floor, thumped against something that clinked metallically. She glared at what she had touched, saw that it was the knife she had clutched out there when Kurt had saved her from a more merciful death, red-shining now, reflecting the blaze.

She snatched at the blade, seized it, clutching. The razor edge slashed her palm, reddended with her blood, but she did not feel its pain. It offered a better, more merciful death than the immolation inevitable now in seconds. She pulled the knife toward her, dropped it momentarily to gain a grip on its hilt, jerked the sharp point to her breast. Poised it an instant while she muttered a prayer, for the peace of her soul and of Milton's. Of Milton's that had been brought back to his dead body to save her from unpardonable sin. Then Emma's muscles tensed for the death stroke, and she shut her eyes to take it.

The knife came alive, jerked from her grip. Unbelievably there was someone in the room, bending over her. Someone! Oh God! Horror was bending over her, horror worse than the knife or the flame. A Thing bulky and formless, its grey orange-margined now by the luminance of the roaring blaze.

It had come for her, come to take her for its own hideous purpose, and it was not a being of this earth. No living thing could have come through that holocaust alive. . . . A lumping tendril slapped across her face, a hot crust on it broke, and wet viscidness squashed over her mouth, her nose and her eyes. She felt another tentacle seethe under her, felt herself lifted, as she writhed, feebly protestant, and her broken leg dangled to stab agony up her thigh, her flank. She was crushed into the noisome, viscid humidity of its foul mass. The stuff flowed over her, swallowed her.

The Thing was moving, was carrying her off. Uttermost terror shrieked in every cell of her anguished frame. Better the fire, oh God, better the fire than this! It was carrying her through the flame. She felt the vile stuff enveloping her grow hot to the fire, heard the sizzle of steam. She could not breathe—could not—

The matrix in which she was contained crawled, and somehow her mouth was free, so that air reached her lungs; dank, cold air freighted with corpse-smell. They were out of the fire then, incredibly out, and the Thing was lumbering with her to its lair. Somewhere in the mass a pulse beat, as if it had a heart. A heart that pounded with some strange excitement, pounded with a rhythm of grotesque life. The pud, pud in her ears was the muted beat of a drum of doom.

The ungainly heaving that told her her captor still moved ceased. She sensed that it had come to its journey's end, that it had brought her to its lurking place, was about to work its will with her. Fear ran icy in her blood stream, sapped all vitality from her battered body as with a sucking plop she came free of the Thing's foul substance and knew dimly that it had laid her down on some hard, unyielding surface. Only pain kept consciousness in her: the jabbing torture of her ruptured tibia; the agony of her lacerated, scorched flesh. The thick stuff still adhering blinded and deafened her. She lay unmoving where the Thing had laid her, waiting. Waiting for the ultimate horror.

And a tenuous hope trailed across the quivering blank of her beleagured brain. Not for herself. For Milton, for her husband who had died and yet was not dead. A hope that his reanimated body had lost the hideous mockery of life with which she had last seen it inflamed. That it was at rest, the body that had been so warm, so near, so dear to her . . . .

NOTHING was happening, nothing at at all. What was it waiting for, the

Thing that had relentlessly pursued her, harried her, that had come through flames to take her? The agony of suspense expanded like a black bubble, bursting her aching skull, till desperation seized her and she drove a fist across her eyes, wiping away the blinding mess.

Above her, redness glowed through a shimmering network interlaced by things twisted, grotesque, reptilian. Bastions lifted darkly about her to support that eerie roof. Where was she? In some black chapel of the damned? In some Luciferean cloister through whose pierced ceiling the reflection of hell's lurid fires flickered restlessly in their eternal dance? Wherever she was, the dull realization penetrated, whatever place this was, she was alone in it. That which had brought her here had departed, on some obscure, revolting errand of its own. She would stay here, it could be sure of that, she would stay here till it returned.

Stay here? Grim humor twisted Emma's dry, cracked lips. Not she. She couldn't walk with this poor shattered leg of hers that hurt so damnably; but she could crawl. On hands and one knee she could crawl. The Thing wouldn't find her here when it came.

Hurry! It may be coming back now, right now. *Hurry!* Turn over. Bite your lips against the screams that tear at your throat as pain runs like liquid fire through every quivering inch of you, and turn. So. That was the hardest part. Now start crawling. Lift yourself on your pushing-down arms, get your one good leg under you and a start. Never mind that other leg—it isn't any good to you. Leave it. Leave it to mock the Thing. *Hurry!* That far-off thud may be its gooey footfall as it returns. But make no noise. Be silent as the grave. Stifle those shrieks—they won't ease the pain and may warn the Thing that you are escaping it. Ohhhhh. That was a bad one! *Hurry!*

Something is dragging behind! Your other leg? Well, you haven't time to pull it off, let it drag. You haven't time, the grey horror will catch you if you stop for that. *Hurry!* Stop that whimpering—crying won't help you. Stop it. You've gone a yard now, a whole yard. Keep going. *Keep going!* how long?—Never mind how long it has taken you to crawl that yard, keep going. *Hurry!*

No, that isn't Gram lying there, ahead, grinning at you. It can't be Gram, she's dead? So are you dead? Don't fool yourself, you wish you were. You couldn't hurt so if you were dead. You wouldn't have to crawl through Hell if you were dead. But *hurry!*

Maybe Milton will be waiting for you when you *are* really dead. In Hell? Perhaps. Hell itself burned in his eyes when he looked at you before he lunged into the parlor and died. Stop thinking—and crawl. *Hurry!* You have forgotten why you were crawling, why you must hurry? Never mind, keep going. Don't turn aside. Don't turn to get past the dark, low, mound across whose end the red light flickers and makes you think it's Gram's skull-like face grinning at you. You've reached it now. Climb over it. Climb! Put your hand on it and push over. It's cold, clammy. It has the feel of cold, dead flesh! The brittle bones of its shoulder crunch under your weight and its hand, its dead hand, jerks up and slaps you stingingly across the face. . . .

It is Gram! Oh God! Oh dear God! It is Gram!

EMMA—the quivering thing that once was Emma in some far-off time before pain and horror conquered the world—screamed as she stared down into the skeleton mask that still was recognizable as Gram's face. Screamed again, and suddenly was silent. She was lifted on a scarified knee and shuddering arms whose hands rested on the frail brittle corpse of her grandmother and she was silent while her own body chattered in the grip of a gelid ague and the freezing shock cleared the fever-mists from her brain.

As reason came back to her she saw that the vermilion-fretted arch over her was a roof of foliage; that the black bastions were the boles of trees, silhouetted against a sky lurid with reflected flame; that Gram's cadaver, swathed in dark burial clothes, had been decently laid out on a pile of dead leaves.

She shook her head, dragged thought away from the racking pain that possessed her. However the old woman's body had gotten here, it had been treated with a curious respect oddly at variance with the ghoulishness of its being moved at all. This was a clearing in the wood, an opening floored by a great rock that had given sustenance to no seedling. Dimly she recalled it, knew she was not far from the Sprool mansion. The glare in the sky was from the conflagration that by now must have completely engulfed it. The road was only fifty feet down this slope before her. the old house was to the right and the village to the left.

Curious—while the whole vault of the sky was aflame it glowed more deeply, more virulently scarlet, to the left—in the direction of Ekwanok—and not from the quarter where the Sprool house was burning. Emma recalled the bonfire around which a mad dance had circled. But that had been completely hidden by Big Tom's shoulder—and now—

Dim, distant thrum of a speeding auto came to her ears, of Kurt's car, running up the road. Then he had escaped from Milton. was still hunting the Things. *The one that had taken her from the flames would be coming back for her!* Fear's livid hand squeezed her heart once more, and the ghastly need for hurry. She must get away from here, get away! But where?

Down to the road. That was her only hope. Down to the roadside to lie there and pray that Kurt would find her before the Thing did. Pray! What good would it do to pray? God would not hear her. Just lie there and—and hope—

By the time Emma reached the muddy ditch of the trail bisecting the doomed Valley of Ekwanok, she had touched the limit of endurance. The very limit. She lay in that ditch more dead than alive, and gave herself over to the waves of unbearable pain that were a moving tide in her twitching, shattered body.

Barely conscious, she lay, a blood-daubed, naked, shattered shape in the muck of the ditch, and knew that the arching heavens were aflame with lurid glow and the dark bulk of the mountains were monstrous blots against that bloody sky. Their coil was very tight, now, around the valley they had doomed, and the horror they had spawned in the long, brooding years was rampant now in the earth-fold between them.

A spark fluttered from the flames leaping, down there in the valley. Some wanton breeze took it, lifted it high and higher. So miscroscopic it was that the mountains did not notice it as it soared. But Emma saw it attain the black veil with which Satan had covered the valley, saw it burn a tiny hole in that veil, and go out, its task accomplished.

Prayer needs, Emma thought—if the wee stirring in that dim pulse to which her life had dwindled might be called thought—only the tiniest possible opening to get through to God. "Please, God," she prayed. "Help Milton and me. Please."

A smile brushed her poor, torn lips and, strangely enough, she sighed as if in contentment. Darkness beat against her brain. . . .

THE murmur of Kurt Tradin's car was louder, nearer. He was between her and the village, and was coming this way. Thus quickly had her prayer been answered! He was coming, he was coming—what was that curious growling mutter, behind the crescendoing roar of his approach?

No matter. Kurt was coming to save her—No, he couldn't be. He had last seen her in the blazing house, he must think her dead, burned. He wouldn't be looking for her, wouldn't see her in the ditch. She must get out in the road, where he couldn't miss her.

He might not see her in time, might run her over? That wouldn't be so bad. Milton was dead.

She should never had brought Milton here. The mountains had nothing against him, they hated only her. Only the blood of the Sprools.

Emma shut off thought that was madness, was scrabbling again, waking pain again as she pulled herself out of the ditch, out into the road. This was far enough, he would see her here. She couldn't get any farther.

The ground was vibrating now to the pound of his wheels. He was coming, coming fast. That strange mutter, like low thunder, was slightly louder, almost indefinably so. What could it be?

Trees along the roadside lightened, their green virulent. Kurt's healight was doing that, his emerald headlight. He'd be here in seconds now, in seconds. Agonizingly Emma struggled to prop herself up on an elbow, so that he would surely see her.

It was like green sunlight now, the glare of his light. There was a curve there, twenty feet down the road, and he was coming head on toward those trees, while here Emma was still cloaked by red-tinged darkness. "He'll have to slow down for the curve," she mumbled. "And he'll be more likely to see me." Excitement shook her. "He's slowing down now."

There was the hiss of skidding rubber, the squeal of tightening brakes. The green light wavered, did not sweep along the trees, and motor throb died away. God, oh God! he's stopping. He's turning—he's going back! "Kurt! *Kurt!*" Her cry, the scream she intended, was a rasping whisper. Her smoke-burned throat could manage no better. She was crawling, crawling in a paroxysm of terror lest he turn and leave her, dragging her injured leg after her. Her tortured progress was infinitely slow, but the light held steady. "KURT!"

Somehow she attained the bend in the road, whimpering, rounded it. Emerald blaze swallowed her. The car was ahead, only steps ahead. Emma fell flat, lifted the ton-weight of one arm, waved. "Kurt."

There was no response from the stalled car. He didn't see her, couldn't hear her. He would turn in a minute now and drive away.

Something threshed on the hillside above her. Emma rolled over to the sound. Something was prowling up there. Her scalp tightened, grisly fingers stroked her spine. The Thing was hunting her! No—it was hunting Kurt. She twisted back to stare at the grey auto, to try to warn him somehow. Realized that the vehicle was empty, that no one was behind its wheel—It must be Kurt on the hillside. He was not about to turn back. He had stopped to hunt the Thing on foot—perhaps had seen one. Of course he had, the one that had carried her off, coming back for her.

Good Kurt. Brave Kurt. He had come to her rescue. But, funny, but she was down here in the road, and he didn't know it. She was down here and she couldn't let him now. If she could get to the car and blow his born he would know she was there and come down to her.

If she could—Emma was off once more on her *Via Crucis,* her road of pain. Crawling through dust, scrambling through mud. Hitching her flaming torment along on jerking elbows, on plunging knee. Banging the torture of her broken leg against stones. Till at last the hot smell of grease was in her nostrils, the stench of burned gas, and she passed into the shadow of Kurt's car, high above her.

Followed, then, the fight to get a hand up to the running board, the struggle to lift the torso and rest her breasts on the metal ledge. The dismay at the discovery that the door was closed. The fear, the awful fear, that it was locked. The reaching of cramped, aching fingers to the handle and the agonized instant before a click told her that it was not.

The door swung open, thudding her to the ground. But it *was* open. Men have climbed Jungrau, Mont Blanc. So, too, did Emma Wayne climb into that auto. Then she lay gasping, quivering on the smeared floorboards.

All she must do now was get up to the seat so that she might reach the horn-button. She rolled, stretched an arm to the leathery cushion.

And her hand touched clammy wetness, sank into the humid, doughy stuff of which the grey, grisly Things were formed!

Here, in this car, in Kurt's car, a Thing hulked on its seat, on its driver's seat. It moved, dropped on her, enveloped her with its shuddersome foulness.

All her fighting, all her terrific impossible struggle, had availed only to bring her straight into the clutches of that which she fled!

CHAPTER SEVEN

Mad—Mad—Mad!

THE obscene, semi-solid mass enveloped her with its clammy, chill foulness, folded about her like an ineffably noisome coverlet. It clamped down on her —and gradually Emma was aware that it was lax, queerly flaccid; that, holding her captive, it was oddly lifeless, unmoving.

Nor, and this too was utterly strange, did it crush her with ponderous bulk, as had the one Kurt had killed on the hillside above the mansion. Somewhere the muted crow of a cock beat to her. Was the Thing, then, indeed compounded of some effluvium of the dreadful night? Was it losing its substance with approaching dawn? Would it vanish entirely with the day?

Would it—an agonized cry sounded in Emma's buzzing ears, the thud of hurrying footfalls. The car shook to the spring of someone to its running-board, and the lewd blanket lifted from her. "Emmy," Kurt Tradin lipped. "Sweetheart."

His face was contorted, his eyes black flame. One cheek was pulped, and oozing droplets of gore. He was coatless and his shirt half-torn from a shoulder, hanging in tatters, his arm a mass of clotted blood, and from it the limp Thing dangled. His great biceps crawled as he threw it aside —*threw it!* Incredibly the grey mass flopped to the seat-back, hung like a cast-aside garment.

Emma's glance stabbed to it, and suddenly she knew! Hysteric laughter burbled in her throat, bubbled from between her torn lips. Kurt's face blazed with a queer light, his arms stabbed to her. "At last! At last, sweetheart, ye're like me. Come, darlin'. Come to me."

Oh God! He was mad, stark mad! That which he had cast aside was a coverall, hooded and plastered thick with putty!

He was the Thing, the grey and grisly Thing that prowled the night and killed. He it was who had plunged through the flames and snatched her from them. The thick wet putty of his grotesque masquerade had protected him from their heat and warded the blaze from her. He —His shaking arms slid under her, lifted her, pressed her against his hairy, heaving chest. His thick hot lips slobbered kisses on her face. She beat at him feebly—feebly—

"My dear," he was mumbling. "My dearest dear. Ye are like me, ye are insane. I can see it in yer eyes. At last ye are insane and fit to be my mate." His head went back, he was roaring with laughter, laughter somehow frenzied, somehow mad as the mad night. "The old fool said," he spluttered, "thet I was crazy and not for you. He wuz right, but he ain't right no longer. I've made you crazy as me." He crushed her against his sweaty breast. "Hey, Jeremiah," he bellowed, and the weird echo of his shout echoed hollowly from the everlasting hills. "Jeremiah Sproo! Look! She's mine now. She's crazy and she's mine. Everybody's crazy, ye white-bearded fool, everybody in th' valley. Look at them. Jeremiah Sprool. Damn you," his crazed shouting shrilled. "I'm not the only crazy one now! Everybody's mad!"

"Mad," the fire-reddened slope of Big Tom caught the word and flung it back at her. *"Mad,"* echo delayed came from the hills across the valley. "MAD!" the crazed universe shouted at her. And "mad" whispered the writhing worms in Emma's own skull. Of course she was mad, and all the insane happenings of the night only the ravings of her own delirium, of her own crazed brain that shrieked the horror to her. Mad, *mad*, MAD.

It seemed to—or was it real?—that redder, more lurid flame glared about her, that the far-off mutter had crescendoed to a wild, imminent clamor. She felt Kurt tense, swing about. She saw—or thought she saw—a horde of fiends, manform and horrible, flooding down the road toward them—brandishing flaming torches that were chair-legs, and riven table-tops, and the flaring palings of once neat fences. It seemed that Kurt snarled bestially, that a fierce, animal howling came from the onrushing pack as they caught sight of him.

REAL! It couldn't be real, this outpouring of demons from a living Hell! It couldn't be real—that Milton —her Milton—loped ahead of the howling pack, an up-ended broom flaunting fire like an orange banner above his head! It wasn't true that Kurt was screaming obscene maledictions at the onrushing, monstrous throng and that they were responding with mewling catcalls, with squeals like nothing ever heard on earth, with maniacal howls. That she herself had joined the blasphemous choir with thin sounds formed in her throat without mental command.

"Look," Kurt bellowed—or in her waking nightmare she heard him bellow. "Look, Jeremiah! Look at them." His hollow, shouting voice broke into ear-piercing, cackling laughter. "Look, Jeremiah Sprool." And then suddenly he whirled to the roadside, plunged into the brush carrying her.

"Emma!" the apparition that was like Milton screamed, "I'm coming. Hold him —I'm coming."

"Mil—" Kurt's stinking hand clamped over her mouth. She fanged it, tasted salt taste of his blood, but it tightened, stifling her answer. She writhed—agony darted through her, numbing.

"Hush," Kurt mumbled. "Hush darling. We've mustn't let them catch us. They'll spoil everything. Jeremiah sent them after us, and if they catch us they'll tear us apart. Hush."

Close-growing trees closed about them, bushes lashed at them. Red shadows danced through thick foliage, and the rush of the following horde was like thunder in the transmogrified forest. Kurt loped through the woods like a thing possessed, clutching Emma to his heaving breast, and the pursuers gibbered and howled behind them. The jungle-horde bayed down the wind after the fleeing man and his captive, and he was silent now as the grave, slipping through vermilion-flickering, arboreal aisles whose flanking trees tossed black branches to a lurid sky.

"Emma!" Milton howled. "Emma, where are you?"

The girl jerked her head, pain seared her neck-muscles. Kurt's palm slipped momentarily from her lips and she screamed, "Here, Mil—" Her captor snarled as he shut-off her scream, twisted to a new direction in his mad flight.

"Hush, darling," he muttered. "Hush." His snicker rippled her spine with loathing. "Yer Milton is dead. That isn't yer Milton but a devil in his body. I know! I killed yer Milton and put him in his coffin."

Oh God! Oh merciless God! Milton was dead and she a captive of his slayer. Feebly Emma squirmed, reckless of torture, and beat weakly at his breast that was steel-armored with muscle. "Let me down, you fiend. Let me down."

Tradin's tireless stride ploughed through undergrowth on which torchlight danced now more dimly. "Soon dear," he gibbered. "Soon. I've got a bed prepared for us, a nice bed of leaves in th' woods, an' Elmer's akeepin' it warm fer us. Elmer. . . ." Suddenly his voice broke into a heart-rending sob, he shook her in his great arms, savagely. "You made me kill him. You made me kill Elmer. Ef I didn't love ye so much. . . ."

"Ohhh, don't! Who . . . who is Elmer?"

"Huh!" The madman's twisted, grotesque head threw back, and peals of shrill, maniacal laughter shuddered through the red-edged trees. "Do ye hear, Jeremiah? She doesn't know about Elmer. She never knew about him. But ye did. Ye knew about my poor, crazy brother locked in my house. Hidden thar. But did ye see him tonight? Did ye see how he helped me make her mad? Did ye see how he killed her horse? An' all week, did ye see how he prowled the woods dressed in th' putty suit I made fer him an' scared whut brains they had out o' them others in the village, whilst I pertended ter hunt him an' we waited fer her ter come? Ye said I was like him, Jeremiah Sprool! Well, I am like him, an' so is she. So is yer granddaughter, Jeremiah, like him an' like me. Crazy. Ravin' crazy. A Sprool fit at last ter be th' mad Tradin's bride!"

THE whole, horrible affair was clear now to Emma's tortured brain. Love for her had made Kurt mad. Love for her and Granddad's gibe. Tortured by knowledge of the maniac concealed in his home, the man had brooded till his mind had snapped when Gram had died. That was why he had written her, why he had dug up Faith Sprool and returned her coffin to the old parlor, why he had costumed his mad brother as foulness incarnate and set him on to harry her. *To drive her crazy, too, so that he might mate with her.*

And then he had learned that she already was married, had set out to intercept Milton on the highway, to kill him there. She had spoiled that scheme, but he had returned to the Sprool house and —Oh God!—had succeeded! "I killed him. I killed yer Milton," the doomful words rang in her ears.

Mad and a killer! From his own mouth had come the confession. And she was to be his bride! Wild laughter clawed in turn at Emma's throat. "Milton," she groaned. "Dead or alive, Milton. Save me."

The sound of the pursuers was a far-off murmur in the darkening forest. Kurt chuckled, started to circle. "They can't find us now, my love. They'll never find us now."

This wasn't happening. Reason fled from her and she was again the whimpering, terrified toy of a grisly nightmare. God wouldn't let it happen. Oh please, God. I'm crazy. Please let me be crazy and just imagining this. . . .

"Drop her, you dog!" A dark figure suddenly loomed out of the forest. "Drop her!"

Milton! It was Milton, or the demon in his body! A gleam from somewhere showed Emma the pallid oval of his face, his scarred mouth twisted in wrath, his virulent eyes.

Tradin growled, jerked aside, dodging Milton's impetuous rush, his flailing fist. Stumbled and fell to his knees, and Emma crashed from his arms to the ground as Kurt leaped to his feet. Agony twisted the girl's throat to a scream of pain and horror as the two figures were motionless for a long minute, crouching and splotched with alternated black and lurid red till all resemblance to anything human was gone. "Yer dead," Tradin yammered. "Yer dead!"

"Got you!" Milt's voice was a growl, an animal rumble. "Got you at last. Are you going to take it from me or from your neighbors, Tradin? They know now what you are. They saw the grey Thing in your car when I yelled. and they're after you. They're hunting you down, *killer!*"

"Ye'd never have cotched me, ye ner th' rest o' yer pack, ef'n I hadn't stopped fer my wife."

"*Your* wife!" Milton leaped, and Tradin lunged to meet him. The two phantasms closed in snarling, yapping, grunting combat. Emma heard the smack of a fist, saw a hooked thumb gouging an eye. The black whirlwind of battle was suddenly detailless in its hideous, dark swirling as vertigo seized her brain, and nausea retched at her stomach.

Someone screamed. A scream shrilled from the maelstrom pregnant with unutterable pain. The whirling mass split and one of the combatants sprawled headlong. It writhed, screaming, on the ground. Milton! Oh God! It was Milton. Kurt leaped to the kill. His shod foot lifted to grind down on Milton's contorted face.

Emma flung out a frantic hand, gripped an ankle, jerked. Tradin, off-balance, staggered. Milton rolled, threw a hand upward, seized a low branch and pulled himself erect. Hung to the bough, reeling and helpless, as the madman heeled Emma's side and jerked away, crouching to leap again—snarling.

Lurid light burst through screening tree trunks and the as yet distant howls of the gibbering pack surged nearer. Tradin froze. His lean visage turned to the sound. Fear flared into his reddened eyes. Again he snarled, lipping his teeth; whirled; and was gone in the shadows.

The instant's respite straightened Milton. He shouted something, plunged after the escaping madman. Their flight and pursuit threshed through the woods, the tumult dying.

The ground heaved under Emma and she was sliding down a long black *glissade* into billowing murk like storm-clouds at the bottom of an abyss. A screech of awful agony, distant but undulled, held her for an instant, then the rolling clouds took her.

FOR a timeless period she was free from pain. But even as she floated in the heart of that dark, warm blackness grief was a leaden lump in her bosom, and green-glowing worms crawled in her racked and aching brain.

Something was pulling her out of the cloud. A voice. A choked and inarticulate voice. Someone's arms were around her and her tortured head was pillowed on someone's shoulder.

"Sweetheart."

Terror gripped her again, and she cried out. "Let me go," she sobbed. "Let me go Kurt," and flailed at hard flesh with futile hands, like fluttering wings of a wounded bird, while her eyelids squeezed tight against the madness twisted features she dreaded to see.

"Easy, Emma. Easy does it." Gentle hands held her wrists. "It's Milton, darling. Milton."

It was Milton! She sobbed against her lips, and his dear arms stilled the shuddering of her torn and twisted body. "You're hurt, Em-girl, you're terribly hurt."

"Yes. But—Oh Milton, are you alive?"

"Yes. I'm alive. I must have a thick head. He sloughed me hard enough to break it in that old parlor where he lay for me, but I only passed out. But I had a damn bad moment when I woke up in that coffin, and hearing him make love to you didn't help my feelings any. Guess I went nuts—I thought—Hell—Your trying to keep me out of that room, even when we heard someone moving around in there, made me think that you knew he was there, that you were going to sneak in there to meet him when you got a chance."

"Was that why you looked at me like that, with hate in your eyes? Oh Milt—"

"That was why. I'm a dog, dear. Forgive me?"

"Of course. Milt—He got away?"

"No." There was grimness in her husband's voice. "No. He didn't get away. He's—" His head pulled around and he was staring into the darkness whence he had come as a far-off howling made the night hideous. "God! The villagers must have found him and . . ."

A last poignant shudder shook Emma as the distant ululation rose to a wild, horrible chorus. Milton's arms constricted more tightly about her. "My poor dear. My poor, poor girl."

"Milt," she managed to say. "Take me away from here. Your car is up on the hill. Carry me to it and take me as far away from here as you can."

* * *

Dawn found them on Big Tom Highway, Milton's car eating the miles away from horror and the valley where madmen still roamed and red fire still raged. "Milt," Emma sighed. "What's to become of us? We haven't a cent. How are we going to live?"

A smile broke the grimness of Milton's face. "We'll live, dear. I have a job. Johnson liked the way I straightened out his mess so well that he's put me in charge of his accounting department. Fifty a week, dear, and a chance to buy stock in the concern. I was coming only to take you back to New York."

Ahead, a finger of the sun broke through the gloomy trees, and the couple drove into its roseate glow that somehow bathed them, as they chugged through it, with a benediction and a promise.

THE END

IN THE NEXT ISSUE

Another Blood-Chilling, Spine-Tingling Tale by ARTHUR LEO ZAGAT!

Out December 26th!

SOULS ENSLAVED

By Henry Treat Sperry

(Author of "Hands Beyond the Grave.")

Three bodies Barton Mowrey had—and the last of them knew naught of the peace of death, but only eternal agony in that world of howling winds and screaming, tortured souls! . . .

HOW shall I begin my tale? How can I tell it, when to write these words must create anew for me the horrors I have lived? Yet I must tell it, for to millions of suffering souls on this earth my message can bring hope of salvation. I alone can speak; and because I have lived these things, you must believe me . . . .

It began a long time back, with my interest in the life after death. My interest, that became at last a powerful preoccupation of which I could not rid myself. After that, came my shuddering fear of ectoplasm . . . .

If you have ever attended a genuine seance, then you know a little of ectoplasm, that weird manifestation for which no scientist has yet found an explanation. You can picture again that dim-lit room, the tense faces circled about the medium as she goes into her trance. Then the ectoplasm appears—a hideous, gelatinous substance that proceeds from the ears and eyes and mouth of the medium. Like a thing alive it projects its snakelike tentacles about the room, leaving behind it weird proof of its existence, perhaps the fingerprints of one long dead. It returns then to the place from whence it sprang. Yet the substance has never, upon autopsy, been discovered in the body of a medium!

If you have seen this, then perhaps you have felt a little of the terror and the nameless fear which always seized me in the presence of this phenomenon. I could never find reason for the fear, could never explain it logically; but because the thing called ectoplasm terrified me, it fascinated me as well. The study of things psychic became my hobby. And in time I came to know, as surely as if it were my destiny, that I must bring all the power of my scientific mind to bear upon this one problem. Somehow I must succeed in subjecting ectoplasm to laboratory analysis!

I thought I knew the dangers inherent in such a task. I knew that scientists had thus far refrained as much in fear of the ultimate effect upon the medium as for any other reason—that they had hesitated to sever a specimen of this living organism from a medium's body, knowing that it might result in death or hideous torture to the subject. Yet I knew not one-tenth of the horrors in store for me—my just recompense for meddling in matters that are not of this earth.

It was at the salon of Madame Fierbois that I first saw the phenomenon, and I went there again and again. She was a kindly, charming Frenchwoman, a truly honest medium, who exercised her powers only in the sincere hope that they might benefit humanity. I came to know her well; and it was she in the end who asked to serve as the subject for the experiment which had become my ruling passion. I demurred; but she was insistent, and at last the day was set.

That same week I met Jeanne Fierbois, the medium's daughter, who had just returned from a convent school in Europe—and thus the two threads of my life were interwoven. She was a fragile, fairy-like creature, as unreal as the life about her. I can truthfully say that the moment she entered the room my heart stopped beating. I had never beheld a more exquisite creature; in that moment I felt her delicate fingers entwined forever around my heart.

From that day I was constantly at Madame Fierbois' home. I loved Jeanne madly. In time I came to feel that she returned, in some measure, my love.

There was but one dark shadow to mar my happiness—the man Aubrey DeJonge. Jeanne had met him on her voyage home, and now he was a constant visitor. He was a strange, dark-haired fellow—obviously a foreigner, though he associated himself with no country—in fact, he seemed to have no past and no birthplace.

DeJonge, too, appeared interested in psychic matters. He discussed them at length with Madame Fierbois, and seemed to know whereof he spoke. But what maddened me was his interest in Jeanne. When I came hoping for a moment with her, I found him always present. Worst of all, I saw that his gracious ways were slowly winning her affection—winning her from me . . . .

He loved Jeanne as much as I—that I could not doubt. But his interest in things psychic, in Madame Fierbois' ability to create ectoplasm, I felt to be affected. It was but a ruse, I thought, to ingratiate himself with Madame Fierbois, to bring himself closer to Jeanne.

I could not know that his interest masked something far more sinister. Nor could I know that my psychic meddling was to bring about my own horrible death.

ON THE day set for the experiment which was to realize my ambition, I could hardly contain myself for my excitement. Excitement—and fear. There were five of us present at Madame Fierbois' salon—the medium, Jeanne, myself and DeJonge, who had come at Jeanne's request, bringing with him a strange lad in his teens who, he explained, was also a medium and much interested in the experiment. DeJonge smiled condescendingly as I rushed nervously about, preparing my instruments.

Then Madame Fierbois slowly entered the trance state. I waited, breathless. After another ten minutes, the ectoplasm began to appear from her eyes and nose and mouth.

I think I stood, frozen, unable to move, for minutes. My first sight of the weird white flow seemed to fill me with a dread and a horror greater than I had ever before known in its presence. I could not force myself to do my task.

Yet at last, somehow, I managed to go forward with my scalpel. I cut off a small segment of the ectoplasm. I dropped it into a test-tube which I had ready, and which I carefully sealed.

I turned then to an examination of Madame Fierbois. She was breathing easily. The remaining ectoplasm had disappeared at my excision, but no blood had flowed. We were all confident that she would soon come out of her trance, with no untoward effects whatsoever from the slight operation.

When I was assured that this was so, I could wait no longer. With my specimen, I hurried from the house. I did not seek to fathom DeJonge's enigmatic smile; I must reach my laboratory and complete my experiment . . . .

I was there ten minutes later. Everything had been arranged in advance, and quickly, now, I set in place the slide bearing my specimen, and adjusted the microscope. With a sharp intake of breath, I bent to look . . . .

But at that moment, a sound jangled through the stillness of the laboratory. It was the telephone on my desk. I whirled, startled.

Ordinarily in such a moment I would have ignored all sound. Yet now I did not. For to my over-tense nerves, that simple ringing of the bell was as the clap of doom.

All thought of my experiment for the moment gone, I rushed across the room, picked up the receiver.

It was Jeanne. I could tell even as she spoke that she was sobbing—sobbing hysterically.

"Barton!" she cried. "Mother is dead!" Then the accusing words tumbled out in torrents: "You killed her, Barton Mowrey!"

For a moment I was too stunned to answer. Somehow I must have known that this would happen—for it was not really surprise that I felt, but only a stunned helplessness.

"Good God," I said at last. "I'll be over at once. Perhaps—"

Her cold words cut in before I had finished. "It isn't necessary. Aubrey is here. He'll—attend to everything. He—*he* is not a murderer." I heard a click as she broke the connection.

Wearily I replaced the receiver on the hook and stood staring about me. Then, abruptly, I remembered. My specimen! The loss of that had killed Madame Fierbois. Her sacrifice must not be in vain. Now, more than ever, I must learn its weird secret.

I rushed back to the microscope. I bent over it and looked down . . . .

I never really saw what the specimen looked like. For in that instant a flash of blinding light seemed to strike at the base of my brain. The whole world and the mystic truth behind it burst before my eyes, was whirling in my head. In that moment before I ceased to know, I understood without the words to tell it all the reason for my fear of ectoplasm. . .

Time was no more; it seemed but an instant later that awareness returned to me. It was a strange awareness too; I seemed to be light as air, to float in infinite space with all sounds a humming nothingness about me.

I looked around. I was still in my laboratory—felt as if I were above the level to which my height should take me. I looked down. . . .

What I saw seemed to send over me a physical chill; yet it could not have been physical. For below me, sprawled on the floor of the laboratory, was the mass that had been my body! I was dead . . . .

WHAT happened to me from that moment on cannot be accurately told in words, for no words of the human language can express the eerie quality of life after the soul has been freed from the body. I saw without eyes; I felt without the body to mirror my feelings; I heard and yet I did not hear, for I had no ears with which to receive the waves of sound. Yet since there is no other way, the pitiable words we know must suffice to tell the agonies of that moment and of those which followed.

For a time I hovered over my body, sick with horror. I did not feel that my time had come, and I wanted very much to live. Without knowing why, I felt that some dread human agency had been acting against me, that I *must* live again to fight that agency. Frantically I tried to reënter my body, thinking that I might in some way stir it back to life. But always I came upon a blank, impassable wall the nature of which I could not fathom.

Then, breaking in upon the fearful silence of my thoughts, there came the sound of footsteps. They were outside the room, dashing up the steps. Now they were at the door. Someone pounded wildly on it.

When there was no answer, a voice cried out to me. It was Jeanne—come to face me with her accusations!

Good God! I thought. She must not see me there! I must find some way to stop her, to bar the door. With all the force of my will I tried then to give myself being, to endow myself with some physical power, however faint.

But all my strivings were of no more avail than a wisp of wind on a mountaintop. I was less even than the faintest breeze.

The door flung open. Jeanne, her dark eyes bright with sorrow, burst into the room. And just behind her, with measured certain tread, walked Aubrey DeJonge.

At sight of my body lying on the floor, Jeanne started backward, clapped her hands to her mouth in horror. For an instant she stood thus, stock-still. Then she rushed forward, bent over my body. She put her arms around it; and with tears streaming down her pale cheeks, she kissed it again and again.

New happiness swept over me as I realized that it was I, not DeJonge, whom she truly loved. For a moment I forgot that her love had come too late—that I was dead, beyond all mortal love. . .!

DeJonge came forward slowly, a half smile upon his thin lips. He bent down, pushed Jeanne a little away—rather rudely, it seemed to me. He examined the body carefully.

"Yes," he said as he rose—and now I knew there was a note of triumph in his voice. "He is quite dead. Suicide, without a doubt. He couldn't stand the responsibility of your mother's death. Come . . ." He took one of Jeanne's hands. "This is a matter for the police. There is no need to involve ourselves. We'll leave him as we found him . . . ."

Anger flamed in Jeanne's eyes at his words. She drew her hand sharply away. "Leave him?" she cried. "At such a time? Never!" She clung to me fiercely.

There was more than anger in DeJonge's eyes then; there was glittering menace and malevolence such as I had never seen before. "So . . ." he said. "You love him still . . . ."

"I love him!" Jeanne cried. "I have always loved him—I know that now."

"And you do not love me?"

There was no slightest tinge of doubt in Jeanne's voice as she answered: "No!"

Even in death, the stark hatred that flared in DeJonge's eyes at her answer horrified me. "In that case," he said, "we shall remain here as you wish. For if you do not love me, I have other uses for you . . . ."

Jeanne started back from him at his words. "What do you mean?" she cried. "I hate you! Go away and leave me here—with Barton . . . ."

DeJonge stepped over to the door, locked it, and placed the key in his pocket. Then he turned about and walked slowly toward Jeanne.

"You do not understand," he said coolly. "You see, *I* killed your friend the good Doctor Mowrey. I also killed your mother. I need not explain just how . . . It is enough to tell you that because I killed them as I did, their souls are doomed to wander lost through all eternity. Now I know that I can do the same to others—and because of that I can possess the world!"

Slowly as he spoke he moved toward her, and slowly Jeanne moved away in terror. Good God! Was the man mad? And yet that was no light of madness in his eyes . . . .

"So you, my lovely Jeanne," he said, "since you do not love me—shall serve as my next experiment. And when I have done with your soul, who knows—perhaps I can find uses for your lovely body . . .!"

Jeanne screamed, backed further away. But DeJonge only laughed.

"Cry out if you wish," he said. "You see, we have an excellent laboratory for our—experiment. The doctor very kindly saw to it that the walls were soundproofed. There are no windows. No cry that you make will be heard in the streets below. . . ." He laughed again.

Jeanne had reached the further corner of the room in her retreat. She too had looked into DeJonge's eyes—and terror was upon her. The blood had left her face; her eyes were wide with fear. Yet she bore up gamely. Knowing that she could retreat no further, she seized a tiny scalpel from the nearby table and held it firmly before her—determined to keep up the futile struggle to the end.

I cried out madly—and my cry was a whisper lost in the depths of space. Frantically my bodiless soul swooped down upon DeJonge, tried as it would have in life to fight with him, to throttle him, to stop his sure advance. But he was not even aware of my presence. He moved forward, smiling . . . .

I rushed back to my cooling body. I summoned all the struggling power of my horror-stricken soul to fight my way back into it. I *must* get back to it—I *must* come back to life! I knew not what fearful fate it was that menaced my beloved, yet I knew that death could be as nothing in comparison. Her soul—lost through all eternity! . . .

But as before my struggles were futile. Yet there must be some way that still escaped my thought. And even as I struggled I felt myself in the grip of a power stronger than myself. I felt my soul being drawn slowly but irresistibly away from the girl I loved. In her moment of greatest need I moved, struggling, away toward darkness, toward a timeless, whirling space. This truly must be death.

I looked back once before blackness swept over me. DeJonge held Jeanne's wrists in his lean dark hands. He had twisted the scalpel, her last defense, from her hand. Slowly he drew her toward him, stilling her struggles.

My dreams will never be free from the memory of the stark terror and fear of the hideous unknown that I saw then on Jeanne's face.

OUT of nowhere, the wind came to howl mournfully, and returned to nothingness. I could see nothing, feel nothing in the blackness, yet I knew that all about me was bleak, hard barrenness. And there dinned upon my soul weird shrieks, howling, cries that were foul blasphemies. And still I rushed onward, impelled by an unknown force, as if I were an integral part of this dark river.

I was on the barren plain of timeless space, alone with the howling of the wind and the shrieks of the damned in pain!

Yet even now I sensed a lessened pressure on me, a gradual slowing of my onward movement. The howl of the wind was dying, had fallen to mere whisperings. The cries of the damned swept away into silence. I stopped, floated aimlessly about. Now I was truly alone . . .

But the darkness seemed almost at once to lose its intensity. Then I sensed another presence near me. I could not see it, and I think it had no form; yet I knew at once, with a rush of joy and hope, that it was the spirit of the kindly Madame Fierbois, Jeanne's mother! At least I was no longer alone in space; perhaps she could help me, help Jeanne . . . .

Then we were speaking to one another. Speaking is not the term, for we voiced no words; yet only by words can I hope to convey, and then but poorly, the meaning of the things which Madame Fierbois communicated to me.

"I have come back from far beyond this place to help you," she said, "because I know you are not ready for death—and because I know the fearful fate in store for Jeanne. You only can possibly save her, for no living person can reach her in time . . . ."

I tried to tell her that both she and I had been condemned to the same fate as Jeanne: that even now Jeanne was struggling to save her very soul and that we must hurry back. But she seemed already to know all these things.

"For us," she said, "there is no need to hurry—for to us there is no time. We shall be able to reach Jeanne quickly enough, though I fear we cannot save her. We must try—but first you must know these things that I know. Had you not died before your time, you would at once have known them . . . .

"Yes," she said, "Aubrey DeJonge, while still alive, has learned the secret of the second body—of ectoplasm! And he has learned more. With the aid of the boy medium who is in his power, he has succeeded in robbing us of our ectoplasm. That killed us—not your experiment. He chose me because he knew me to be peculiarly susceptible when in the trance state—you because he hated you. But he knows now that he can do the same to others. He can thus attack the world—enslave humanity with the threat of the fearful fate in store for them—of their death at his command, and worse. And this is what he means to do . . . ."

She explained to me, then, that all humans have three bodies—the first, the material body that we know in life; the second, or transitional body by which the soul, after death, makes its way to the life beyond; and the third, which is the soul.

"The second body," she told me, "is composed of what we call ectoplasm. It leaves the body after death—though only in the case of mediums in the trance state is it ever discernible. Only by means of it can the soul enter or leave the material body.

"For me this is not true, for I was a medium. I had friends beyond, was always close to the dead; I can still pass through to the true Beyond. But to other humans it spells unnamable horror. For them the loss of the transitional body at the instant of death means eternal agony!

"Because you died thus, Barton Mowrey, unless you can return to life you are forever lost! You will stay for all eternity in this fearful darkness. You can never go beyond this howling black nothingness!

"Jeanne will be lost here too—yet you can never meet. A million others will be alone forever in the darkness. The threat of this fate hangs over all humanity in DeJonge's strange power . . . ."

I cried out to her in shuddering horror at the thought. Must we not then hurry to save Jeanne? Was there even now any hope that I might leave this fearful place and live again? . . .

"I think there is hope," she said. "But you must do each thing I tell you to do. Come, we shall go together . . . ."

OUT of the night we came, swifter than light, leaving that fearful nothingness behind us. We were in my laboratory once again.

Jeanne's struggles had ceased. Her clothes half torn from her young body, she lay, bound and helpless, on a table. Above her bent DeJonge, a fiendish light in his eyes as he anointed her head and breasts with the devil's brew which would further his designs. Beside him sat the boy, his medium, summoned there for his devilish work. My useless body still lay upon the floor; none save these three, it seemed, yet knew that I had died.

I knew now, without knowing how I knew, just what DeJonge would do to Jeanne—just what his methods, compound of sorcery and psychic science, were. This anointing oil he used—a little of which he had managed to spill upon Madame Fierbois and myself without our knowledge—had the strange effect of stilling for a moment the functions of the body as if in death. Soul and ectoplasm then would leave the body—but at the moment of their leaving DeJonge would act. In that instant when the ties that bound soul and ectoplasm were weakened, he would direct the second body of the boy medium to seize upon the ectoplasm of the one attacked, severing it from the soul and uniting it with DeJonge's own!

And with Jeanne he would do more than this. With her second body imprisoned and her soul left to wander in blackness, he would make use of her material body as he wished! Through the power of her ectoplasm which he had seized, and by a swift counter-application to minimize the effect of the anointing oil, he meant to bring her body back to life! The soulless body of the whitefaced girl who lay there helpless would be his slave to do with as he desired.

Already DeJonge's plans were nearing completion. The boy was in a trance, and as I watched, the loathsome ectoplasm began to pour from his eyes and mouth. DeJonge touched this, then began to speak. He spoke in Latin, calling on the evil shades of the outer air for aid in what he meant to do. And I knew that the end of that exhortation would spell a dread eternity of horror for the girl I loved!

If a bodiless soul can go mad, then I was in that moment a raving madman. Always Madame Fierbois told me the things I must do, yet it was as if she directed me without my knowledge, so mad was I with the lust to kill the body and the soul of Aubrey DeJonge.

To gain the first shred of material existence, I must identify my soul with the ectoplasm of the boy—I must gain it over the desires of his own soul, which controlled his second body! I swooped down, like the madman I was, to do so. Yet even in death my soul recoiled from the horrible substance. I felt myself being driven away . . . .

But Jeanne's terrified face was still before me—the fate in store for her a burning thing in my memory. I summoned all my will-power. Shuddering, I forced my soul into the hideous mass. And I knew again, dimly, the feel of living as I had not when my soul roamed alone.

Only now could this have been accomplished. Only when the boy was in a trance, his second body pouring forth and the ties that bound soul and body weakened, could I have found this haven for my soul. Yet the struggle was not done.

His soul, weakened though it was, still battled against me. It fought as one when the last hope is gone—yet it fought.

I mustered all my strength and courage. I tried to feel *alive*—to force it to submission by the very fact that I had being again and would not be put aside.

But it was Madame Fierbois who won for me. Somehow, in that moment her soul seemed to convince the soul of the boy that I was no enemy despite my fierce struggle—that its true enemy was Aubrey DeJonge, my real antagonist. It realized in time, as the boy could not have realized when conscious, that I sought its aid and not its enmity.

With that knowledge the boy's soul lay dormant. It could not assist me, but its acquiescence was enough. I knew now that I controlled the boy's ectoplasm as if it were my own . . . .

Abruptly then, I rushed upon DeJonge. At first I fought him as if this second body were the first. I wrapped the ectoplasm about him. I saw stark horror in his eyes as I sought to throttle him with the snakelike tentacles.

Yet even then he seemed to be breaking free, and I knew this way would not suffice. To save Jeanne—I realized now—*I must get at the soul of the man.* . . .

Thinking this, I caused the ectoplasm to enter DeJonge's body. At a word of direction from Madame Fierbois, I was able to find and come in contact with his own second body.

There was a blinding flash about me. Abruptly I knew that the ectoplasm of the boy was leaving me to return to its rightful owner. And I had entered DeJonge's ectoplasm, identified myself with it. Or rather I, who had been robbed of my second body, was finding it in DeJonge, confined in his own. It was that which I had entered. And having entered it, I began the struggle with the soul of DeJonge for the right to live!

Words alone cannot suffice to tell of that fearful struggle. All about me was blackness; yet in the evil thing I faced I saw stark terror mirrored as I swooped to the attack.

Before the fierceness of my first onrush, that other soul seemed to strive to vanish, withdraw into some dark nothingness of its own. But I followed, sought it out.

I forced it, calling on the dark powers of hell for aid, to come forth to battle. And I saw now that it was no longer the soul of Aubrey DeJonge, but burning hate itself, and all the evil of the world since time began, that fought with me. And now it was conquering me!

Frantically I struggled. My soul too, seemed almost to lose identity, to become cold fear and horror itself. Slowly I was slipping, was being forced from my second body. Slowly I felt myself moving backward—backward into that bleak waste of howling winds and damned souls from which I had but now returned.

I called on Madame Fierbois and her

friends in the Beyond for help. I called on God Himself to save my soul. Yet still I went backward, and the thousand burning eyes of hate and evil were all about me, enveloping me.

But my cry had not gone unheeded. Abruptly my soul was no longer alone in darkness. Light and hope and courage were beside me, were fighting for me.

The burning eyes of hate went dim, slipped far away into the darkness of hell. Before me in the soul of Aubrey DeJonge was now only gibbering fear. Fear that struggled desperately for a moment, then too was gone. There was nothing there now save silent submission and despair.

I had won.

Now that the soul of DeJonge had for the moment ceased to have power to control his second body, I could truly become myself again. With a powerful effort of my will, with a prayer to God and the spirits of good about me, I brought my own ectoplasm out from the thing which confined it—from DeJonge's ectoplasm, which now lay quiescent, masterless. And my soul and ectoplasm flowed out from DeJonge's body. With my soul as master, my second body flowed toward my own physical body, entered it.

There was a flash of blinding blackness. Abruptly, full human consciousness returned to me. My once-more living body was rising from the floor where it had lain! I had come back from the dead!

Again I saw through eyes, felt floor beneath my feet, and heard sounds about me. Across the room, the boy was slumped apathetically in his chair. Jeanne still lay bound upon the table, but I saw in her eyes new hope and joy.

Then I saw DeJonge. He stood, feet outspread, seemingly waiting for me . . . .

Like the madman that I was, I was across the room and upon him. I struck out at him fiercely, disregarding the blows he rained on me in return. Once he seized a scalpel and slashed at me; I felt the sharp burn of steel in my chest, but I did not stop.

His blows weakened. He backed away from me, mumbling incoherently. I caught him in a corner and rained blows upon him again.

It was not until five minutes later, when police burst down the door of my laboratory, that I came to my full senses and realized that during that time I had been pummeling a witless thing. . . .

SO I came back like Lazarus from the dead. Yet unlike Lazarus, I alone of the living know that I truly died. Not even Jeanne knows the whole truth. I do not dare to tell her, for she might think me mad.

No, it is best to keep my own thoughts hidden. For we are very happy, Jeanne and I. People say that they have never seen so ideally-mated a couple. It is best not to risk marring such happiness.

Buried in my scientific labors, I meddle no more with psychic things. But sometimes I can not help but think of them . . . and thinking, I remember, and a great fear comes over me. . . .

The boy medium is a normal boy again, his own master. But Aubrey DeJonge has never regained his reason. He is known as a harmless lunatic, and people pity him.

Yet none pity him so much as I—for I know the fate in store for him. I know that somehow in my weird battle for freedom his second body was harmed, so that he cannot die as others die. His soul will wander for eternity in that bleak barren waste of howling wind and shrieking souls, never to find rest. His fate is that which he planned for Jeanne and for myself. And I pity him, with all the compassion in my heart . . . .

HONEYMOON COFFIN

By
Ben Judson

The grey-green specter came from darkness, to force young William Arnold's clutching fingers about the white throat of his own beloved bride. Had he become indeed a bloodthirsting madman—or did the very fiends of hell possess his soul and body?

THE gaping young face before me blanched, livid with terror. The denim-clad youngster darted his bulging eyes from mine to the somber mansion crouched on the knoll across the river, and back to the dollar bill I held in my hand. He shook his head wildly. A sharp gasp caught in his throat, like the death-rattle of a corpse—and he fled back down the road, his naked feet flaying the dust after him.

I checked an impulsive snort of irritation, frowned on the half-submerged timbers before me. The debris of the bridge would afford a risky passage on foot, but the car was doomed to remain on this side of the little river. Since the boy had refused, we would have to pack our own luggage along that Indian-trail of a path to the house. How wild the old place had grown within that short but ecstatic month! The place that but a few weeks

Terror Novelette

before had been home to me! . . .

I turned to the luxuriance of tumbling, chestnut-tinted hair by my shoulder. Constance, my wife, was staring directly ahead, across the churlish stream, across the quarter-mile of coarse grass and scraggly oak, to the gloomy, castle-like abode that was to be our home. Her lovely eyes were moody and afraid.

"Not too tired to hike it?" I asked, caressing the soft damask of her cheek.

She drew her face close to mine, and the rose-color seemed to fade from it, like the twilight creeping down behind the old house. Her regard became childlike and fragile in its seriousness, and I could feel the warmth of her breath trembling against my lips.

"Bill," she quavered, "don't let us go on. It frightens me—the place sits there so silent like death!"

I gazed into the troubled depths of her eyes. It bothered me a little that at this time, when we were almost on the doorstep of our home, we should meet the first disturbance of the peaceful enchantment of our honeymoon!

"But this is where we're going to live, honey!" I contented gently.

She sighed, and then smiled bravely. "I let my feelings get the better of me. The gloomy house, the frightened look on the youngster's face, and the broken-down bridge—all seemed to forebode something awful!"

I smiled reassuringly, patted her soft hand. "Don't worry, dear," I said, and laughed. "I'll protect you. . . ."

I got out of the car, pulled the bags from the rear compartment. I carried them, one by one, across the shaky, spindle-like timber that linked the banks of the cavorting stream. Then, gripping Constance's diminutive hand, I guided her over the narrow span.

The luggage clamped under both arms, I trudged along the rock-studded path. Constance pressed close behind. The bladed growth whipped at our legs, and my breath came in heavy gasps as we panted up the uneven incline.

Behind us the darkness gathered thickly. The house stood out in bold silhouette on the brow of the hill, like a gaunt, winter-starved beast crouching in ambush. Its windows seemed gaping, lifeless eyes, and the verandah yawned like the stone maw of a cannibalistic gargoyle, ready to crush any living thing that might venture within its toothless gums.

Like my recently deceased father, the place seemed to have died in testy and decaying old age. It had been a lonely spot for me after my father's death. As soon as a decent interval elapsed I had fled the saddened mansion and the memory of dad's pale, sunken cheeks and staring, sightless eyes.

And lovely Constance Defoe fled with me as my young bride, helping me to forget the gloomy stillness of that death-haunted room, where my father had lain cold and unsmiling. By our marriage the two great estates of the Defoes and the Arnolds were joined. That is, they would be when Constance's aunt, Mathilde Grull, died.

But Mathilde Grull was a comparatively young woman. George Defoe's will gave his large patrimony to his daughter Constance, but only upon his sister-in-law's decease. In the event—God forbid!—that Constance died before her aunt, the estate would go to Miss Grull. But my patrimony was as large as the Defoe estate, and we had no need of Constance's unsettled inheritance.

I wondered if Doctor Nayr had rehired the servants as I had requested in my letter. The unlighted, cheerless vacancy of the windows of the place gave little hope that he had complied.

Burton Nayr had attended my father's death. A cat-footed, long-faced old soul, he had been a steady frequenter of the Arnold home ever since I could remember. But I had liked him, in spite of his long face, and called him Uncle Burt.

THE *clop, clop* of our feet sounded sharply over the masonry of the porch. I set the bags beside the entrance, and raised my fist to knock.

The heavy door receded slowly before my poised knuckles. A hunch-backed, parchment-faced monster dressed in black bowed us in.

"Doctor Nayr has been expecting you," he informed us in rumbling tones. His square, flat face leered at us as we entered. Then he glided soundlessly past us and retrieved our baggage.

The doctor was pacing the living-room. There was no change in his long-drawn expression as he quietly greeted me. Then he saw Constance.

"Ah, Constance, my dear!"

I was astonished to see the sparkle pop into his eyes. Somehow I did not like that glitter. It seemed obscene and unnatural in his usually morbid countenance.

"I have some news for you. . . ." He paused, nipping the end of his tongue between his teeth. "Your Aunt Mathilde passed away three days ago."

I could hear the sharp intake of Constance's breath. I myself was startled.

What claim could death have had on a woman like Mathilde Grull, a woman scarcely past the prime of her life? She had been beautiful, too—enough like Constance to pass for her double, only a little older.

"Accident?" I demanded.

"Fell and struck her brow while riding. She died almost instantly. I was there to sign her death certificate." Doctor Nayr passed a comforting arm over my wife's fragile shoulders, and somehow I resented it.

"When is the funeral?" Constance asked in a quiet voice.

"She was buried yesterday."

"Oh."

There was no more said, but I realized what lay behind Constance's calm acceptance of the fact. There had never been any love between Constance and her aunt. There was a rumor that George Defoe had jilted Mathilde Grull when he married Mathilde's sister. An enviable fortune had gone with that marriage. And Mathilde had hated Constance as bitterly as she had hated her mother.

The ogre of a butler appeared, announcing that dinner was served. Nayr sat at the head of the table, and Constance and I on either side of him.

The wainscoting of the dining-room was stained dark. Sable velvet curtains were drawn over the windows, and a single candelabrum placed in the center of the dully glowing table linen ineffectually lighted the place. We seemed to be seated in a small oasis of light, surrounded by an utter void of darkness. From the umbra where the light joined the void, the ghostly-faced butler materialized from time to time, serving us with a silent precision that was mystifying and uncanny.

Nayr crouched over his plate, masticating with a solemn uneasiness. Occasionally, when he glanced up at Constance, the glitter of the candles caught in his eyes. It was at these moments that the masklike obscurity was torn from his face; and in that flickering glitter I read no light of heaven.

I began to feel restless and morbid, wishing almost that I had yielded to Constance's plea that we turn back at the bridge. I fought off the feeling, gulping down intemperately the wine that Durgan, the butler, kept brimming to the lip of the glass. But the heady warmth of the liquid served only to sharpen my apprehension.

During coffee I broached a question that had somehow been troubling me.

"Uncle Burt," I said, "I noticed dad's painting has not yet been hung in the library. Is it still in his room—the room he died in?"

Nayr's slow glance raised to mine. Was it fright that drew his eyes down again?

"No," he replied, "it is—still in his room."

"I'll bring it down after dinner," I said.

"No, no," he rasped. He jerked his startled look up again. "Your father requested that it be left in that room. And he asked that no one be allowed in the room for a year!"

"Why," I exclaimed, "I heard nothing of that!"

"It was his last wish. You weren't close enough to hear it. His breath was very weak towards the end."

SOMETHING in his furtive regard told me Uncle Burt was lying, lying because he was afraid. But what was it that he feared? I couldn't understand. I let the matter rest at the time, determining secretly to have a look by myself into my father's room.

We gathered in the living-room after dinner, seated before the great open fireplace. The season had turned well into autumn, and the gloomy, high-ceilinged room began to grow uncomfortable with chilliness. I called Durgan to lay a wood fire for us.

Maybe it was my imagination, but when the butler shoved his mummy-like hand into the fire to replace a fallen log, the flames seemed to lick *through* his member without giving him the least sensation! The incident gave me quite a start, and an eerie feeling pricked along my spine. Constance noticed it too; I heard the almost inaudible gasp of astonishment from her direction. Durgan turned his baleful, vacant gaze on her for an instant, then vanished noiselessly into the remoter shadows of the house.

I slipped away, apparently unnoticed, when the embers had warmed the three of us to a comfortable languor. Mounting the old marble staircase stealthily, I paused in the darkness before the door to my father's bedroom. I had a premonition of what would happen; I tried the handle carefully.

It was locked!

It was not this fact that roused my wonder. It was the fact that Nayr should forbid me entrance. The doctor had had his little superstitions, but they were superstitions for which he could account with some scientific explanation, however absurd it might seem to me. Could he fear a room, because a man had died in it?

There was a master-key on my ring; at its command the door opened easily.

I stood at the foot of the old four-poster bed and struck a match. The shadows raced like birds of ill omen on silent, nightmare wings from the tiny point of flame. I stared above the dresser where the picture had been. But there was no picture there.

The match flickered out and dropped to the floor. I turned softly toward the hall. As I stepped out of the room, I started.

Doctor Nayr stood by the door, the candle in his hand throwing into relief the horrible whiteness of his face. A violent tremor of fearsome amazement shook my body. It was as if I had seen my old father standing there in his grave-clothes!

"The painting isn't there!" I muttered.

Nayr's brow purpled, thunder-clotted with wrath. "I told you the room wasn't to be opened!" he snarled.

I started to ask, with an angry jerk of my head, "To whom does this house belong?" But I desisted. Nayr drew shut the door, and relocked it, pocketing the key. Then he turned to me, and the passion had ebbed from his countenance.

"The painting is at the cabinet maker's," he explained. "It is being reframed."

He waved me downstairs with a testy jerk of his finger, following behind with the candlestick.

The matter was not mentioned again. Nayr took his leave shortly, and we dismissed for the night the servants he had hired—Durgan and a sable-faced Negress who served as cook and housemaid. Locking the windows and doors, Constance and I retired to our adjoining rooms.

It was about midnight when at last I fell asleep. . . .

THE feeling of fear stole over me in my sleep. It is difficult to explain, that struggling return to half-consciousness. I flogged like a spent swimmer gasping for the air at the surface. But some unnameable terrifying undercurrent seemed to draw me down to I knew not what depths of suffocating horror.

I awoke with a soundless cry of fright gibbering in my constricted throat. A long and bony finger of warning seemed to point to some presence hovering over the footboard of my bed. But I dared not open my eyes, for fear of proving the warning real.

I knew then that something had flown from me during my sleep, that something alien to my being and this earth had usurped its place. I knew that my doom had been fixed before I had become conscious of its presence. But even that was not what held my body rigid, sent the blood leaping through my aching temples.

It was the Thing that I knew stood grinning at me from the foot of my bed, though I had not yet opened my eyes!

Slowly I forced open the lids. Through the slit in the curtains at my left, the moonlight cut a livid wound in the naked darkness. Not a sound, except the pulse-beat in my ears, disturbed the deathly quiet of that room. But it was not this that started my eyes from their sockets.

A nebulous mist hovered in the darkness, emitting a fitful, greenish light. It was not like the moonlight, for it seemed to glow of itself, like the pale phosphorescence that feeds on rotted timbers.

Out of this shape, this hideous yet human shape, burned a pair of malignant, vulpine eyes. The glare of those awful eyes caught mine. They seared into my brain, divesting it of all volition.

Its blathering lips mumbled soundlessly, as if chanting some grisly blood rite. It advanced slowly over the footboard, and the grey-green featrues took on definite shape and line.

My fists clenched until they bit blood in the palms; my breath jerked in a terrified, high-pitched gasp.

It was the face of my dead father that was staring at me!

Was I another Hamlet, to be harrowed to idiocy by an unavenged parent? God, if the thing would only speak, instead of mumbling gruesomely to itself!

Maybe this thing wasn't true, maybe, Oh God—but the prayer refused to escape my lips. Something within me, yet not of my own being, smothered my will. I could *wish*, but I was unable to further the wish into action. My body belonged to a power other than my brain, like a puppet jerked willy-nilly by the strings of Satan.

I sat there, cringing back against the head of the bed, squeaking in my throat like a terror-sick child.

Suddenly a cloud passed over the moon, obliterating the gash of light that entered through the window. The phantom light, with equal suddenness, grew correspondingly brighter. In truth, it was no more vivid than a hazy glow; but the increased brightness seemed to strike into my face with the violence of a speeding comet.

A high, quavering yell ululated abruptly from my tortured lungs. The phantom hesitated momentarily at this terrified outburst, and at that instant I seemed to regain a part of my volition.

I leapt from bed with a spasmodic thrust of my legs, and dove for the light switch. Light and life seemed at that moment to be identical; in that hell of darkness I could find only death. It was with the desperate lungs of a drowning man after a straw that my hand struck the electric button on the wall.

The room flamed with the unaccustomed brilliance. I looked around, half expecting to see the ghastly shape creeping upon me, solid and real. But it was gone, vanished.

Weakness assailed my knees, and I crept to the bed. But I was calm, calm with the equanimity of a dying man who is certain of his destination. Like Faustus. I knew my soul could no longer be counted in my possessions, though I had received no recompense for its relinquishment. Yet, for all my calmness, I knew that within me abided a far worse evil than that which had visibly accosted me. What a precious thing, as dear as life itself, is volition!

I lay back in bed, leaving the protection of the light about me, towards morning yielding to a fitful slumber.

WITH the return of dawn, something of my normal self seemed restored. The fright of the preceding night's experience appeared absurd.

I tumbled from bed and gazed at myself in the dresser mirror. The same stubborn chin, the same square-set face, though a little wearied and drawn for a bright morning . . . but the eyes, how changed!

Something in those grey eyes fascinated me. They were not mine.

What was it that was lacking in those fixed orbs? Then I remembered. My father's eyes had set like that when he died!

I dressed hurriedly, and sought out my wife. Surely, she would comfort me, pluck me back from the pit of insanity.

Constance was waiting breakfast for me. There was a wholesomeness about her embrace, and the smell of freshly steeped coffee, that suddenly made me glad of life, and removed me far from the harrowing unreality of the preceding night.

The sun slanted through the drawn curtains, falling across my wife's face. A lovely blue sparkle played in her eyes, and I was happy for it. Then I told her my story of the night before.

"I felt there was something evil about this house," she whispered. "Even before we crossed the river! . . ."

I cast my eyes down, so that she could not see into the depths of their terror. "I wish I had believed you," I said. "But, darling—we can leave now."

I wanted to shout, *"Yes, for God's sake, let us hurry!"* But that alien being within me stifled the words in my throat and pinned me to my chair. The room grew black around me, a terrific dinning pounded in my ears. An insensible presence seemed to ooze over and envelope me.

"No, no," I muttered. "We aren't children!"

I felt my lips move, heard the syllables issues from my own throat, but I wasn't conscious that I had caused their utterance. It was as if I knew what I was going to do, fought against it, but my organs responded independently of my will.

What could I not do in this involuntary state! What crime might I not commit! I wanted to shout a warning to my wife, "Leave this house, leave it without me, before it is too late!" But the *thing* within me suppressed the power to do anything but what *it* willed.

Constance must have perceived some of the elemental disturbance flaying within me, for she started abruptly from her chair, and ran over to me. She pressed her cool little hand against my brow, tried to gaze into my averted mad-sick eyes.

"Bill!" she cried, and her voice trembled, "what has come over you? Are you sick?"

"No!" I answered gruffly. I raised myself to my feet and turned away from her.

CHAPTER TWO

The Specter's Will

AN HOUR later I found myself sitting in the library, seemingly waiting . . . Waiting for what? For death?

Thinking these things, I came abruptly to my feet, and whirled around. My forehead cracked against the skull of someone advancing to my chair.

I reeled back. "Doctor Nayr!" I cried.

"Constance phoned me you were ill," he explained, rubbing his brow. "Sit in the chair, and let me examine you."

He felt my pulse, drew open the lids of my eyes, and peered within. Constance entered the room, watched him silently.

Then he straightened, and whispered in her ear. Her eyes widened with concern.

He made me relate, in minute detail, all that had happened during the night. His long face gazed at me seriously as I spoke. I smiled weakly as I finished.

"You must think me pretty childish."

Nayr shook his head slowly. "I have heard of such cases," he rumbled gravely. "If such things as spirits exist—and we must admit the *possibility* of their existence—you are one who would be very likely to perceive them. You are probably a very sensitive medium."

He rose, pulling a vial filled with a white powder from his bag. "On the other hand," he added, "it may be simply a case of nerves and indigestion."

Turning, he asked Constance to procure a glass of water. When she had disappeared, he bent close to me, muttering in a low, meaningful tone.

"Whatever you do," he instructed me, "do not forget that *you are not insane.* If you follow this, we *may be able to save you.*"

I gasped at him, thunderstruck. Constance returned with the water, and the doctor dumped the white powder into the glass. When it had dissolved, he handed it to me.

"A sedative," he remarked.

He left shortly, and I slumped into the chair, feeling even more troubled.

I dozed through most of the remainder of the day; but my napping was fitful and troubled. I would fall into unconsciousness, repeating over and over in my mind, I am *not* insane; and I would come to, asking myself the question: *Am I sane?*

When dusk finally settled over the gloomy house, I felt more wearied than when I had risen in the morning. I wandered into Constance's room, and she drew me protectively into her arms. I clung to her bosom like a frightened child.

"Go away with me now," she murmured. "The car is still across the river."

But I turned obstinately from her, muttering, why I knew not, "We can't go *now.*" It was not my own voice that spoke.

It was about ten when we turned into bed, Constance insisting that I must have rest. I glared through the darkness of my bedroom, waiting for, almost hoping for, the return of the nebulous mist. But wearied at length with waiting, my eyes closed involuntarily. . . .

I AWOKE at an early hour of the morning, as I had the night before. There was the same setting: the splash of moonlight by the window, the tomblike silence and pregnant blackness of the room. I might well have imagined it a continuance of the earlier experience.

But I awoke in a different cast of mind. I had already been initiated into the terrors of a first meeting with the unknown. Thus, when sleep left me, I opened my eyes directly, and gazed towards the footboard of my bed.

I knew it would be there. And almost. I knew what it expected of me. An extended finger beckoned me, as the luminous apparition backed towards the door.

I sat bolt upright in bed, shaking my head violently. I wanted to scream, *"No, no, I won't do it!"* But the sound caught in my throat in an inarticulate gurgle, like that of a man being strangled. The imprint of that bony hand seemed to constrict my throat, as if it had been that which had cut short the scream.

If it would only speak, leave off that horrible gnawing of its foul lips, cry out, at least, "I am thy father's spirit!"

But it glared silently at me, its light-rimmed eyes boring into my mind, crushing my will and drawing me on. I knew instinctively what was about to happen. Already my hands reached forward, the fingers curving like ravenous, bestial talons. I slithered forward, crouching like a primordial brute, stalking after the kill.

God have witness, I fought it off! What horror is there more appalling than the knowledge that one is about to commit a brutish, unnatural crime!

I was going to strangle my wife!

Strangle her, in cold blood, with those eager, bloodthirsty hands of mine! And some deep, untainted corner of my brain battled in agony. Battled against the Satanic will that was lashing forward the jelly-like lobe which propelled my stealthily advancing feet and set my features in a wolfish frenzy of blood-lust.

But the finger of death beckoned me on! The door communicating with Constance's bedroom yawned silently at the phantom's command. The weird light retreated towards my wife's bed, drawing me, slowly, slowly—as inevitably as death.

The torturous seconds seemed to lengthen into hours as I crept, catlike, over the tufted carpet. I would have forced those claws, hardened to steel by the straining muscles of my forearm, onto the flesh of my own throat, had I been able. But it was as if I, the one that willed the right and wrong of things, had died abed.

Now I could feel the tender, warm skin under the grip of those hated talons; now Constance stirred restlessly in her sleep, the prelude to returning consciousness. A burning tear stung my eyelids and splashed onto my hands, splattering as if it had struck flint. And with that ironic tear, the last vestige of my revolt against the horrible thing I was performing seemed to fall away. . . .

The mumbling of those foul lips on the opposite side of the bed grew almost audible, as of a scavenger whetting its chops in anticipation of an appetite soon to be satisfied. The compelling eyes seared agonizingly into my brain, constricting my fingers into a narrowing vise of death.

The sobbing of Constance's labored breathing came faintly to my ears, like an anguished cry for help born along in the winds of a sea-tempest. Her terror-filled eyes, now opened, stared up into mine, starting from their lids. Her bosom heaved in the anguish of suffocation, and her fragile body twisted and jerked.

I gripped harder. Slowly those terrified, pleading eyes glazed over. The writhing subsided. Blackness raced upon my senses, and I felt the murderous talons I called my own relax their death-grip.

I reeled backwards. Constance lay mute and white, her eyes wide open and staring. I looked about me.

The phantom had vanished!

From some remote corner of the house a faint laugh echoed, mocking and Satanic.

MY KNEES buckled under me then, and I sunk onto the bedside, weeping bitter, anguished tears. Only a few hours ago I had soothed my aching head against that still, tender bosom!

At last, dazedly, I picked up the body of my wife, crushing her delicate limpness to me. My feet plodded forward.

The bedroom door opened softly, mechanically, as if anticipating my entrance. Into the hall, down the marble staircase my feet bore me. The darkness closed in about me, but my eyes stared vacantly ahead.

Ahead of me the cellar door receded, and I descended effortlessly into the subterranean depths. Another door, massive and oaken, swung inward. I stepped inside a vault whose air hung dank and close.

One thing remained vividly in my memory, the one thing which gave any semblance of reality to the nightmare through which I moved. As I entered the vault, I felt the nightgown which enveloped Constance's form tug against my grasp. I heard the rip as the material parted, where it had caught on a nail projecting from the doorpost.

Somehow, I clung to that incident as a prisoner clings to the tiny shaft of light that streams in his cell window, that is his only connection with life that is sane and normal. Yet the incident rendered me panic-stricken.

My only hope was that this ghastly adventure *was* but a nightmare. Yet so small a thing as a bit of torn cloth threatened that hope!

I deposited the body gently on the floor, turned and retraced my steps upstairs to my bedroom. The doors closed as mechanically behind me as they had opened, and I seemed to think there was nothing singular in this phenomenom. I dared not peep into my wife's room, but marched directly to my own bed.

Stumbling onto the mattress, I lay there, until my eyes drooped in a fitful dreaming. Below me, through a vast chaos of shadows, a pleading, spent cry begged my succor: and through the chaos a horrible laugh mocked faintly. The laugh issued from my own lips. . . .

THE cry from the depths of the chaos changed in tone, until it echoed the mockery of my own insane laughter. My body shivered, as if suddenly chilled, and I opened my eyes.

Morning had come, thick and grey. I lay, stiff as a day-old corpse, my eyes wandering furtively about the dismal chamber. The muscles of my hands and forearms felt sore and knotted, as if they had undergone some superhuman test of strength.

It was even as if I had passed from one life to another, and could not decide which was real: the nightmare I had just experienced, or the macabre consciousness I was now realizing.

Is this insanity, I wondered—not being able to tell illusion from reality?

How can one know, how can one *ever* know, the truth of things? God if I could but find some *proof.*

I started up in bed. There was a way—but it terrified me! Suppose I could prove last night's dream a reality, suppose Constance were *not* in her bed—

I got up. My frame was seized with a violent trembling as I approached the door that separated my room from Constance's. The knob rattled in my grasp as my hand hesitated to push aside the barrier. Then abruptly with a gigantic effort, I flung open the panel.

She was there, thank God! She was there, gently breathing with the sweet abandon of sleep. The vapor of my fears seemed suddenly to lift, and I felt weak with the relief that comes after panic.

She roused gently, turning her mist-filled eyes to mine. An astonished sob erupted in my throat, and I drew back.

Was *this* the Constance whom I had kissed to sleep the evening before? It was she; yet she had changed somehow, as if a dozen years had elapsed between that time and now, softening her beauty, drawing fine lines at the corners of the eyes. The same chestnut hair spilled over her fragile shoulders, the same pouted lips begged a kiss of me, the same moody eyes questioned my confusion. But there was a difference, a greater difference than the appearance of a few lines. . . .

Maybe the change was in me, maybe those gray eyes of mine saw differently. There had been cause enough! I rushed to the mirror.

My hair had turned completely white!

WILD speculative thoughts tumbled about in my head. Had less than forty-eight hours passed since Constance and I had returned from our honeymoon? Or had years slipped by, with my diseased brain having no record of the passage?

I turned again to my wife, an inquisitive, distressed expression on my face. Should I tell her of my dream? I almost decided in the negative, thinking to spare her the horror of that experience; but already she was speaking to me. And her questions deftly extracted from me an account of all the terror I had known.

"I'll call Doctor Nayr again," she decided with a worried, searching glance into my eyes.

Before we sat down to breakfast I slipped unobserved into the cellar, and crept, my heart pumping feverishly, to the vault.

A bat squeaked in the darkness over my head; the flurry of its wings beat momentarily against my cheek. There were faint rustlings from impenetrable recesses, like the dropping of rotted grave-clothes.

I knew I would find it. Maybe that was what made it all the more horrible when I did find it. My fingers reached aspen-like into a blot of light—

From a nail drooped an inch-wide strip of black silk!

I plucked the gauzy material from the iron tooth, and jammed it nervously into my jacket pocket. All my hopes shattered chaotically about me.

Where was Constance; upstairs, waiting breakfast for me, or behind that planked door, her soft, warm loveliness frigid in death? Had I talked to Constance this morning, or was *that* my dream?

My hand quivered on the handle as the weighty panel surged in. The beam of silver crept forward over the cement of the floor like the glance of a hesitant eye. But there was no body on the cold pavement!

The eye of light wandered uncertainly about the narrow vault. At the further end of the chamber it picked out a long, boxlike object resting on two saw-horses. I advanced quickly to the object.

It was a coffin!

Would I find within that receptacle the gown from which had been torn the remnant of silk I had jamned into my pocket? My knees wavered menacingly under the thrust of my sagging body. I fought back the dimness that assailed my senses, and slowly raised the coffin lid.

It was empty. A pent-up sigh steamed from my tortured lungs, and the lid clamped shut as weakness relaxed my fingers. I turned dully, and made my way out of the vault.

* * * * *

We gathered in the library, Doctor Nayr, Constance and myself. The doctor's pale face grew longer than ever as I related to him my fresh experiences. I told him of the coffin I had discovered in the vault—surely that could have been no dream—and he stared at me pityingly.

The look of skepticism on his face enraged me. "I will show it to you!" I cried. "It's down there, in the cellar!"

We descended, both of them gripping one of my arms, as if I would escape them, or fall like a child and hurt myself. Their concern chafed and baffled me, and I tore loose from their grasp, to fling open the door to the vault. The candle Doctor Nayr held flung its hesitant gleam along the walls.

There was no coffin there!

I saw the two saw-horses, but their burden had vanished! A frustrated scream gurgled from my lips.

Then I remembered. My hand dove into my coat pocket, to pluck forth the bit of telltale silk.

But that, too, was non-existent!

A funereal numbness overtook me. My body sunk to the floor.

"The piece of black silk," I jabbered, "that was torn from your nightgown—"

Constance gazed at me astounded. "My nightgown wasn't torn!" she exclaimed. "And it wasn't black, it was peach-colored!"

I remembered, then, talking to her in the morning. Her gown had been peach-colored.

"But the body!" I screamed. "It was clothed in black!"

"What body?" the doctor demanded. "There was no body!"

I broke out sobbing like a frightened child. They grasped me by the shoulders.

"Don't let your mind go to pieces!" the doctor commanded sternly.

As I labored up the cellar steps, my mind revolved, "I must get away from this place—it is driving me mad!" Then my brain jerked numbly. "I am mad!" I thought. "I will deed the property to Constance, and then have them place me in a sanitarium."

They had the papers ready for me when we regained the library. Had I suggested deeding the place over, or had they? I couldn't remember having spoken about it.

Durgan, the square-jawed butler, witnessed the signature. I noticed that the ink seemed to crawl over the paper like a worm, of its own volition.

"Now take me away," I sobbed.

The doctor shook his head sadly. "No," he objected, "you will be better off here, where we can watch you."

Suddenly my desire to go away seemed to dissolve. "Yes," I acquiesced dumbly. I let them guide me to my bedroom. There I lay down, fully dressed, and the doctor drew the heavy curtains, casting the room in utter darkness. Soon after they had departed I fell into a disordered slumber. . . .

CHAPTER THREE

Wedded to Death

I AWOKE, gasping for breath. A heavy, poisonous air seemed to press onto my chest, to enfold my being as if it would crush the life from me.

My eyes snapped open. They stared directly into the burning orbs of the fiend who had before possessed me!

The livid face of the monster was within a foot of my own, and the fleshy lips were grinning horribly. It backed away, pulling me unconsciously forward with its magnetic stare.

God, was I going to live through another crime, however illusionary it might prove with the advent of dawn? I tried to close my eyes, to keep out the horrid sight, to deny its presence by strength of will. But I felt my volition seeping from me, and my lids refused to shut.

The hall door opened, and beyond it I could see a grey illumination flooding in the window from the overcast sky. It was still day, then! I must reach the light. I thought. Then, perhaps, I would be able to destroy the hallucination. I hurried after the specter as it disappeared into the hall.

It was gone, though, when I reached the hallway. But no sense of relief flooded over me. I knew the phantom was there, although I could not see it.

My feet propelled me on, to the head of the staircase, down the marble steps. Where was I bound? My body seemed to know, although my brain did not.

At the foot of the stairs I turned into the library. My hands were clutching forward, as they had done last night, ugly and clawlike. For whose throat were they meant this time? Could *this* be a dream?

Suddenly I saw myself in the mirror placed opposite the doorway. Fiends out of hell! Could there be any more horrible monster?

My face was twisted into a hideous, blackened aspect, more befitting the name of blood-crazed wolf than man. I had seen a picture of the *loup garou*, a terrifying, vulpine-faced Gorgon, with the arms and body of a man. But this monster which glared back at me was infinitely more horrible.

A sudden, harsh scream rent the stillness ahead of me. A woman quailed before me, her slender hands clutching protectively at her throat. It was Constance, her eyes glued on my features.

It must have taken but a few seconds to cross that strip of carpet that separated us. But in those few seconds I passed through all the tortures of hell.

Oh God, in those seconds I suffered enough to pay for all my sins and those of my ancestors! Could I do nothing to arrest the performance of that blood-crime I was about to commit?

Suddenly my arms shot forward, my talons gripping the quailing flesh. The drooling and slobbering of my lips came to my ears, as if my bared fangs had already sunk into the warm, pulsing neck. Constance's eyes were fixed, iced with terror, though death had not yet struck the light from them. The death-rattle coughed in her throat, and she sank onto her knees.

She did not attempt to fight me off. That made it all the more appalling. But the more heart-sick I became, the more vicious the strength that crept into my slowly contracting fingers.

I felt the cartilage of her throat collapse. My claws sunk into the putty-like flesh, and her body went limp. I released my grip. The corpse slithered to the floor. Ugly blue marks showed on the ivory skin where the neck lolled back.

This was no dream!

How did I know? I did not. But I do know, that *this seemed more real to me than the time earlier in the day I had spent in consultation with Doctor Nayr!*

I might wake up shortly, but how could I know?

I went over to the desk. Pen and paper were laid out. I seated myself, and took up the pen mechanically. The ink traced words on the tablet.

How natural that I should write these words, though I hadn't known their meaning until I had read them off!

I strangled my wife in a fit of insanity.
Now I shall kill myself to atone that crime.
William Arnold

"Now I shall kill myself!" I murmured, as my hands crept to my throat.

A faint, exultant laugh mockingly reëchoed my whispered sentence. My mind no longer fought off my desire to kill. My knotted fingers embraced my windpipe; their pressure closed in slowly like the coils of a cobra. Sense faded into the twilight of near death, and my eyes closed with the languor of sleep.

Then something metallic crashed against my forehead. I reeled backwards.

In the instant of consciousness that was left me, my eyes started open. A man, with a candlestick raised in his hand, crouched over my sprawling form, his face square and expressionless.

It was Durgan, the butler!

Then consciousness eddied away.

A SENSE of release was the first perception that stirred my reanimated mind. I came to with the exultation one experiences upon being liberated from long confinement. But not in a physical sense did I imagine myself freed, for that perception had hardly yet returned.

My eyes opened, but I could see nothing, for blackness closed in heavily about me. The air I breathed was hot and foul.

I attempted to wriggle out of my uncomfortable position. My body was stretched out stiffly, and my arms crossed on my chest. I twisted, but narrow walls held my form straight; I tried to raise my arms, and they struck a low wooden ceiling. Pushing back my head, I felt it strike another partition; my feet drummed against another hollow-sounding barrier.

Six close-fitting walls kept my torso rigid. Sweat poured onto my brow as I sucked in the vitiated atmosphere of my tiny cubicle. I remembered the suicide note, and the face of my executioner.

I was in a coffin, buried alive!

Alive? I began to wonder. Could this be death? Was that the curious feeling of relief I had experienced upon the immediate stirrings of consciousness?

But dead or alive, I knew I must escape the wooden prison that held me. I arched my back, pressing savagely against the coffin lid. An eternity seemed to pass while I struggled thus, my spine threatening to crack at any instant.

Suddenly a bolt snapped, and the lid sprung open.

I was in the little subterranean vault where I had—or dreamed I had—deposited Constance's mangled body. My coffin rested on the two saw-horses, and at the head and foot of the box, two candles glimmered.

But my coffin was not alone. Resting by its side was another, lid clamped shut!

Gingerly I slipped down from the oblong box in which I had found myself, and strode around to the second coffin. I fumbled with the catch.

What would I find beneath that somber lid? My fingers trembled, and it was with a struggle that I forced my eyes onto the outstretched figure that was shortly revealed.

The lid slipped from my hand, and clumped onto the rim of the box. My knees staggered beneath me.

It was Constance I had seen, pale and immobile like a waxen image! The blue marks showed about her neck, where my fingers had crushed the breath from her.

But she was dressed in the black nightgown!

My mind groped hesitatingly about, trying to solve the macabre jigsaw, but reason blurred in the confusion of the ghastly puzzle. Twice I had strangled my wife, and now, unless this too were a dream—*or something far more sinister than a dream*—what solution could I draw?

I closed the lid of the coffin in which I had found myself, and crept to the door of the vault.

Up the cellar steps I tiptoed, onto the first floor of the somber, mute house. Night lay like a pall over the darkened rooms, like the eternal blackness that invests the stillness of a sepulcher.

A sepulcher—was it to that abode I had taken my young wife? Were we all dead now, the phantom, Constance and myself? What was I—an unquiet spirit who couldn't be sure of its nature?

As I groped into the library I half expected to find a body there—the body of the mortal William Arnold, that worldly part of me of which my present self had been the animating part. But the matches in my pocket, which flickered genuinely enough, discovered only an upturned chair.

On the desk, however, was something which vitally claimed my interest. It was the suicide note with my name appended at the close. Could the incidents of a *dream* hang together so neatly? . . .

THEN I heard it—the peal of faint, mocking laughter, jarring through the house in a crescendo of funereal triumph. A shudder ran the length of my spine, but it was not a shudder of fear. My whole being began to quiver with hate, hate for the demoniac apparition that had taken from me my sanity, Constance and our tender, promising love.

A low growl seethed over my bared teeth. My body crouched in the pose of a stalking jungle cat, and my talons gripped forward like the claws of death. Again a fiend seemed to possess me, whetting the bloodlust within me—but this time the fiend was myself, intent on the destruction of the mocking triumph!

I charged swiftly through the darkness, scenting like a panther the origin of that laugh. Down the cellar steps I crept, for the echo of the horrible cachinnation seemed to quiver in that subterranean blackness. Cobwebs licked my tortured face, but I canted through them, unconscious of their embrace. A bat catapulted into my outstretched hand, and I crushed its frightened squeak into a leathery pulp.

Behind a low door, to the left of the vault entrance, my ear caught muted stirrings. In there was the wine cellar, a dank, cobwebby place, its passages dark and twisted as the catacombs.

Stealthily I lifted the ancient hasp, and pushed against the mouldering barrier. The door gave in slowly and noiselessly, and I glared at the fantastic scene.

With his back toward me, Durgan, clad in a long black frock-coat, stood over an upturned wine cask. On either side of him a candle burned, shedding its dull effluence into the crannies of the dank room.

Facing Durgan, who was mumbling out of a crumbling, yellow-stained book, were two other figures, one in shimmering white, and the other in the greenish-black luminescence of the phantom!

There was an unrestrained, lustful grin on the phantom's loose-hung lips. Its baleful, greedy eyes glowed hot like embers, fastening themselves on the white-robed form beside him.

A slight gasp sucked in my throat as I saw the figure in white. It was Constance, standing immobile, her eyes shut, her cheeks deathly pale! One fragile hand resting in the paws of the monster beside her; there was no sign that she was conscious of the ceremony.

I recognized the guttural words that spilled from the invisible lips of the butler. *He was performing a marriage ceremony!* The apparition who bore the likeness of my father, was taking to wife my Constance!

The phantom must have heard my gasp of astonishment, for it looked up quickly. Have you ever seen a ghost *quail in fear?* The specter did just that, backing quickly away, its terror-struck eyes glued on my grim countenance. Constance, released from the grasp of her specter-groom, opened her eyes, and looked up dazedly.

The muttered words ceased abruptly Durgan, seeing the consternation on the face of the groom-to-be, whirled about.

The butler's trip-hammer fists swung up in protection, but he was too late. I lunged forward. A bestial roar escaped my lungs; my hand doubled into a missile of titanic destruction. The frenzy in my blood lent the blow I delivered an uncanniness and a force that was butchering. Durgan's mouth crumpled under the impact, and he slid inert to the floor.

I turned, to charge on the cowering form of the apparition—and stopped short! Constance was standing in my path! Her eyes gazed upon me, vacant and lifeless. Behind her the black-robed ghoul crouched, his fiery orbs burning into the base of her skull.

Dull words came tumbling from her colorless lips. I froze before her, regarding her vapid expression.

"You must go away," she enjoined tonelessly, as if she had no control over the sounds she articulated. "I am no longer yours. I am dead—you are living. In this world of the dead, all mortal ties are broken. The bond of marriage does not exist beyond the grave. I am promised to another who had claimed me for his bride. Go—go to the coffin in the vault: there you will find what belongs to you!"

HORROR shook my frame. Misgivings trembled in my mind. I had seen the body of Constance in the casket; now, this *other* Constance repulsed me, claiming her right of divorce by death. Could I truly believe I was met with the ghostly beings that rise from the grave?

I don't know now. All I can say is this: That terrible doubtings shook my mind; what I experienced in that house was so real and horrible that to this day I can merely state, *I doubt.*

It wasn't Constance that was speaking, I knew. It was the monster behind her, speaking through her lips. What awful power was it that it owned?

But dead or living the monster should never possess this beautiful, cold apparition in white who had once been a warm, eager lover to me. This much I promised myself.

The specter must have sensed my intent. In his hand I saw a knife gleam!

We lunged together at the same instant. The knife raised in the ghoul's paw, then slashed down upon my neck. I ducked, and caught the monster's wrist in my hand. We thudded to the floor, snarling and clawing like two beasts fighting.

Blood streamed from my cheek where the knife had grazed the skin. The specter fought with demoniacal fury—straining, straining to bury its flashing weapon in my body. The folds of its stinking garments enveloped and stifled me. But their fetid odor seemed to marshal all the hate that had grown within me since the ghost had first plotted its cunning against my weakness—and that hate lent me strength.

I felt the bones crumple in its wrist, and the knife dropped from its grasp. Then my talons sought the monster's throat. They sunk like glowing steel into wax. The body jerked spasmodically, the fleshy lips blathered horibly in the gasping struggle. At last the heaving torso went limp. I released my grasp.

The thing lay still. It would never move again. I ripped the cunning mask from its face, and gaped at the dead, twisted face.

It was the face of Doctor Nayr!

A gasp of surprise sounded behind me, and I spun about. It was Constance. With the monster's decease, a vital, meaning light had sprung into her eyes. The oppression of the specter's hypnotic power was gone!

I grasped her tottering figure to my breast, and led her from the room. Then I picked her up bodily, and carried her upstairs to her room. All through the remainder of that gloomy night I kept vigil over her exhausted, sleeping form. . . .

POLICE COMMISSIONER RIDER'S burly jaw dropped with surprise. Durgan, the butler, squirmed in his seat, his chin a welter of crimson bandages.

"Do you know him, Commissioner?" I asked.

"Do I know him!" Rider snorted. A relieved smile curved his lips. "Sure, he's the con who lammed out of the state pen a month ago! The warden was fattening him up for the chair, until the Bishop—that's what he went by in the underworld—decided to take a powder. He used to be a parson or something, before he made up his mind there was more dough in the confidence game."

The commissioner hunched his chair closer to the butler. "Come, sugar," he wheedled, "tell daddy the story, *or I'll break your damned jaw in half!*"

"William did that already," Constance murmured.

Durgan glared sullenly at the commissioner. A half-hearted attempt at a leer twisted the pulp of his mouth. "Why not?" he muttered. "It was a hell of a swell joke. The doctor had a pan of brains bigger'n any cop!"

"Skip the farce!" Rider growled.

Durgan glanced at Constance, then hatefully at me. "When I blew the pen," he began, his voice modulated and low as if he were enjoying the telling of a tall story, "Doc Nayr took me in. I told him I was out of work and needed money for train fare, so he set me to pulling weeds in his garden. I planned to knock him off and grab his wallet before I pulled out, but he got suspicious of my face and looked up my record. Then he told me he had a job for me, with real money in it. He promised to hand me over to the cops if I didn't take it. The job looked good, and he had the drop on me, so I didn't make any fuss about it. Then he put this monkey jacket on me."

"How did Miss Grull get mixed up in this—job?" Constance asked.

"She was in it from the first. She and Nayr were trying to get both estates. So Nayr faked Miss Grull's death. Then she could start passing herself off as you, Mrs. Arnold. . . . She looked a lot like you." He turned to the commissioner.

"The idea was to get Arnold to sign over his property to his wife, so it would all fall to Miss Grull when his wife died. With Miss Grull passing herself off as Mrs. Arnold part of the time, and the doctor's disguise, they hypnotized Arnold into thinking he was crazy, so he'd sign the property over. In the same way they figured to get him to kill his wife. After that, if he didn't kill himself—a murder and suicide by a madman—we aimed to do it for him. That would leave them with a clear field, and Miss Grull and Nayr would split the property between them.

"But the doctor double-crossed his partner. When he saw Mrs. Arnold he fell for her, hard. He was batty as hell anyhow; and he got some crazy idea that if he could get Arnold to kill Miss Grull, thinking it was his wife, after Arnold was dead everything would be fine. He'd give out the word that Mrs. Arnold was dead; and he'd keep her locked up, saying she was Miss Grull and had gone a little cracked from the whole affair. Nobody outside the house had been told the fake story about Miss Grull's death. Being the family doctor, he figured he could get away with this. And he'd naturally be made executor of the estates, so he'd have the money and Mrs. Arnold both.

"I guess he must have thought he could keep on hypnotizing Mrs. Arnold till she was in love with him—or if he couldn't, he could keep her locked up anyway. So he called off Arnold before he'd quite killed his wife; then he hid her in the wine cellar and sicked Arnold on Miss Grull. Arnold killed her, all right. . . . Only trouble was, I didn't sock Arnold quite hard enough afterwards. I meant to kill him. . . ." Durgan glared at me.

"The old doctor was sure batty," he added. "He even had me marrying him to Mrs. Arnold, thinking he'd have her then for sure. But Arnold busted in. . . ."

"There are a couple of things I want to know," I said then. "What happened to the picture of my father and where is the piece of black silk I had in my pocket?"

"The picture's in the wine cellar, in a sort of dressing-room the doctor fixed for his make-up when he started playing ghost. He used it as a model for his face, so as to look like old Mr. Arnold. What a costume! Got me scared too . . . I don't blame you, Mr. Arnold, for going crazy. He put some kind of paint on his robe so it would glow, and covered his shoes with rubber so he could sneak around without being heard."

"What about the piece of silk?" I repeated.

"Oh, that—he snitched it out of your pocket when he examined you in the library. And he told me to take the coffin out of the vault. When he got you thinking you were insane, he made you sign the deed."

Rider took him away after that. There was still a smile on the butler's pasty face as if he thought he had been very smart.

Mathilde was buried in the coffin in which she rested in the vault. Nayr was interred in the other, in which I had been placed for dead.

Shortly after, we sold our estates, and moved far away from that place.

So, after all, there were no ghosts responsible for all that had transpired. It was all due to devilish, human cunning.

But sometimes, when I look into the mirror and see my white hair and the stark vapidness that has lurked ever since in my eyes, I wonder. . . .

THE END

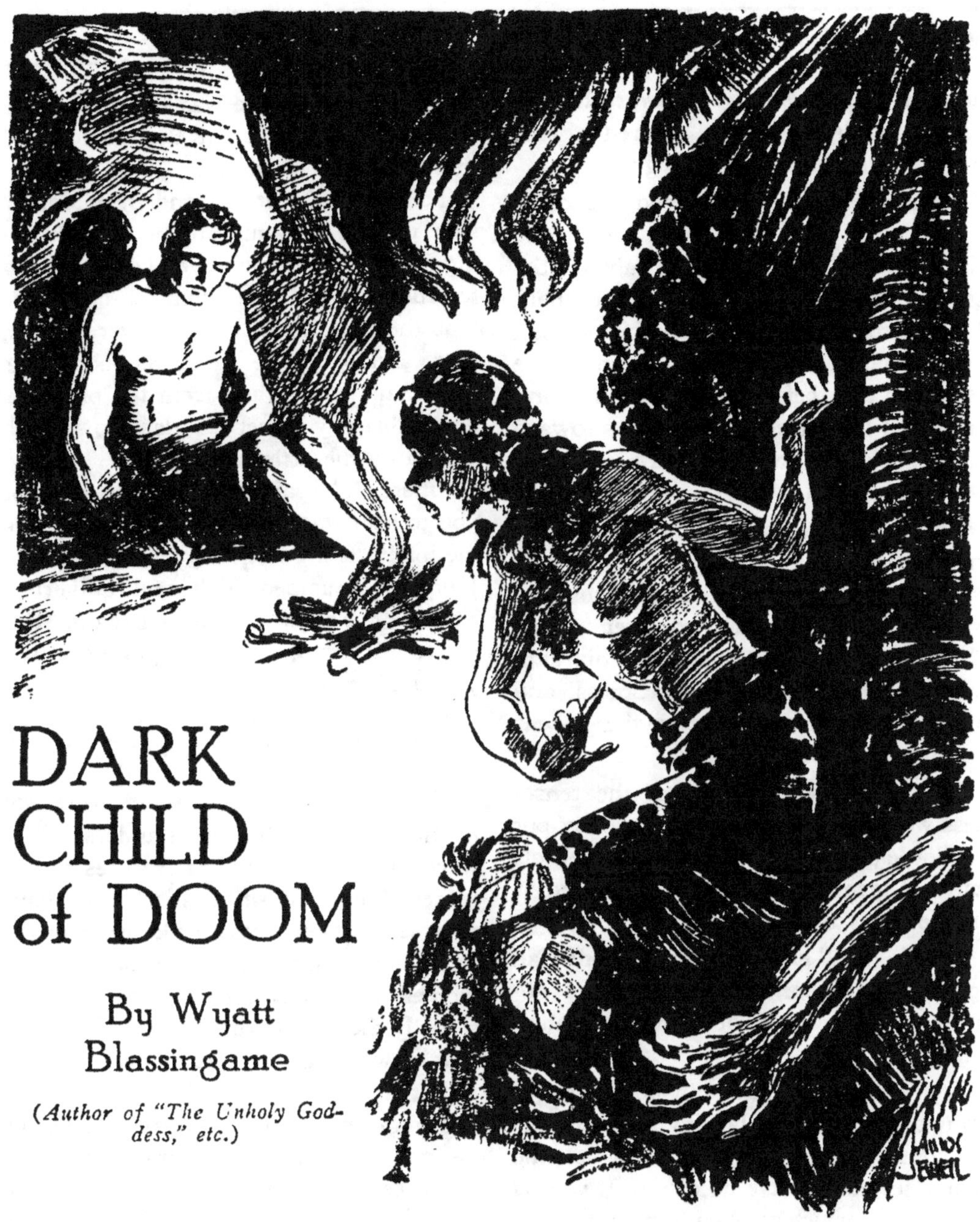

DARK CHILD of DOOM

By Wyatt Blassingame

(Author of "The Unholy Goddess," etc.)

On that lost Pacific island Tom Mainor found peace and love—till the wolf-man's curse set the slavering mark of the beast on all that the stranger white man held near and dear!

IT WAS as if I had seen a ghost. I stood stock still, staring at him. It was five years now since Tom Mainor had gone out on an exploration through islands south of Bali. Then, with his entire party, he had dropped abruptly out of sight. We had long since given them all up for dead. Yet it was Tom Mainor who stood there now, in the flesh, at the bar of the Adventure Club.

He was evidently drinking heavily and his face was flushed. But it was an abnormal flush, as though a thin coat of blood had been smeared over the pallid face of a corpse. As I went toward him he lifted a bottle of Scotch, poured a stiff drink and tossed it down straight.

Mainor and I had been good friends in the old days, and I was damn glad to see him alive. But something about the drawn, ghastly look of his face, and about the way that he gulped that whisky, took the joy out of our meeting. Even before I reached him, before I spoke to him, and he turned those black, hollow eyes toward me, I knew that the man was afraid.

He jumped when I touched him, and swung furiously toward me, the bottle gripped in his hand. I saw that his hair was turning gray at the roots, though he wasn't but a year or two over thirty. Under the flush of the alcohol his skin was sunburned almost to blackness, and under that, permeating everything, was the ghastly white of terror.

When he saw me some of the tenseness went out of his body. He slowly put the bottle on the counter, and extended his hand. I gripped it and almost jumped at the coldness of his touch.

"Hello, Ed," he said. "Boy! I am glad to see you! Here, have a drink." I noticed that the bottle of Scotch was half empty.

It must have been an hour before he got around to his story. During all that time he continued to drink steadily, but the liquor seemed to have no effect. It was as if the terror which gripped him, and which made even the skin of his hands white under the sunburn, was too great for the alcohol to touch. We had taken a couple of chairs in the empty card room, with the bottle and glasses on a small table.

I learned that his ship had been struck by a typhoon, and driven the Lord knows how far off its course. The storm was blowing itself out when the ship hit a coral reef and went down. Mainor did not know exactly what happened after that. He clung to a life preserver, and somehow, somewhere was washed ashore. There were natives on the island, and they took care of him.

This much I learned, and then Mainor shut up like a clam. But he kept drinking and his deep-sunk eyes kept jumping fearfully around the room. I could see that the muscles in his face were drawn taut, and when he lifted the bottle his fingernails were white from the pressure. Then abruptly he set his glass down with a thud on the little table.

"Listen," he said. "It won't be good for you to hear this, and you will never thank me for it. But I've got to tell somebody!" His voice jumped high and quivering. Then he got control of himself again. "I've got to tell somebody," he repeated. "And you used to be my friend. . . ."

I said, "I still am."

"All right," he said. "Listen!"

THE people on that island were not like other South Sea Islanders. They were tall, with clean-cut features and a golden skin, the most beautiful race I have ever seen. They dressed like most of the Islanders, though. Both the men and the women wore only a loin-cloth and occasionally they went without that. I learned that I was the first white man ever to visit that island.

A more courteous and generous people never lived. Yet from the first night when I lay resting in the hut and listened to the far-off booming of drums, I knew that something terrible, something hideous and supernatural hung over the island. I could smell it in the air, mingling with the odor of the palms and of a curious sort of wild jasmine that grew there. And a nameless, invisible horror ran like blood through the throbbing of the drums.

I had been there perhaps six months, perhaps a year—I had no way of keeping track of the time—when I got my first hint of the Thing which I had smelled in the clean sea air, and heard in the throbbing of the drums. I was lying in the sand watching men spear fish out near the coral reefs. Half the villagers were on the beach that morning, but they were not laughing as usual and there was a curious tenseness in their actions. All night and all morning a drum had been sounding a weird cacophony in the mountains behind the village.

Then I saw the man coming. He was a tall, slender youngster of about twenty, whom I had grown to like. and as he walked along the beach a harsh, absolute silence fell over the crowd. I was suddenly aware of the running murmur of the surf, and of the wind stirring the palms. The crowd drew away from the man as they might have from a leper.

He was walking with his head erect, shoulders flung back. But there was something unnatural about the way he moved. He walked stiffly, laboriously, as though he were forcing himself.

Then he was close enough for me to see the expression on his face, and my body jerked with unreasonable fear. His eyes were set and staring. His mouth was half opened, lips pulled back across his teeth. I could see his nostrils expand and contract with his breathing, and I could see that his eyes were glazed. I thought suddenly of a condemned prisoner walking toward the electric chair.

With slow, shuddering reluctance he came to a halt not more than forty feet from me. Without warning, the drum—a mile or more away on the mountain—went mad. The sound became an insane, dancing fury that rose to a wild, crashing crescendo.

The man on the beach began to revolve slowly and his arms moved out from his body as he turned. He seemed to spin, not by any action of his own, but as a top revolves when the string is unwound.

He was whirling like a dervish when the drum crashed, and stopped. The string which whirled him seemed to snap. His body jumped into the air. Still spinning, he struck the sand on his face, rolled over twice to lie flat on his back, arms outflung.

The spell which held me broke then and I sprang up and started toward him. An old man caught me by the arm and pulled me back. "No," he said. "Lezor will come for him."

HE HELD me, and the villagers stayed where they were until off the mountain and through the palm-roofed village and onto the beach came the man, Lezor. I knew him. A tall, dark man with black hair that fell about his shoulders, and black eyes that were like lambent flames, and a thin high-browed face that was dominated by a mouth savage as that of a wolf. He came across the beach and the natives made a wide and silent path for him. I could hear the crunching of his bare feet in the sand, and the murmur of the surf. Without a word he leaned over, picked up the stiff body and flung it over his shoulder. He turned and went back across the beach toward the mountain. . . .

All day I asked what had happened and always I got the same answer. Lezor had killed Nacano. The two men had quarreled. Nacano had attacked Lezor, who had escaped and gone to the mountains. After that there was no end for it except Nacano's death. The drums had killed him.

I had heard of such things in Africa and in Haiti, and blamed the death on the psychology of fear. I cursed myself for not having run out to Nacano, spoken to him and broken the trance before it was too late. I did not know then what I was to learn later, and I believed that I could have saved him.

It must have been a half year later that I married Teela. She was a tall, slender girl with skin the color of a rising moon, and there was a tint of bronze in the darkness of her hair. Her face was a soft oval. There was the pink of coral in her cheeks, and the scarlet of coral in her lips. I had given up all hope of ever returning to New York. No ship had ever touched this island, and perhaps none ever will. I was young and Teela was beautiful, with the golden fire of her skin, the soft fullness of her breasts—and when she moved it was the way a palm tree sways in the wind.

I had come to know Lezor well by then, for he too was in love with Teela. Lezor had spoken no word to me, but an old man of the village and Teela's mother had warned me that if I married the girl I should die the death of the drum. I tried to laugh at them, but remembering Nacano, the sound that I made was harsh and nervous in my throat.

I could see that the entire village was afraid, and throughout the wedding ceremony there was a sense of dread and of terror. The whole village, however, took part in the festivity, except Lezor. He came later.

There was something weird, something frantically terrible about the tall, gaunt man with the flaming black eyes and the black hair as he stood there flatfooted, staring at us. And once again I thought how like his mouth was to that of a wolf. When he spoke his words were not audible more than a yard away.

"You will not die the death of the drum, stranger," he said. "Teela chose you and she is yours, and now the curse is on you and the curse is on her, and the curse is on your child. Through your child I shall get my revenge." He turned then; his bare feet made a dull whisper in the sand as he started away.

I started to leap after Lezor, jerk him around and batter that animal-like face with my fists. Then I remembered I was a white man and I laughed. The whole thing was superstition and I was being absurd.

So completely had I forgotten that, during the time the mid-wife was with Teela, I did not once think of Lezor. There was a drum throbbing weirdly on the mountains, but only subconsciously did I hear it. It was shortly after sun-up that the drum stopped abruptly and I realized for the first time that it had been beating. A moment later I heard the midwife calling to me.

When I heard her voice I remembered with a sudden cold and shuddering fear the curse of Lezor. There was a note in the midwife's voice which I had never heard in the voice of a human being. My hands were clenched and beads of sweat stood on my forehead when I passed through the fringe of palm trees, and came in sight of the old woman standing in front of the little house.

Her cheeks were a mass of wrinkles, and above them her old and colorless eyes peered at me. Her teeth had rotted away years before so that her lips fell in across sunken gums. It was a face incapable of expression.

"It has happened," she said.

I went toward her then and I could feel a nerve quivering in the left corner of my mouth. I tried to speak but there was no sound. The old woman said, as if I had asked a question, "Lezor cursed the child."

"Where is it?"

Without a word she turned back into the hut. A moment later she came out, holding something in her hand.

FOR perhaps a full minute I stared at the thing without believing. And yet I must have always known that it would be so. It was not a human child that the old midwife held in her hand, though its body and head were shaped like those of human children. The head was too large and its face which should have been red and puckered, was a ghastly grey. Its eyes were closed like those of a whelp. I did not move when I saw its mouth, though I felt in that moment a vague premonition of the horror which was to come. For its mouth was the mouth of Lezor—the mouth of a wolf. Matted dark hair covered its head and body. The child raised one balled fist toward its face, and I saw that its hands were shaped like the feet of an animal.

The midwife looked at me with her bleak, expressionless eyes. "Do you understand what has happened?"

I shook my head.

"The child will never be like others. The curse has fallen on our people before. Within twelve days the child will be able to play like a little animal. Within a day or two after that he will be a monster who knows only one thing: how to kill. The law requires that the people of the village give you fourteen days. Then they will come to kill you and Teela and the child. They will come to kill me also, but I shall not be here."

Looking back I wonder at the calmness with which I accepted her statement. It did not seem strange to me then that the islanders should destroy the mother and the father of the thing which the midwife held. Somehow, with the sudden ceasing of the drum I realized the hopelessness of what I faced.

I do not clearly remember the two weeks which followed. I remember that now and then I would enter the small house and look at the child and the mother, and the old crone sitting silently in the corner. Then I would go out again shuddering with revulsion.

The child grew larger day by day. It was the fourth day, I think, that he began to make growling sounds in his throat. There were already teeth in his mouth and when he growled his lips curled back.

A change came over Teela also as she suckled the thing supposed to be our child. After its birth she was nervous, tense, even as I was, waiting desperately for the horror which was to come. But about the fifth day she began to smile, and when I saw her it made me sick deep in my stomach. For it was not the smile I had known a few months earlier. Her teeth must have been growing and when she smiled her upper lip pulled back showing the pointed ivory. There was a hungry, savage look growing in her eyes.

It was on the thirteenth day that the old midwife killed herself. She did it with a calm fatalism that added more than any other one thing could have to the horror of the day. If I hadn't already come to believe, to know, that the curse put upon me by Lezor would kill, I would have known it after the midwife's death. But from the moment I had looked at the child I had not doubted.

That same day Teela and the thing that she had borne and I started for the mountains. I went instinctively, I think, rather than from any desire or hope that I could escape the villagers. What Teela thought I don't know, for she had come to look more like the child than like her former self.

THE Thing—I could never think of it as my son, and I can't believe that there was really anything human about it—scampered along ahead of us the way a puppy gambols. It was about the size of a large bobcat then, with long clawlike fingers, big wolfish teeth—and its body was covered with stiff, black hair. It was the eyes, however, that set the cold and slimy fear prickling my spine. For in its red eyes I could see that the Thing hated me and that its hate grew more vicious with every hour.

The mountainside was rocky and steep. I was beside Teela and the Thing was about twenty yards ahead and above us, facing the right, when it stopped. I saw its nose begin to wrinkle, the lips to curl back from the long teeth. A savage, blood-hungry look came over its face and I thought of a starved dog. Then it began to move forward on its bare feet, cautious as a stalking animal.

There was a little whimpering noise beside me and I turned. Teela was staring after the child with dilated eyes. Her breathing was husky in her throat.

Above us the Thing was moving stealthily toward a clump of high grass beside a rock. Very suddenly it dived and at the same instant a panting, hoarse scream split its throat.

When it came erect there was a smile on its hideous face, and in its hands the still body of a rabbit. The animal's head hung queerly to one side where its neck had been broken, and the fur of the throat was stained with blood. Abruptly the child's head bent and long teeth fastened in the rabbit's throat.

I couldn't stand any more. "Stop it!" I yelled. "Stop it!"

The big head and the wild eyes lifted. The Thing began to back away from me, slowly. It growled deep in its throat and hatred vibrated through the sound the way the throb of a ship runs through its hull. I was cold and shaking inside, almost sick at what I had seen. I said, "Drop that rabbit. You can't eat it raw."

Something caught my shoulder, whirled me around. I saw black eyes in which wild fury leaped and I staggered backward. Cold iron shivered in my chest and my muscles were shaking as I stared into the contorted face of Teela. "Leave him alone!" The words sounded like the scream of a mother wolf. "He killed it! Let him eat it."

It must have been a full minute that I stared at her, unbelieving. Her face was twisted, long eye-teeth showing above her lower lip. Her breasts rose and fell with the fury of her breathing. Her right hand gripped my shoulder and the nails were buried in my flesh, but it was a long while before I noticed the pain. Then I pulled away from her and turned once more toward the Thing. It had disappeared.

We pushed on up the mountain and a half hour later it overtook us. There was blood smeared on its face, but the hands had been licked clean.

Night in the tropics comes quickly. While the sun trembled on a mountain top the sky was a white tent and the half moon was almost invisible against it. Then with a rush darkness spread over the heavens; the moon got mellow and bright.

Teela and I kept climbing and the Thing kept playing like a puppy about us. Its energy seemed inexhaustible; it scampered over rocks, dashed off in every direction to come loping back, to whimper about Teela, growl and show its teeth at me.

After an hour or two we found a spring which bubbled up between two rocks and went tinkling in a small stream down the mountainside. We stopped there for the night and ate of the food which we had brought. And it was then that I saw Teela take the dead bird from the bag I had carried and eat it raw. But I said nothing to her, for her eyes were fastened on me as she ate, and there was a hatred beyond expression showing in them.

The Thing didn't come near the small fire I built behind a rock, but I could hear it growling from the shadows near by. And when it growled, Teela answered. It was as if they were talking in those strange and horrible sounds, and the conversation set the blood moving icily through my veins. For I knew now that I was hunted not only by the natives of the village. *My own wife and child were planning my death!*

I DIDN'T understand the words they used, if those sounds could be called words. But their meaning was furiously clear. Now and then when Teela answered the Thing in the darkness her face turned toward me. I could see the look in her eyes and the way her lower lip twitched behind her eye-teeth. And time and again I could see the red eyes of the Thing glowing from the shadows.

I was sitting with my back against a large rock. The fire was only a foot or two in front of my outstretched legs and beyond the fire Teela squatted. Great rocks arose on every side, but in places the moon seeped through them to make liquid pools on the ground around which the black shadows towered. And twice I saw the Thing glide through these lighted places to vanish into darkness. Each time its face was turned toward me. The sight of that face above the deformed and hideous body set the muscles aching along my jaw.

I didn't want to sleep. I was afraid, horribly afraid. But it was more than fear that made me fight sleep, though I knew that eventually I must lose. I couldn't forget that the woman crouched across the fire from me, listening and answering those blood-hungry sounds from the darkness, was my wife. And I had loved her. God help me, but I still loved her, though I knew that she hated me now, and though the very sight of her changed face made me feel sick at the stomach.

We had climbed hard during the day and now my whole body was tired and aching. My eyelids felt heavy and tugged down at my cheeks, but I struggled to keep them open. Across the fire from me now Teela stretched flat on the ground, though I could not tell if she was asleep. A low wind made the coals of the fire glimmer. Far off somewhere a night-bird was singing. My eyes got heavier. . . .

Abruptly my head popped erect. My eyes jerked open and a cold shudder ran through me. At the edge of a pool of moonlight less than thirty feet away was the beast-thing, *my child,* glaring at me. Its mouth was still smeared with blood.

Stiff with fear, I looked at Teela. Her body had not moved, but I thought her eyes shut quickly.

My hands clenched on my hips then, clenched until the finger-tips sunk into the flesh. Oh God, I thought, this can't be true! It can't!

And yet I knew that the Thing in the darkness was my child, and that it planned my death.

"Very well," I said aloud. "If it wants to kill, we'll see. . . ." I knew that I could kill the Thing in an even fight. It wasn't any human child, but it hadn't gained its full strength. I could still whip it. If I waited a day or two it would grow and I would be the child in its hands.

I got half erect then, pushing against the large rock. As I moved, Teela stirred slightly. I stopped and suddenly I felt empty, hollow inside. Slowly I sank back to the ground. I couldn't kill the Thing. I knew that. I was an American and I couldn't kill my own child.

After a few minutes my eyes began to grow heavy again and with the desire for sleep a mounting terror crawled through my body. I knew that the Thing in the darkness was not asleep. Now and then I could see its eyes glowing like those of a cat from the blackness beside some huge rock, and I could see the hunger and the hatred in them. I fought the desire for sleep as I might have fought some drug that cloyed my blood.

Once I arose and put new sticks on the fire. It caught up, and I could hear the dry wood crackling. The circle of light spread wider, but Teela did not move. I would have built the fire even larger, but I was afraid. I knew that by now the villagers were looking for us. A fire would guide them. What our fate would be if they caught us, I did not know.

Time crawled like a sluggish worm through the darkness. I sat propped against the rock to keep from sleeping. The position was uncomfortable and my tired muscles ached. My head kept drooping downward toward my chest, then snapping erect again as fear lunged through me.

Gradually the tiredness began to seep into my brain. My eyelids tugged down until my lashes touched my cheek. My head wavered forward. . . .

I CAME awake fighting like a madman. I could feel the pain in my face and body, but it was dull and far removed compared to the horror which surged through me. Terror was a living, wild, and furious beast clawing its way through my vitals, and my fists beat without sense of direction.

I must have fought for half a minute before my staring eyes began to focus in the half second intervals they were allowed, before my fear-paralyzed brain began to record emotion.

And then I knew that the thing I had dreaded was happening. The deformed creature was at my throat, its claws tearing my shoulders, its hideous mouth fighting for my jugular vein. And beating at my body, raking the flesh from me with long nails, trying to hold my hands away from the Thing at my throat, was Teela!

I battered at the face, drove it backward, but Teela's hands still clung. She swept long nails across my cheek, leaving bloody tracks.

With a snarl the Thing dived. Its teeth fastened low in my throat, began to gnaw upward.

I caught at it, tried to tear it away. The teeth held, slid upward. Warm blood was spewing over my chest, but I could not feel the pain because of the terror which gripped me. *A half inch and those teeth would be in my jugular vein.*

I dug fingers into the matted hair of the Thing, tried to push it from me. Teela clawed at my wrists, jerked them away. The teeth jumped upward, clamped.

It was a paroxysm of horror and fear that hurled me over backward. The teeth held, went tighter.

And then, as suddenly as light may leave a room, the teeth left my throat. A howling, blood-curdling shriek rose like a trumpet of flame into the night, shaking high with pain. The cry of a wounded animal. A second later I was flinging myself erect, pawing at my body, writhing under the agony that scorched me in a dozen places.

Instinct sent me leaping from the fire into which we had rolled. For five long seconds I stood, body twitching from the pain of a dozen burns.

Across the fire the Thing whirled and leaped, paws beating at its coarse, black hair. Then it stopped spinning and came to crouch beside its mother at the edge of the firelight.

The Thing growled, deep in its throat. Teela answered, and both began to move on tiptoe around the edge of the fire toward me. I stood shivering, watching wide-eyed, mouth open, unable to move.

Even if I were able I couldn't kill this Thing and this woman. They were my wife and my child. I couldn't kill them, but. . . . They came on slowly, making that blood-hungry noise in their throats.

Perhaps I never really heard the sound. Perhaps I only imagined it, but it seemed to me that from far down the mountain I heard the low rumble of drums—the men of the village on the hunt!

Teela and the creature beside her were less than five yards away now. I whirled, leaped into the darkness and went racing down the mountain toward the men who hunted to kill me. At least they were human!

As I ran I heard Teela and the Thing, pounding after me. And I heard Teela's high, furious shriek, *"It will catch you, will kill you if it must follow you back to your country!"*

It was only luck that kept me from breaking my neck as I went down the mountain.

It was luck also which brought me safely past the men of the village who were searching for me. I didn't try to avoid them. Whatever it was they would do to me, I knew that it would be better than the death that lay in the hands and the teeth of my wife and child. I remembered Teela's words: "It will kill you if it must follow you back to your country." Somehow I didn't doubt those words, *and I still don't doubt them.* That I passed safely through the men who searched to kill me, did not relieve the awful certainty that the curse would follow me.

When I came into the village, empty except for the women, I meant at first to sit and wait for the men to return. I still believe it would be better to die the way they would have killed me than the way I must die. But I couldn't help hoping that I might escape. I am an American, and though I had seen enough to make me know the truth of the magic which had been put upon me, I kept telling myself that it was only some weird coincidence that had caused these things.

There were canoes pulled up on the beach. I took water and some food and went to one. I shoved it off and paddled away.

It was five days later, after the food and water was gone, that I lost consciousness. I don't remember being picked up by the ship which brought me back home. But I—I'm afraid. I can't forget Teela's curse.

TOM MAINOR went silent. His eyes darted nervously around the room. He licked dry lips, reached out and took a drink from the bottle. It was a stiff drink, but it was not the liquor which made him shudder.

I thought then that Mainor was slightly crazy; that the days without food or water had affected his mind. I talked with him a while longer, trying to laugh off his fears. But it didn't do any good. He left the club after finishing the bottle. His hand was icy cold when I shook it and promised to drop by his apartment the next day. As he went out of the door I could see his fingers twitching at his side—and though his walk was unnatural, it was not that of a drunken man.

I went over to the bar and joined Peters and Dave Wade in some juleps. That story had given me the jitters and I wanted company. Wade had gone to the phone to call some girls and arrange a party when the policeman came in. I didn't see him until he was beside me.

He was a big, sandy-headed man, but his face was a bit pale now. He looked from Peters to me and said hesitantly, "Er, er, either of you know a man named Tom Mainor?"

That wasn't any way for a normal policeman to speak and something sent those cold jitters over me again. I said, "He was my best friend."

"Come out here a minute," the cop said. My legs moved with the stiff, unnatural gait of Mainor as I went toward the street.

The body was at the mouth of a dark alley less than a hundred yards away. I can't tell you exactly how it looked because the first glimpse made me sick and I turned away. But not before I saw the look in his dead eyes—not before I saw that his throat had been split open and that there were coarse black hairs in his mouth and hands. . . .

CORPSES FOR WITCH'S MOUNTAIN

By Franklin H. Martin

What secret horror lay behind the whispered legend of midnight doom that stalked the tortuous road up Witch's Mountain? Was it some unknown demon of darkness that forced, one by one, the fear-frozen group of people to hurl themselves down into the storm-lashed maw of the canyon? Or was it the weird eyes of the gigantic film director, whose black whip writhed like a living serpent, waiting to feast on the living flesh of fildom's great!

A JAGGED streak of lightning cut a livid rip in the sky's pitch-black ceiling off to the north. The mounting rumble of thunder, then the swish of rain—driven before a sudden wind that whipped down from the mountains. Doris Gladden shivered a little as she stood with the little group of people under the portico of the administration building of Majestic Films, Inc., and looked at their tense faces. She seemed

to read on each the same look of half-fearful expectancy. The door behind them opened and two men came out to join the group. One, a giant in stature, was dressed in boots, riding breeches and a baggy tweed jacket. A mop of tangled black hair, unkempt, uncared-for, almost touched his shoulders. Impatiently he slapped the leg of his boot with a slender black riding whip.

This was Graubeck, the director. Some said he was divinely inspired. Some called him a madman. People fawned on him, listened with bated breath when he talked—and hated him on first sight. He was hated most by those who knew him best. But all agreed he was a genius. . . . The other man, slim and dapper and suave, was Douglas Hopping. Hopping, the famed producer, nominally Graubeck's superior.

Graubeck strode to the edge of the portico, stood out where the rain beat down upon him—stood with great chest expanded and black, leonine head thrown back, letting the storm drench him. His voice rumbled thunderously. "Magnificent!" His great arm swept in an arc to encompass the black, stormy horizon. "This is elementary. Real, terrific—beautiful!"

"Yes, of course." Douglas Hopping's voice was mild, soothing. "But do you think we should start out on location now? The storm may last until—"

"What the hell?" Graubeck bellowed. "I'll drive you—all of you—into the face of this storm, for days. Until you begin to feel, *feel*—you understand?" He slashed his bootleg with the slender whip, as if actually driving those trembling people through some elemental battle with the lashing rain, the crackling lightning.

But that meant they would start out at once, in this storm, up the side of Witch's Mountain. Witch's Mountain—a dark, lowering peak, a place shunned because of its treacherous passes and sudden, dizzy drops and sheer cliffs—but even more for its strange, sinister history. There was a legend that the mountain was accursed. Many and weird were the stories that seemed to prove it.

"We start at once!" Graubeck bellowed.

Doris Gladden, slim, blonde and fragile-looking, edged close to Paul Dorsey's broad shoulder. "He—he frightens me," she whispered.

Dorsey, Graubeck's ace cameraman, grinned down at her. "That's just his act. Beautiful. He likes to play the storm-king. But there's really nobody like him."

Graubeck whirled dramatically, faced the group huddled back out of the rain. "Doris! Can you feel—like that? You know the abandon of the storm, eh? Or maybe you're like the rest of these half-dead orchids, ready for the ash-heap!" Again the swish of the whip against bootleg.

Doris Gladden shuddered. There were ugly rumors that Graubeck had used that slim black whip on other stars. In private sessions, where the woman emerged wild-eyed and terrified, and gave magnificent performances! For people whispered he beat them to arouse them to the emotional heights he demanded, and the super-excellent performances which he alone got. No one could be sure, but Graubeck's latest sensation, a lovely, placid-looking girl, whom he had turned—miraculously—into a thing of fire and ice, had worn specially designed gowns that hid her lovely back—gowns that would prevent the camera's eye from catching the sharp red welts on the white skin. And Doris Gladden was to be Graubeck's next star. In a few minutes they would start for Witch's Mountain on location.

Her eyes, wide and blue and troubled, stared at the huge man.

"Answer me!" Graubeck blasted. "Can you *feel* the storm?"

"Yes!" The girl answered softly, quickly. "Oh, *yes!* I can feel it."

Graubeck cursed. "Then let's go! Come on!" He made a sweeping gesture with a muscular arm.

THE little company ran out from under the portico and climbed into the large bus waiting in the driveway. They breathed the stormy air gratefully, for there had been a five-hour conference in the director's office. Now they were facing a six-hour ride in order to get on location by dawn. The rest of the company would go in buses and trucks. Only a few rode with Graubeck and Douglas Hopping in the director's bus. Doris Gladden, the new star: Paul Dorsey, the ace cameraman, with the brown eyes and dreamy expression of an artist but with the fists and shoulders of a middle-weight fighter; Charley Wyeth, old-time "bit" player, grey-haired veteran of a thousand anonymous parts through two decades; Sandra Boyden, dark, exotic and smouldering—a perfect foil for Doris Gladden's blonde loveliness; Marvin Cleek, Doris Gladden's leading man, tall and dark, with roughly handsome features and a Texas drawl. And the driver.

They were going to film a Graubeck masterpiece from a grimly realistic novel dealing with primitive mountain folk. The picture—to be called "Wild Mate"—Douglas Hopping, the producer, had given Graubeck full rein to handle—to put the human puppets whom he directed and moulded under the blast of his blow-torch fervor and turn out another epic.

Graubeck made no gallant gesture at letting the two females of the group enter the bus first. He lunged through the door and dropped into a seat, letting them follow him aboard. One by one they all got in. The old trouper, Charley Wyeth was last. He was lifting his ancient traveling bag up on the rack. It slipped from his grasp and fell to the floor and flew open.

There was a moment's breathless silence. All stage and movie people are superstitious. Each has his pet jinx. But on the Majestic lot there was one evil omen that all knew and feared, from the newest extra to the president. When starting on location, if a member of the cast dropped his suitcase and it came open, bad luck rode the wind. People on other lots laughed at the idea—but with Majestic it was a foreboding sign of disaster—even of death.

Grey-haired Charley Wyeth scooped the bag up, turned a stricken face toward Graubeck. "I'm—I'm sorry. It slipped."

Graubeck's black eyes glinted like a snake's under his overhanging shaggy brows. "So *you* dropped it, eh?" he snarled accusingly.

"I'm sorry," Wyeth mumbled again.

Douglas Hopping cleared his throat. "If you think we ought to postpone our departure, Graubeck, we can still—"

"Hell, no!" Graubeck bellowed. "We'll start. I'll meet bad luck—even tragedy! Let it come. I'll welcome it, if it will only explode you bloodless clods into some kind of feeling! Let's go!"

The driver put his gears in mesh. Slowly, walking almost on tip-toe, hushed, like people at a funeral, the cast took their seats. Old Charley Wyeth slumped alone into a back seat. Sandra Boyden turned her head to glare at him. Her dark, slumberous eyes fastened for a moment on his lined face with a look of intense loathing. Her red lips formed the words, "You clumsy fool!"

Marvin Cleek shook his dark, handsome head. "That was a bad one, old-timer," he drawled.

Doris Gladden deliberately went back and settled herself near the old man. "You couldn't help it, Charley. It's a silly superstition, anyway."

Charley's worried face was miserable. "No, it isn't. It works. I've been around movie lots for more than twenty years. I'm sorry."

"Don't brood on it," the girl smiled.

Doris Gladden went up and sat down beside Paul Dorsey. "Poor old Charley," she said. "He's all broken up."

"He should be," Dorsey grinned. "Think of the doleful effect it had—even on Graubeck."

"It's sad about Charley Wyeth," the girl whispered. "He started the same time dad did, but he just never got any place."

The cameraman looked up in surprise. James Gladden, the girl's father, had been Hollywood's most celebrated director, up to the time of his mysterious disappearance, two years before. There were whispers about his sudden dropping from sight, some talk of scandal, fantastic stories of strange intrigue. But nothing had ever been proved or disproved. He had just gone. No word had been heard of him since, except for vague rumors.

Usually Doris didn't talk about her father, Dorsey knew. She had gone ahead with her own career as a budding actress. She had worked hard, intelligently. And now she was getting her first big chance—directed by Graubeck, himself.

The girl seemed oddly restless. She stared out of the bus window, dark from the night outside, alive with a quicksilver flow of sheeted rain.

"Don't worry, Beautiful." Dorsey grinned. "Everything will be all right. This is the start of big things for you."

She gripped his sleeve with a sudden clutch of fear. "Paul, I'm—worried. It's as if some terrible thing were hanging over me. I never felt this way before. It isn't because of—that silly evil omen either. As if poor Charley dropping his suitcase could harm us. I'm—I'm just plain frightened."

The bus rumbled and jogged along. Through the windows nothing showed but a smear of wet, black night. There was little conversation. They sat still, rigid, staring straight ahead. Paul Dorsey's hand closed around Doris Gladden's in a reassuring grip, and he was surprised how cold her fingers were. "Don't let it get you, Doris," he grinned. "It's the storm, and Graubeck, and maybe some disturbing memories—and that damn' suitcase superstition."

"No," she whispered. "It's none of those things. It's something else. I don't know what, but it's here—and I'm afraid!"

CHAPTER TWO

Madman's Laughter

THE big luxurious bus swayed from time to time as it rolled over the rough mountain road, and sometimes the motor labored and the floor took on a steep angle. They had to climb a steep grade on the way up to Old Witch, but from the windows it was all one trackless, black void.

It was Graubeck's own special bus, equipped with every convenience of a Pullman car, with washstands and even a well-stocked ice-chest. Graubeck wormed around, opened the ice-chest and took out a large leg of cold fowl and a chill bottle of wine. He jerked the cork with one powerful twist of his fingers, began drinking from the bottle and gnawing on the pheasant leg. Only after several bites did he turn around and wave toward the ice-chest, making some gruff, unintelligible sound apparently meant to be an invitation for the rest to help themselves.

But nobody stirred.

"All right!" Graubeck growled, mouth full. "Rag dolls. No souls, no bellies. Don't feel, don't eat, don't breathe. Clods, all of you!"

"May I get you something to eat?" Paul Dorsey asked.

Doris Gladden shook her head. "Thanks, no. I'm not—hungry. I don't feel—" She stopped. The bus lurched suddenly and halted. The abrupt silence accentuated the lash of wind-driven rain on the roof. The storm was increasing in violence.

Graubeck lowered the pheasant's leg from his mouth and peered around the driver's screen. "Well? Get on! Why are you stopping here? Afraid of the storm?"

The white-faced driver tried the starter until Graubeck yelled again. "Stop grinding the life out of that thing. See what's wrong!"

Taking a flashlight from a tool pocket and draping his slicker over his shoulders, the driver stepped out into the rain. The occupants flattened their faces against the windows to see where they were, but the darkened rain-streaked windows told them nothing. The tilt of the bus told them they were on an incline.

"Ignition might've gotten wet," Marvin Cleek guessed, "splashing over these mountain roads."

Sandra Boyden whirled from the window. "This damn mountain! I hate it!"

"Hate a lot of things lately, don't you?" Marvin Cleek drawled.

"I hate *you for one,* you big four-flush-er!" Sandra's face was, for a split second, gaunt with bitterness.

Graubeck clapped his hands in ironical applause. "You're improving, Sandra. But I can see why you don't want to register in front of a camera. Emotion makes you ugly, wizened as a witch."

"If I were a man I'd cut your heart out!" Sandra screamed, in a hysterical fit of temper. "You great, fat slug—you unspeakable baboon!"

Graubeck for once seemed to be enjoying himself. "God," he said deliberately, "you're not even a woman. You're an alley-cat. Now shut up!"

"What is the matter with everyone?" Doris Gladden demanded. She put her finger-tips to her temples. "You're all so jittery I could scream!"

Abruptly, old Charley Wyeth pulled his slicker from the rack. "I think I'll get some air." He walked down the aisle to the door.

Marvin Cleek threw a disgusted glance at Sandra Boyden. "Me too, pardner. The atmosphere in here is sort of thick."

"Just a minute, Marvin!" Sandra snapped. "I want to tell you something." She went out on Cleek's heels, clawing at the back of his coat.

Graubeck bellowed out the door to the driver, "When are you going to fix that motor, you dim-witted rabbit!"

Doris Gladden appealed to Paul Dorsey. "Can't you see? Everyone is acting so strangely. It isn't like Marvin and Sandra to fight like that. They like each other very much. Even Graubeck isn't as brutal as this usually. You can notice the effect even on poor Charley. What is it?"

Dorsey grinned. "Well, maybe it's the mountain. There's a legend about it, you know. They began to call it Witch's Mountain years ago—" He stopped and his eyes became worried. "Why, Doris, don't look so horrified. Everyone is just on edge. Nerves—that's all."

There was a quick, blinding flash of lightning.

From the blackness outside came a lusty shout that trailed off weirdly. Then, a moment's electric silence, broken only by the patter of rain—and on top of that a shrill feminine scream. The scream was repeated and echoed, freighted with a wild terror that made Doris Gladden stiffen in her chair and dig her nails deep into the flesh of her palms.

"Wh—what was that?" she breathed.

Douglas Hopping roused himself from his reverie and stepped to the door, called out uncertainly, "Is something wrong?"

Graubeck thrust him aside. "Hey, you!" he shouted to the driver. "Give me that flashlight."

The driver, standing by the raised hood of the stalled motor, half turned toward the black void that had been the origin of the blood-curdling shriek. He shot the flashlight beam in that direction, but it showed only a yellow cone of slanting rain.

Charley Wyeth's face emerged beside the bus door. "What is it?"

GRAUBECK lumbered out into the rain, snatched the flashlight from the driver's hand, and directed the beam on the wet, rocky ground in front of him. "What's wrong?" he trumpeted. There was no answer. He advanced, playing the light, illuminating only a few feet of ground before him with each step. And then the light fell upon a slumped figure, folded face down, like an Oriental in prayer. It was Sandra Boyden, and the rain was lashing her bent back, pressing her thin clothing close about her form, limning each curve of her soft shoulders and rounded, shapely thighs. The gigantic director reached down, clamped one huge paw around the girl's shoulder, and jerked her to her feet.

"Snap out of it!" he growled. "What happened?"

The girl turned her face toward his, her dark eyes wide in the flashlight glare, her face stamped with sheer terror. Graubeck shook her roughly. "What is it? Where's Marvin?"

"I wanted—wanted to tell him something," she gasped. "I had to tell him something, because I had an awful feeling I wouldn't see him again—ever."

"What did he do?" Graubeck snarled. "Run off in the rain, rather than listen to your whining?"

"No—no!" Her voice rose shrilly. "He went off the cliff—fell. I saw him go over—just as the lightning flashed!"

Graubeck played the flashlight around, stepped back quickly with a half-smothered curse. Not five feet from where they stood was an abyss, a canyon that reached down abruptly to black nothingness. The director cupped his hand and shouted, "Hey, Marvin! Marvin Cleek!"

There was no answer, save a storm-smothered echo, and the swish of wind-driven rain. Slickers thrown around them, the others piled out of the car. Graubeck reached out suddenly and jerked Doris Gladden back with a yank that pulled her to her knees. "Look out!" he warned. "There's a sheer drop here."

He moved cautiously forward, played the flashlight along the edge of the cliff. When Doris Gladden saw the steep black drop she covered her face with her hands and a tremor shook her slim body. She had been within inches of the rim when Graubeck had yanked her back.

Graubeck lay prone, head out over the edge of the cliff and pointed the flashlight down. "If Marvin Cleek went over there there's nothing we can do," he said, getting to his feet. "It's a drop of two hundred feet, at least."

Sandra Boyden dropped to her hanls and knees again, began crawling toward the edge of the precipice. In a wild, stricken voice she started to wail, "Marvin! *Marv-in!*"

Graubeck reached one hand under her arm-pit, lifted her roughly to her feet and started her back toward the car. The others followed dumbly. Dorsey's arm went around Doris Gladden's shoulders as she stumbled toward the lighted vehicle. She hesitated, leaning against him.

"Paul—this is terrible! I had a premonition. I told you so."

Graubeck stopped in front of the gawking driver. "Hey, didn't you fix that motor yet?"

"You took my light," the man said sullenly.

The director pushed the flashlight back into the driver's hand and hoisted Sandra Boyden's half limp form through the bus door.

"Better turn around and go back to town for help," Douglas Hopping suggested.

"What the devil for?" Graubeck grumbled. "If Marvin Cleek was fool enough to fall over that cliff nothing can help him now. We're going on up the mountain."

"And leave him?" Hopping gaped.

"It would do a lot of good to stay here!" Graubeck snarled. "Somebody can come back in the morning. Soon as that motor's fixed we go on up the mountain!"

"Listen, chief," Paul Dorsey said. "Maybe there's a way down that cliff. We might find it, if we looked around. There should be a tow rope in your chariot. That would help."

"I looked over that cliff!" Graubeck snapped. "I'm saying we get going."

"But Mr. Graubeck," old Charley Wyeth protested, gently. "Maybe poor Marvin is—"

Graubeck's heavy hand gave the old actor a vigorous shove. "Do I have to stand here, and listen to a bunch of sniveling puppies! Sit down, all of you."

The driver, his slicker dripping water, climbed into his seat. The starter purred. The motor caught.

"Up the mountain!" Graubeck barked.

Sandra Boyden flashed to life from her slumped posture in a deep seat. Her dark eyes were wide and staring, her fingers hooked like talons, her exquisite features strangely twisted. "You can't go and leave him like that!"

Graubeck's thick fingers closed around the whip that dangled from his wrist by a little strap. "You never could act, Sandra. Sit down and shut up."

"But," Hopping said mildly, "it is irregular to go on and leave him. How will you explain it, not trying to find him?"

"His body is two hundred feet below, on the rocks!" Graubeck snarled. "I saw it. We can't reach him—and I've got nothing to explain. It's this alley-cat"—he jerked his head toward Sandra Boyden—"who has plenty to explain. She and Cleek were sweethearts, until he got tired of her nagging—God knows he had reason! She followed him out. He went over the cliff and she didn't. Well—what's your guess?"

"I didn't do it, I tell you!" Sandra screamed. "We were still sweethearts. There's a curse on this mountain. And there's a curse on you, too, Graubeck. Everyone who comes in contact with you has bad luck. What about that kid—your protege—who committed suicide? How about—another in an insane asylum. . . And now Marvin Cleek—he only walked over the edge of a cliff." She stabbed a long-nailed finger at him. "You're cursed, Graubeck. You know it—*cursed!*"

"You pushed him over!" Graubeck snarled. His great shaggy head turned slowly to look at each occupant of the bus. "What just happened is the result of a quarrel between two puny, neurotic morons. I've got an important job to do, and this lovers' mess, or death itself isn't going to interfere. Get me? I'll get somebody to handle Cleek's part. Hell, I can get a dozen! But we're going up the mountain and make that picture!"

"You can get a dozen to take his place!" Sandra shrilled. "But I can't! You don't want human beings. When you're through with them they're crazy. You put your stamp on them—your curse!"

DORIS GLADDEN'S mouth felt dry. She was trembling, and she stifled an inexplicable desire to scream. She knew she would, if Sandra's crazy tirade didn't stop. Things were bad enough without that. She got up and put her hand on the dark girl's shoulder. "Please, Sandra, control yourself. It was an accident."

"No!" Sandra's mouth was twisted with fury. "No! It was Graubeck's curse. You should know about that, Doris. Graubeck was the last one who worked with your father, just before he disappeared. He worked with him on this very mountain. What became of your father?" She laughed bitterly. "Ask him!"

Her finger jabbed accusingly at the big director. And Graubeck's huge paw caught Sandra Boyden's shoulder, slammed her back into a seat.

Doris Gladden's whole body trembled as she confronted the hulking director. "What do you know about my father?"

"Just what everyone knows," Graubeck growled. "He disappeared about two years ago. I suppose I'm responsible for every crazy fool who runs away, eh?"

Douglas Hopping cleared his throat, timidly. "I'm afraid I'll have to assert my authority, Graubeck, and order you to turn back. Something must be done about Cleek."

"Oh, you must, heh?" Graubeck's deep voice was sarcastic. "You don't fool me, Hopping. What do you care about Marvin Cleek? You know it's too late to do anything. What you're worried about is the so-called curse of this fool mountain. Well, we don't turn back, see? We keep going, so we're up there at dawn—ready to shoot the first scenes."

Hopping mumbled some half-hearted objection. It was drowned in Graubeck's bellowed order to the driver. "Get going, you!"

Again the car began its labored, jouncing journey through the black stormy night, up the steep twisting road of Witch's Mountain. Sandra Boyden slumped limply in her seat. All animation was gone from her body, but her eyes, resting on Graubeck's back, were alive with a blazing flood of vitriolic hate.

Doris Gladden resumed her seat, like a person in a daze. Everything was so strange, so suddenly terrifying. These people, staring, white-faced, were not at all as they had been, only a few short hours ago. They were like figures in a nightmare. The sway of the bus was making her feel light-headed. The black, stormy night, beating and lashing against the bus windows seemed to take on a new significance; a weird, terrible presaging of doom.

She tried to tell herself that they were just going out on location, that this was the beginning of her big chance. But there was an indefinable undercurrent that beat on her senses like the distant throbbing of tom-toms. It pulsed to a single note. Doom. Doom.

Paul Dorsey was sitting beside her, patting her hand. "Don't pay any attention to what Sandra said, Doris. Graubeck didn't have anything to do with—your father's disappearance. I'm sure of that."

"Wh-what made Marvin Cleek walk off that cliff?" She tried to keep her voice and thoughts steady.

"It was an accident," Dorsey soothed. "He just walked that way, and didn't see the canyon in the dark. It was horrible. Don't think about it."

Doris looked up at the cameraman's face, and queer tingling sensation ran up her spine. Paul Dorsey was smiling, but it was not his usual, friendly smile. There seemed to be a diabolical twist to his lips, and a strange, almost demoniac light in his eyes.

Suddenly Sandra Boyden leaped from her seat. She screamed shrilly, once, and her clawed fingers raked Graubeck's face. The big director drew back his hand and dealt her a blow on the side of the head. She collapsed in her seat as if all her bones had turned to string.

Doris Gladden shrank back, turned toward Paul Dorsey. "Why don't you stop him? Why do you let him strike a woman like that?"

"She was hysterical," he explained. "He had to do it."

"So you're afraid of him, too!" the girl accused.

"Take it easy," Dorsey advised. "She needs to be treated like that. Graubeck is really wonderful. Wait and see. He'll make you a sensation."

"It's true that he kicks women around, then," the girl said slowly. "He really does treat them like dogs, lashes them with that whip. He won't do it to me, you hear? He won't make a star of me that way!"

Dorsey was still smiling, with that odd, diabolical twist to his face. "Don't worry, Beautiful. Don't worry about a thing. . . ."

The progress of the big bus seemed to become more labored. The motor pounded and gears grated as the driver dropped it into second. There was a sputtering rant to the engine's pace as the driver raced it with clutch thrown, as if trying to pick up the missing cylinders. The bus stopped.

"Now what, for God's sake?" Graubeck bellowed.

Once more Sandra Boyden started up. "I'm not going to stay in this accursed thing!" She lunged toward the door. "You're not going to drive me mad, Graubeck!" Her weight against the door rail threw it open. For a second no one moved. And Sandra Boyden jumped out into the black, stormy night.

"Go after her!" Doris Gladden begged Dorsey.

The camerman was on his feet as she spoke. He jumped toward the front of the bus and went through the door. Wind-driven rain lashed through the opening. They heard Dorsey's voice calling. Doris Gladden tried to follow, but she felt very tired. Her arms and legs were very heavy. She dropped back into her seat.

Then came another shout—a shrill, high-pitched scream. So sharp and sudden that it seemed to cut into the girl like a knife.

Old Charley Wyeth passed the girl's seat, running down the aisle to the door. He stood there, peering out into the savage night. Several times he called. There was no answer, save the wind and rain. Charley Wyeth started to step off the bus, but Graubeck's hamlike hand shot out and jerked him back. The director stood in the door and sent his booming voice out into the drenched blackness.

Still no answer.

"What happened?" Wyeth asked.

Graubeck glowered at the little old actor for several seconds, then he threw back his head and began to laugh. His laugh echoed like the boom of a storm surf, but there was no mirth in it. Rather it was the fiendish cacophony of a madman. It hammered against the girl's ear-drums like a physical pressure. Doris Gladden shivered, involuntarily. She blinked at her eyes, trying to clear her strangely blurring vision. The lights of the bus began to whirl before her eyes. She seemed to be spinning into space. . . .

CHAPTER THREE

Graubeck's Spell

WHEN Doris regained her senses the bus was in motion again. There was a sharp odor in her nostrils. She opened her eyes to see Old Charley Wyeth bending over her, holding a bottle of smelling salts under her nose. She shook her head. She had the sensation of just awakening from a bad dream. She looked around wildly. Up at the front of the bus Douglas Hopping was hunched over, chin on chest. Graubeck was sitting straight up, his great shaggy black head and shoulders towering above the back of the seat.

She and old Charley Wyeth were the only ones in the back of the bus. The others were gone.

"What happened?" she asked the old actor. "Where did Paul Dorsey and Sandra Boyden go? What happened to them?" Her tongue felt dry; the strange metallic taste of fear was in her mouth.

Charley Wyeth shrugged. There was a hint of a grim smile on his lips as he said: "Guess Old Witch got them, just like Marvin Cleek."

"What do you mean?"

"This road runs along the edge of a cliff," Charley Wyeth explained. "At some places it's a sheer drop only a few feet off the road. There is a legend around that if you walk near the edge on certain nights something makes you jump. Foolish, of course. Yet—"

"Then you think all three of them—Marvin Cleek and Sandra and Paul Dorsey, all walked off the face of the cliff?" There was incredible awe in her voice.

He was silent for a full minute. Then he said in a husked tone: "I—I don't want to think about that. But—it looks that way."

The girl pictured that first step off into nothingness—in the dark! The awful hurtling through wet black space, down and down. . . . She covered her face with her hands.

"Graubeck's going on up the mountain." Charley Wyeth's voice dropped almost to a whisper. "He says he's going to start making a picture at dawn, no matter who decides to step off the side of the mountain."

"He's inhuman!" Doris breathed, through white lips. "How did the bus happen to stop like that, twice, each time so near the edge of the cliff?"

Charley Wyeth shrugged. "Do you think they all ran out that way—just to leap straight over the edge?" He crouched close to the girl's side. "But listen: I—I'm scared as hell. You know that—I had the feeling to run out the last time we stopped, too. Something sort of pulled at me—to run out!"

The girl's wide eyes studied the old trouper's lined face. She shuddered. "I hate to admit it," she said, "but I did too. Something—something awful—made me want to go out there. Like a hand that reaches cold fingers into your soul. . . ."

"It's something to do with Graübeck, I think," Charley Wyeth said huskily. "He was just a tramp reporter on a Los Angeles paper ten years ago. A big, roughneck leg-man, too thick to write his own stories. Had to telephone them in. Then he got something on somebody and got a job in pictures. Blackmail, practically. All of a sudden, he changed. He got very strange. Used to live up here some place in a little cabin. Got interested in black magic—they say he sold his soul to the devil. . . ."

"That's crazy, preposterous!" the girl cried. And yet, there was something about this horrible night. . . .

"I'm only telling you what they say," Wyeth went on, gently. "He makes people into stars—and then they run away or go crazy, or commit suicide. I've been around more than twenty years, Doris. I've seen a lot. They say there's a curse on Graubeck, just like there's a curse on this mountain. I used to laugh at those things when I was young—I believe them now."

"It's like a horrible hallucination!" Doris got up, made her way jerkily to the front of the bus. Graubeck turned and looked at her as she approached.

"I—I want to go back," she told him. "I don't want to—to go on."

Graubeck stood up slowly, towered above her. He measured each word as he spoke. "Go back and sit down." The thin black riding whip swayed from its strap on his wrist as he raised his arm to point. His black eyes gleamed like witch's fire beneath the straggling bushiness of his eyebrows. "You're going to start work tomorrow morning. And you will do just as I tell you. I'll make you respond as a musician makes his instrument respond—make you answer my will in every fiber of your body and soul!" He leaned toward her. "I will make you feel things, as I feel them. I will give the world my magic—through you!"

What was that compelling hypnotic power that dragged her, helpless, to him? The weird, hypnotic light in his strange eyes; the slumbering vibrance of his rumbling voice? She steeled herself against him. This man was half beast, half devil. He warped human beings—made them creatures of his diabolic will—until they could hear the unearthly voices urging them on, to dash blindly into the night, to run, torture-driven, over the canyon edge.

They had all been under his spell. Marvin Cleek and Sandra Boyden were puppets of his own molding. Paul Dorsey, the cameraman, had looked upon him as a deity.

This sinister brute in human form had twisted their minds and souls the way a storm wind twists a grove of saplings. He leaned over here, like some obscenely gross, hulking statue, glaring out of slitted jet eyes; and the whip, hanging from his wrist, swung back and forth with the sway of the climbing bus.

Perspiration beaded the girl's upper lip as she stared at him from fright-frozen eyes. She fought back an impulse to scream, to fly at him and claw those sagging jowls with her nails—as Sandra had done, just before she had dashed out to plunge to dark destruction.

"You're *not* going to do that to me!" Despite her efforts at control her voice quavered. "You're not going to put your spell on me. Do you hear? I won't look at you! I won't listen to you!" She twisted to face Douglas Hopping, to appeal to him. But he sat like a rag doll, head forward, chin resting on chest. Eyes blank and staring.

"Yes," Graubeck rumbled, and his voice was soft yet strangely penetrating, "I will mould you—my way!"

A prickling sensation started in the tips of her fingers, ran up her arms. This was all unreal and grotesque. She almost prayed it was a horrible dream, yet she knew that it was not. Somehow Graubeck must have the sinister power to turn people into driveling madmen. And he was staring at her now. It was her turn next. . . !

She turned, lunged toward the rear of the bus. Graubeck's great rumbling voice echoed around her ears. She put her hands up to keep it from her brain, but it seeped in through her skull, reverberated in her whirling senses. "I will mould you —*my way!*"

OLD Charley Wyeth crouched in the rearmost seat, watching her with wide, frightened eyes. "You see? You see what he does to you?"

The lurching sway of the bus threw the girl off balance. She pressed her face against the cool glass of the window and tried to fight the feeling of dread and terror that was enveloping her like a rising tide. Her eyes, wide with fright, stared out at the jet night through the streaming pane. A constantly rolling curtain of black nothingness—like the inside of a dark terrible tunnel.

Then she saw a face!

Out of the wet stygian smear beyond the window, out in the storm-burdened night, she saw a face. The face of Paul Dorsey. White, with great staring eyes, it looked back at her for a second, as if floating in space. The mouth was open, as though calling her name, "Doris!"

But there was no sound, and the face was gone in the same manner it had loomed out of nothing—like a flash. Paul Dorsey, who had plunged over the rim of the cliff, miles and miles back along the dark, mountain road. The girl pressed her cheek against the glass and stared at the dark curtain of night until her eyes ached. The doomed look in his eyes—the awful set expression of his mouth! That was the way he must have looked as he started to plunge down, down into—. Doris pressed the palms of her hands to her aching eyes. A frightened moan escaped her tight-pressed lips.

"What—what is it?" Charley Wyeth's voice was a husky whisper above the drum of the motor.

"I'm not going to stay in this bus," she told him. "I won't ride up the mountain with that fiend! I'm through. You hear me? I'm through!"

"You mean you're going to get out?" Wyeth grated. "You're going to jump out, like the others did?"

"I'm not going to stay here," she repeated. "It's driving me mad."

"Good Lord!" Wyeth groaned, his blue-veined hands shaking. "Maybe Old

Witch is calling you—like it called the others. . ."

"No." She breathed the word through clenched teeth. "I'm not going to jump over the cliff. He—he hasn't put his mark on me yet. I'd rather trust myself to Old Witch than stay with him."

"You sure—you're not under his spell already?" Wyeth whispered.

"No. Not yet." Her little chin became firm.

"Then I'll go with you." The old bit actor's hands trembled. "I'll raise this window and we'll jump out. We can get a foot-hold on the rear fender. He'd never let you get past him to go out the door."

"You'll go with me?" Her trembling fingers rested gratefully on Wyeth's thin wrist.

"Sure, Doris. I'll go with you. I knew your father. I knew all of them, when they were starting. I even know this mountain. . . . Soon as the car slows down for a steep turn I'll open the window and we'll drop off. We can get back."

"Back?" she repeated dully.

"Yes, back to town. It's a long walk, but—"

The car seemed to slow down. Charley Wyeth knelt on the back seat and lifted the large, specially-built window. The wind drove a wet spray of rain over them. It was impossible to see anything except a few feet of wet rocky road in the glow of the headlights.

"Jump!" Wyeth urged.

Doris Gladden threw one last look over her shoulder. Graubeck, in the front seat, was staring straight ahead. She threw one slim leg over the sill, then the other landed on the rear fender. She pushed herself clear. Gratefully she felt the thud of her feet on the hard, wet road. Charley Wyeth followed. For a moment they stood in the driving rain and watched the big lighted bus lumber on up the road, climbing a twisting grade.

A sudden wild desire to shout seized Doris. The rain lashed her face and body. She screamed, "Good-bye, Graubeck. Good-bye. you damn' devil!"

The tail-light of the bus faded to a red pin-point. And then, blackness.

"Come, my dear, we must start," the old actor suggested, gently taking her arm. Something—she didn't know exactly what—suddenly terrified her. She whirled, faced him, a vibrant, living shadow in the stormy night. Then, without warning, a sudden madness seemed to grip her. Blood pounded wildly against her ear-drums. She uttered a single, piercing peal of laughter and whirled, began to run.

"Please, for God's sake!" Wyeth called after her. She heard, above the tattoo of her own hastening feet, his faltering pursuit. And then—dark silence.

She ran faster, her feet stumbling on rocky ground as she left the road. Nothing ahead or behind, above or below, but blackness and wind-whipped rain. A swirling, and a night that was like inky cotton. And its very substance seemed to shriek, "Faster—*faster!*"

"Stop!" Wyeth screamed behind her. "That's what the others did!"

The girl laughed as she plunged headlong through the stormy dark. Graubeck hadn't gotten her. He couldn't get her!

Suddenly her feet went from under her. Her hands pawed emptiness, clawed desperately . . . blankness. . . .

CHAPTER FOUR

The Mountain Curse

COLD rain beat on the bare flesh of her arms and neck. Everything was black around her. She was lying face down on rocky ground, her fingers clutching jutting stones. Then she turned, heard Charley Wyeth's voice. "Sorry, Doris. I had to tackle you. Had to throw you on the ground. You were headed for the big drop."

"Oh, Charley . . . Thank Heaven. I don't know. I think I was a little crazy."

"Your nerves were shot," Wyeth told her. "Come on. Get up and give me your hand. We'll get going."

Doris scrambled to her feet, felt again the bite of rain against her face. "Where can we go? In this awful storm we won't be able to find our way."

"I can find it." There seemed to be a new note of excitement in the old actor's voice. "You'll be surprised how well I know this mountain."

She felt for his hand in the dark. Together they started to walk. The rain lashed them and the wind whipped across their faces.

Gratefully, after a while, the girl felt the relative smoothness of the paved road underfoot. She gripped old Charley's hand, leaning her weight against the chilling wet wind, struggling along at his side, eyes half closed. The night was filled with a thousand shrieking sounds.

She thought once she heard Sandra Boyden's voice as it had trailed off in that last terrible frightened scream. Then Paul Dorsey's voice seemed to ride the whistling wind. Then it was Graubeck's rumbling bellow. But all faded into a derisive whistle of the elements. Half conscious, half alive, she stumbled on, hanging grimly to Charley Wyeth's hand.

"This way!" He spoke close to her ear against the tumult of the storm. "We climb a little here—off the road."

Stumbling, groping, she stayed with him. Then the moan and whistle of the wind died a little, and the rain was not lashing at them.

"There's a big cave in here," Charley Wyeth said.

She heard the scrape of a match. The flare of its flame showed Charley's face gaunt and grey, wetter than a drowned man's. Lined—but somehow triumphant. The match-flame spread. Charley had lighted a candle.

"What place is this?" She was looking around dazedly.

"A cave," he told her. "I've been here before. I've been here often." Then he began to laugh, a strange high-pitched laugh. And something in that laugh made Doris cringe and stare at him in wonder.

Charley Wyeth put the candle on the floor of the cave. He sat down, cross-legged in front of it. Doris sank limply across from him on the other side of the candle, and stared across the flickering light at the man who had guided her there through the storm.

"I can't bring myself to realize these terrible things have actually happened," she said. "The whole thing seems unreal, from the time we started—"

"I dropped my suit-case, and it flew open," Charley Wyeth reminded her. "That didn't make them feel any better. When I dropped my bag—"

"Don't blame yourself," Doris broke in. "Some terrible evil was abroad. Marvin and Sandra are gone. And Paul is gone. Paul and I were in love, Charley. Just when it seemed that everything might turn out so well. We had both worked so hard. It was an awful shock when dad disappeared. Now Paul is gone . . ." The girl's voice trailed off.

"They always said this mountain was bewitched," Charley Wyeth said. "But I've been coming up here for years. This cave nobody knows about but me. I've got candles here, you notice. I even have some food cached here, too. You hungry?"

"No, thank you." She passed the back of her hand over her wet forehead. "I don't think I'll ever eat again."

Charley Wyeth got up and walked into the shadowy corner of the cave. The girl heard him fumbling around with something that made a heavy scraping sound. He approached the lighted area carrying a square tin of corned beef in his hands. "Come on," he invited. "Come and watch me feed the dog."

"The dog?" The girl's face and voice were puzzled. *"Dog?* I'm so tired, Charley. I'll wait here."

"This—is a very special dog."

She looked up at him, and the odd expression on his face unconsciously made her recoil. "What is it, Charley? What are you talking about?"

"Come and see." He picked the candle from the floor, and Doris scrambled to her feet and followed him.

He walked toward the rear of the cave. The ceiling became lower and the flickering light of the candle-flame cast shadows in odd, jumping patterns. At the back of the cave there was an L turn. The floor sloped slightly downward. Charley Wyeth put the candle on the floor and began to pull back a screen of cut pine limbs and dead branches.

Behind the screen of boughs were the stout steel bars of a cage. Something moved behind the bars, and Doris' startled eyes fixed on skinny, dirty fingers which wrapped themselves around the steel grating!

DORIS GLADDEN'S lips opened, but sheer, sickening terror froze her voice. Inside that cage was a thing that looked strangely like a man, a figure tall and gaunt, bearded. He was dressed in ragged singlet and trousers. The uncertain light of the candle cast his bearded face and form in weird lights and shadows, made his eyes gleam like a wild beast's.

Charley Wyeth chuckled. He tossed the can of corned beef between the bars. The gaunt figure pounced upon it with animal-like ferocity, seized it and smashed it with his two hands against the rocky floor of the cave. The can split with the blows and the ragged creature dug the meat out with his fingers, stuffing it in his mouth, eating with ravenous gulps.

"A very special kind of dog!" Charley Wyeth smiled, and there was something in that smile that made Doris slink back, gasping. "See him? He used to be a great man, a big shot. Look close, Doris. Look very close. And see a man transformed into a beast!"

As Wyeth spoke the girl's name, the man in the cage straightened. The broken can of meat dropped from his fingers. He stepped close to the bars. "What did you say, Wyeth?"

At the sound of the gaunt man's voice Doris swayed toward the cage. She stood, gripping the steel rungs, staring. Then she covered her face with her hands. "It's too much!" she wailed. "It's a horrible dream—Paul's poor dead face in the black night. Then dad's voice. . . ."

"Doris!" The man in the cage was straining against the bars. "Doris! It is your dad. Hold the light close, child. Can't you see? My own eyes are a little dim. I've been in this place months, years . . ."

The girl held the candle close, staring at the face of the gaunt, grey-bearded man. Then the candle slipped from her fingers and she collapsed limply on the floor, her two hands twined about the bars. The candle rolled along the floor and Charley Wyeth picked it up, held it high over his head.

"It's your daughter, all right, Jim Gladden," he laughed shrilly. "She was going to start making a picture up on the mountain tomorrow. She was going to be a star, Gladden. A real star!"

The tattered, grey-bearded man kept calling the girl's name, over and over. She looked up and struggled weakly to her feet.

"Dad, I'll get you out of there . . . but

I'm so tired. It's been so terrible tonight. I don't know yet whether I'm having a nightmare, or whether I've died—and in the worst hell anyone could know. . . ."

Charley Wyeth's shrill, insane laughter blotted out the man's answer. It echoed like the babel of a crazed mob against the narrow rock walls of the cave.

"This time we reverse the usual procedure," he cackled. "You go through hell first—then you die!"

CHAPTER FIVE

From Beyond the Grave

THE girl stiffened, whirled, and threw herself upon Charley Wyeth. "Open that cage! Let him out! You hear me?"

Charley Wyeth backed away from her, shaking his head, making animal-like little chuckling sounds. "It can never be opened, my dear. I threw the key over the cliff. Over the big drop, where Marvin Cleek and Sandra Boyden, and your own sweetheart, Paul Dorsey, went—over where *you* are going soon!"

"Why?" The girl stood before him, hands outstretched in a gesture of supplication. "Charley, you can't realize what you're doing!"

"Oh, yes?" Charley's cracked laughter cackled again as he waved his arms wildly. "I've thought about it for years." He craned his neck toward the bearded man in the cage. "You told me I was a terrible actor. We were friends once, years ago, but you'd never give me a chance. You said I couldn't act. Nobody would let me act, no one would give me big parts. For twenty years I've waited. Tonight I play the lead. You understand? I play the lead in my own play. I, Charles Wyeth, the laughing-stock of the cheap road-shows becomes the star! And the director, as well!"

"But Charley," the girl begged. "Why have you got dad locked here? What did he do to you?"

"What did he do?" Wyeth yelled. "He kept me down. I begged him for years, but he wouldn't give me a chance. Only bits. Charley Wyeth, the 'bit player' whose name was never known. While he became the world's greatest director. Tell him how I acted tonight! Go ahead, tell him. I even fooled Graubeck. I fooled you all, because I am a great actor."

"Yes, I know," the girl said. "But please—"

"All of them, coming from nothing," Wyeth raged. "I watched them become great, while I did bits in mob scenes. Your father knows why I've kept him here, feeding him like a dog. I've played some great rôles before him, right here in this cave. But he keeps saying I cannot act. Tonight I showed the world. By dawn tomorrow the whole world will be talking about the way I played it. Grandly, subtly—magnificently!"

"Wyeth is mad, Doris," Gladden said from behind the bars. "He's been like this for, years. Harmless, until the day he lured me here."

"Mad?" Wyeth laughed. "You think so? Was it madness to fix the detour signs so the bus kept making a wide, sixty-mile circle around the edge of the mountain? Was it crazy to shut off the gas from the rear tank every sixty miles, so the car stopped each time near the same spot—right by the side of the cliff?"

"The same spot?" the girl repeated.

"Of course," Wyeth gloated. "And just a few feet off the road is the precipice. You thought it was Old Witch calling. Anyone who walked away from the road couldn't help going over—down hundreds of feet."

"You did all that?" Doris's face was knit in incredulous horror.

"It was all deliberate," Wyeth laughed wildly. "Even when I dropped my suitcase I did it on purpose. I watched everyone become terrified. When the bus stopped I dropped capsules, so everyone in the back of the bus would want air. I pretended to be frightened too. I gave a magnificent performance, Gladden."

"Don't you see?" Doris begged. "We must get my father out of here." She dropped to her knees before Charley Wyeth. "You were wonderful. Now—"

"No!" Wyeth made a sweeping gesture. "The climax has yet to come. I am going to play my biggest scene—with you!"

"With me?" The girl was trying desperately to soothe his wild raving.

"You will be my leading lady, for the big scene," Wyeth said. "Charles Wyeth, assisted by Doris Gladden. . . . Your father, the great James Gladden, can watch, but I will direct it myself. He can watch—from behind the bars!"

"Good Lord, Wyeth!" James Gladden seized the bars and strained mightily. "You aren't going to do that!"

"Why not?" Wyeth shrilled. "You've directed other scenes like it. But this will be real." He walked slowly toward the girl, his face wreathed in a horrible, satanic grimace. "I bided my time. I could have taken you out there in the storm. But I wanted your father to see the performance."

The girl lurched backward, threw up her arms. "No. No! Stop! You're insane!"

"You don't think Charley Wyeth can play a big dramatic role, eh?" Wyeth cackled. "You will soon know better. If you run from the cave you will go over the cliff. Nobody could miss it in the dark. Your lovely face—your spine, your arms, your legs—will be smashed beyond recognition. People will say that the terrible Graubeck has driven another of his stars mad. I only will know the truth!"

DORIS GLADDEN stood staring blankly at the gibbering madman before her. Her clothes were torn and disheveled, so wet that they clung revealingly to her figure. She pulled a soggy, twisted shoulder-strap up as she felt his hot eyes lingering on her exposed flesh. Under his mad glare she went cold all over. This awful thing was to be the end of a night of incredible terror.

"Here is the scene," Wyeth drooled. "Us two, in this cave on Witch's Mountain. A storm—and death in the air. Your two friends have died. Your lover dashed to pieces on the rocks. You have nothing left to live for—and you play your last scene before the very eyes of your father!" He was imitating the tone of a director, instructing a star before the shooting of a big scene. He stopped and laughed. "Does that sound familiar, Jim Gladden? Does old Charley Wyeth know how to act a big dramatic scene? Watch!"

For a second Doris Gladden held her ground. She fought against a great emptiness that rang in her head. Charley Wyeth's emaciated hands were extended as he advanced. His eyes grew wide, lighted with a hot, animal glare.

The candle-light swam before her eyes in lazy circles. Her limbs seemed no part of her. She felt herself slipping—slipping. Soon she would sink to the floor of the cave, all the fight gone out of her body, an inert, helpless form. A prey to mad Charley Wyeth's first and last horrible leading rôle.

"Doris!" Her father was shouting her name, battering the stout steel bars of the cage. "Doris!"

The sound of his voice roused her from her terror-inspired coma. She glanced wildly toward him, then looked at the menacing figure of Charley Wyeth. Something seemed to snap at the base of her brain. "I'm going out—out where Paul is!"

Charley Wyeth's cackling laugh drowned the echo of her cry. "All great scenes should have death in the offing!" he exulted. "It raises them to magnificent heights! What does Graubeck know about making them *feel?* Only the breath of Death on the cheek can do that!"

Doris Gladden stiffened, turned. She opened her mouth to call a frantic farewell to her father, then suddenly recoiled, a sensation of clammy terror running through her young body. Old Charley Wyeth, his eyes agleam with the insane spark of madness stood before her, his claw-like, blue-veined hands outstretched, his thin old fingers hooked, trembling. They reached out.

She tried to duck past him, to dodge, to shake off that terrifying grip, but the strength of blood-madness lay in those hooked talons. The girl felt their cold, damp touch slide up her bare arm; felt the flimsy stuff of her dress give and rip under those clawing fingers. A scream stifled in her throat; she could hear his rasping, hoarse breath close in her ears; feel it hot against her face. And then, like writhing white serpents the fingers of one hand closed about her slender throat as Wyeth's other hand tore bare her white breast. . . .

The throbbing of her pulse pounded in savage rhythm, loud in her ears as the pressure of those talons increased. Air—she must have air! Weakly, half-fainting, she sagged against the wiry madman, and then, miraculously, his grip loosened, a strange smile of triumph twisting his thin grey lips. . . .

With a sudden sinuous movement she writhed from his grip, fended off his seeking hands and ran madly, stumbling, gasping, toward the dark cave mouth.

"I—I'm coming, Paul!" she shouted. "Paul, it's I—Doris. Soon I'll be with you—we'll be together, out there in the darkness. . . ."

Again she had that strange pounding in her veins, that feeling of mad abandon that had seized her as she ran through the black stormy night. Nothing would stop her this time. She would run until there was no ground beneath her feet, and deep, dizzy blackness enveloped her as she plunged down, down. . . .

Out of the cave she lunged, into the lash of wind and rain, stumbling in the dark, running.

She could hear the pound of Charley Wyeth's footsteps behind her—almost upon her. Unintelligible words echoed in his cracked, crazy scream, half-drowned by the fury of the storm. The very shriek of the angry wind seemed to join with his cries and mock her.

Not that! Not that! If her bursting lungs held out she would soon pitch forward into the waiting black void. Safe from mad Charley Wyeth, in the arms of Death—with Paul!

"I'm coming, Paul!" she exulted. . . .

IT SEEMED that she could see him, coming toward her with outstretched arms. His face was like that unreal apparition, the phantom she had seen through the dark night, after he had gone over the cliff. Soon she would join him. The ghostly form loomed nearer. Her arms went out as she ran. Then she slipped downward, crashed into something solid. . . She thought she felt arms around her, and heard Paul's voice saying, "Doris! I've found you!"

"Paul. I'm with you. We—we're both dead—is that it Paul?" Everything was hazy and weird and mixed up.

But his arms felt very real. His voice sounded alive, reassuring. The lash of the wind and rain was real, too.

"When Sandra went over I tried to stop her," Paul said. "I slipped, stumbled over rocks, hit my head. The bus was gone when I came to. It seemed to be going past again as I got to my feet. I couldn't understand it. I called out."

"Oh, Paul!" she gasped. "I saw your face. I thought it was a phantom. I thought you were dead."

"Why did the bus circle?" Paul asked. "I thought I was seeing things. Then I thought I heard your voice. I've been searching in the dark for hours. Then I saw the light over there—what is it?"

"It's a cave," Doris told him. "Charley Wyeth fixed it so the bus circled. He's got all the detour signs switched on this mountain road. He made the bus stop. He did everything. He—he has father caged up in that cave!"

"All right, all right," Paul soothed. "You're hysterical. Don't think about your father."

"But he's there!" Her voice rose. "Charley Wyeth did it!"

Paul Dorsey's arm pulled her toward the cave. The light of the candle inside showed a dull gleam in the black, stormy night. "Why did he want to do that?"

Doris Gladden clung tightly to his side. Together they plunged through the rain toward the cave mouth. "He is mad. He wanted to play a big dramatic part," she explained. "He has wanted to for years and years. He hated everyone who succeeded. Hurry! Father is there."

A figure stood near the dark entrance. It was Charley Wyeth, straining his eyes in the storm to find the girl. As Paul and Doris loomed out of the wet blackness, the old bit actor fell back a pace. He stared once, with wild, goggling eyes at the pair.

"We're back, Wyeth!" Paul Dorsey stepped toward him.

"They're back!" Wyeth shrieked. "They both went over the cliff. Now they're back. It's Witch's Mountain!" He let out one more unearthly scream and darted past them.

Paul Dorsey started after him, but Doris clutched his arm. "Let him go, Paul. Don't go out there again. . . I think I know where he's going."

For several moments they stood in the dark cave mouth, listening to Wyeth's headlong, stumbling progress through the dark. Then it seemed that a shrill human cry was mixed with the moan of the wind and rain. . . and then, once more, only the sounds of the elements. . . .

Doris Gladden's voice was tired. "I think Charley Wyeth himself has answered the call of Old Witch."

The candle was still burning on the floor of the cave. The huddled figure on the floor behind the bars raised its head, blinked uncertainly. "Who is it?"

"It's Doris, Father. And Paul's with me. Paul will get you out of there, and in the morning we'll all leave Witch's Mountain together."

"It doesn't seem real," the gaunt, grey-bearded man mumbled.

"It is, though," Paul Dorsey said. "Real as—as the body of Charley Wyeth we'll see in the morning. We're through forever with the curse of Witch's Mountain!"

THE END

BLOOD ON BLACK KNOLL

By G. T. Fleming-Roberts

(Author of "Kinsman's Curse," etc.)

Above the headstones on Black Knoll a dark-winged horror lurked—ready to swoop down for its nightly toll among the sacred, defenseless dead. . . .

NORMAN BLAKELY had said to the conductor, "You be sure and tell me when we get to Black Knoll Junction, because I wouldn't know it from a hole in the ground."

Standing now on the deserted station platform as the train pulled out, Blakely began to realize the truth in his words. A hole in the ground—Black Knoll was little more than that! Across the track, the only visible street lamp illuminated the darkened front of Thomas Riggs' Variety Emporium. Bank and drugstore separated the Emporium from the Giles Riggs Furniture Company—a two-story frame building that offered to merchandise undertaking services as well as tables and chairs.

Back of these business enterprises, Blakely supposed he would find a scattering of houses, then the prairie—desolate miles of it, with fertile black soil transformed into gumbo mud by the steady drizzle of late fall rains.

A thin stream of water—it seemed that no matter of collar adjusting would quite shut it out—trailed along Blakely's spine. A chill followed the same course. He entered the station.

The two men inside supported a glowing iron stove between steaming boots. The sad-faced one, whose right ear was lopped where a short pencil wedged it out, would be the station agent, Blakely decided. He surveyed Blakely suspiciously from hat to shoes.

The other man was comfortably stout with a face that resembled in coloring and shape nothing so much as an ivory cue-ball with a splash of black lacquer for the hair. His smile, too, seemed painted. His black suit became his cadaverous complexion. It was irritating to have him sit there looking at you and at the same time doing sums on his fingers as if he were calculating your worth—in pennies!

"Rainin'," the station agent solemnly informed Blakely. Blakely nodded affably. It was a beginning, anyway. If they so desired, these two men could probably give him all the information he needed on the murder of Simon Vroon. Blakely scuffed a match on the floor and lighted a sodden cigarette. He dropped on the waiting bench and was conscious of the fact that the ivory-faced man gathered in the skirts of his black coat as if he feared contamination.

"Salesman?" the station agent pumped. "You'll not find much business in this town, I'm afraid. Folks is too pore."

Blakely smiled faintly, slowly shaking his head—much to the annoyance of the ivory-faced man who was showered by the water swirling from Blakely's hat. "My business," Blakely said, "is with the dead rather than the living."

Ivory-face slid farther from Blakely. The agent lifted his eyebrows, looked apprehensively behind him, and said: "You and Giles, here, ought to hit it off. Giles has been plantin' the folks about town for the past two years, and his old man did it before him. Introduce you two." The agent swelled with social importance. "Meet Giles Riggs—Rigg-or-mortis, we calls him, on account of *that* bein' his profession along with other things. What'd you say your name was, stranger?"

Blakely told him, shook the snow-cold hand of the undertaker. "My job is to dig 'em up rather than plant them," he smiled. "That is," he added hastily, "I dig up old murder cases." He paused to catch the startled expressions that crept into the faces of his new companions. "I don't pretend to solve them; just sugar-coat them for the great American newspaper public. I'm especially interested in the murder of Simon Vroon, the jewel collector who was killed here about three years ago. You'll remember that though there were a number of suspects, there was no indictment. The stolen jewels were never found. It is my opinion—"

BLAKELY was to keep his opinion to himself. A sudden gust of misty air rushed into the waiting-room as the door was thrown open. A man entered.

He was tall with shoulders that stooped beneath a heavy face. He staggered rather than walked into the center of the room. Giles Riggs and the station agent got halfway to their feet, staring wide-eyed at the newcomer.

The man clawed at his bluish lips as if to aid the utterance of words. *"Blood,"* he shuddered. "Blood all over Constable Billings! The bat—"

A frantic gesture from Giles Riggs put a stop to the man's sentence. "Cecil Thrumb!" he exclaimed. "You're sick!"

And when the undertaker pronounced these words, Blakely saw something within Riggs' face that made him shudder. After all, if Riggs "planted" only the folk of Black Knoll he *must* look covetously upon every potential corpse!

The station agent took Cecil Thrumb by the shoulders and pushed him to one of the benches. "Easy now, Mr. Thrumb. What's all this about Billings?"

Cecil Thrumb grew marble-eyed. "Tom found him—Tom and my sister. He was hanging, that's what! Hanging on the barbed fence around the churchyard, his arms all spread out and hung over the pickets. Bled to death—though God knows where the blood went to. There was a little on his throat where the *teeth marks* were, but most of it was gone—gone as if—" Thrumb glanced at Blakely and lowered his voice to a husky whisper—"gone just as if it had been drunk up by something!"

The station agent had gone shades lighter. He glanced up at Blakely, winked and tapped his forehead significantly.

Goggling with horror as he was, Thrumb had not missed the gesture. "That's not right, Jim Smith!" he said. "I got as good sense as anybody. And you needn't look at me like that, Giles! I'm not ready for one of your coffins yet. It was your brother Tom Riggs who found the constable with all the blood sucked out of him." Another cautioning glance from Giles caused Cecil Thrumb to pause. Then, "I don't give a damn!" he roared. "You and your Chamber of Commerce always shushing a man when he wants to speak his mind about this town in front of strangers! Black Knoll's doomed. The black wings of death are hovering over us right now. It's the curse —the curse that always falls when somebody disturbs the dead!"

Through the open door, Blakely saw the fogged glow of an oil lantern bobbing across the tracks. He could hear a raucous-voiced woman arguing with a man as the two approached the station.

"I'll have no part of it, I tell you!" the man was shouting. "Your brother is a long way towards being right when he says things like that ought to be left to the Almighty. Isn't there proof enough? Constable Billings being killed that unholy way is enough for me. It's hands off!"

The woman, a powerfully built, Nordic type blonde stamped into the room. She stood just inside the door beckoning authoritatively to the man with the lantern. "Just come in here, Tom, if a worm like you can stand the light!"

Thomas Riggs, proprietor of the variety store, entered the room. He was a short, cringing sort of man, small-boned and scrawny. He eyed the other occupants of the room sheepishly. "We couldn't stand it," he said apologetically. "Couldn't stand there where Constable Billings is stretched on the fence. There's nothing human about this!"

"*We* couldn't stand it!" Mrs. Riggs shouted. "It was you, Tom, that started blubbering!" She looked around the room, eyes lingering on Norman Blakely. "You, young man, look as though you had *some* sense. I'm Hattie Riggs, Cecil Thrumb's sister. I've just seen murder. Now, what's to be done about it?"

Blakely said, "You'd better call up the county sheriff and report the killing. And while you're waiting for him to get here, suppose I run over and have a look at the body. I'm used to that sort of thing. The churchyard, you said, Mr. Thrumb?"

Thrumb seemed too horrified to speak.

"That's right, young man," put in Mrs. Riggs boldly. "He's hanging on the west fence. You can't miss him."

Blakely went to the door, turned around and asked: "Anybody going with me?"

Giles Riggs coughed, looked at his brother.

"You, Mr. Riggs?" Blakely asked.

"Er—no," replied the undertaker. "Can't stand wet weather. Rheumatism. . . ."

Blakely laughed derisively and stepped out into the drizzle.

HE HAD no more than crossed the tracks, walking in the direction of the church steeple which he could see dimly silhouetted against the dark sky, than he heard cinders behind him scrunching beneath hurrying feet. He turned, stood waiting, as a stooped shadow came running towards him. It was Cecil Thrumb, Hattie Riggs' brother.

"Just couldn't do it," he mumbled as he came up to Blakely. "Just couldn't see you startin' out for that graveyard not knowing what you're up against. It's a hellish business. Rather than let it out and ruin the tourist trade, they'd let you go up there to God knows what." He shoved Blakely into the shelter of an old box-car that stood on the siding. Then he drew a long breath.

"This neighborhood is infested with bats," he began. "Not the ordinary run of bats, but *something* much larger. That's why Billings went up there tonight. He scoffed, wouldn't believe what we had seen with our own eyes. Won't any of us go near that cemetery because—because we've seen a bat up there—a bat fully six feet across the wings!

"One night when I was driving the old buggy back from the next town, I saw it! It was a bat perched on top of one of the grave-stones. There was an unholy bluish light about its head. I gave the old mare a cut with the whip, and when I *did* look back, it was still there, flappin' its black wings! And I'm not the only one to see it, either. Hattie's seen it, and the postmaster, too. And some of the graves have been disturbed. Something's been digging! That's what killed Constable Billings! That bat *sucked* the blood right out of him!"

Blakely was convinced he had to do with a madman. He laughed easily. "That's all nonsense. Bats are harmless creatures, and they never get that big. It just couldn't be."

Thrumb threw his hands above his head. "All right!" he shouted angrily. "I'm through. I did my part in warning you!"

He whirled abruptly, stalked off mumbling something about know-it-all young men from the city. Blakely strode on through the rain. . . .

The town took its name from the knoll upon which the church stood. The knoll was little more than a hump of relief in the monotonous stretch of prairie. The church building had long been in disuse. Unpainted pine boards shuttered the doors and windows. Soft ground had yielded to the weight of the structure and the steeple leaned at a precarious angle.

Blakely entered through the rusty iron gate, rounded the church, and looked down upon the graveyard below the hill. Ancient headstones were patched with moss; shrubs, vines, and weeds mingled in tangled abandonment.

Blakely forced back gloomy thoughts. He took his flashlight from his pocket and turned it on. The cold, white ray sheathed the raindrops in gleaming silver. He proceeded across the burial lot, fanning his light ahead of him. Twice, his groping feet stumbled into sunken graves, breaking through the shallow sod into the filthy pit below.

Blakely stopped. Ahead of him, the white grave-markers were more scattered. His light found the iron fence and moved slowly along the pickets.

Suddenly, the beam stopped, trembling upon a crooked cross of a shadow that sprawled against the fence. Blakely broke into a run, zigzagging between the gravestones, keeping his light on the shadowy form.

A cry of horror escaped Blakely as he came abreast the shadow. It was the body of Constable Billings. The very fiends of hell could have thought up no more torturous method of killing a man. The constable had been thrown with his back against the fence. His wrists had been impaled on the iron spikes that topped each picket. His head had been forced back till his neck was wedged between the iron posts.

This barbarism alone would have caused death—but there were in addition two small pink wounds on the man's throat. It was as if some animal had feasted there! Blood from the wrists had stained the rusty fence a deeper red, and there were drops of blood on the constable's coat front as if the death-beast had slavered while gourmandizing.

HORROR held Blakely rigid. For minutes he stood there, mouth dry, scalp creeping. Then his teeth clenched, his lips became a thin line, his eyes narrowed. Six foot bats! Nonsense! Here was the mark of madness—of butchering lust, insatiable blood-thirst. But there could be nothing supernatural about it.

Yet Constable Billings had been a strong man—a hundred and seventy pounds, with not an ounce of surplus fat. It must have taken three men to kill him thus—unless—unless there was after all something beyond normal ken. . . .

Blakely shook his head angrily. Rot! He forced himself into impassiveness as he brushed back the constable's mop of black hair. His finger wandered over the scalp, moving to the back of the skull. There he found a lump the size of a hen's egg. Struck from behind, the poor devil hadn't had a chance to defend himself. But why had he been killed by so fantastic a method? The killer could have more easily thrust a knife into Billing's heart.

Blakely turned, started away. There was nothing he could do until officials took charge. He headed back towards the church, his mind touching upon various theories too impractical to be applied.

He had gone but a few feet when abruptly his foot broke through sod, struck slippery muck. He pitched forward to the ground. The hand that went out to stop his fall plunged into black space. He groped, found crumbling soil and pulled himself back from the pit into which he had so nearly fallen. He lighted his flash, spraying the ground with its beam.

He had come nearer to falling into a new grave. Or was it new? There was something about the air that came up from the pit—an odor of corruption and filth. . . .

Chills raced along his spine. The flashlight shook in his hand.

Half covered with black mold though it was, he could nevertheless make out the outline of an old coffin. Its lid had been hacked away with an ax, and the ghastly, rotting contents revealed. Moldering grave-clothes, even the decaying flesh itself had been ruthlessly slashed!

Blakely staggered back. The hand that brushed cold sweat from his brow also knocked off his hat. It remained there in the mud, unheeded. Like a man far gone in liquor, Blakely staggered towards the church. It was all beyond sanity, far beyond even madness—for what strange mania would prompt a madman to butcher a corpse? . . .

Ahead of him, a large white monument seemed to glow with faint phosphorescence. Blakely scarcely noticed it as he approached the stone. Then the blue light became more concentrated, casting an ungodly halo against the black horizon.

Blakely stopped in his tracks. The blue beam mounted higher and higher. Good God! Why hadn't he seen it!

A great hunched form had mounted the monument. Blue light gleamed upon a hideous, hairy face—gleamed upon glassy, staring eyes, upon crimson lips crossed by long, ivory fangs!

"A vampire!" The word screamed from Blakely's throat. He whirled in his tracks, damp air sobbing into his lungs. He had seen huge, batlike wings slowly unfold as the beast prepared to launch itself!

Blakely fled—fled back towards the open grave with its butchered cadaver, back towards the poor, bloodless thing that had been Constable Billings. He stumbled, felt his throat go tight with fear. Heart throbs that threatened to pound through his chest brought him to his feet. He raced on, taking the fence at a single bound. Then he was pelting down the road.

Behind him came the *flap-flap-flap* as of huge bat-wings beating the air. Terror twisted his head around.

Nothing—nothing but the wind playing with the skirts of his trench-coat. Nothing more.

CURSING himself for a coward did not help. He did not stop until he had once again sighted the railway station.

There he paused, catching his breath. He'd look like a fool breaking in on that crowd with all the color frightened out of his face. He calmed himself somewhat, crossed the platform, and softly opened the door.

Floorboards squeaked. The agent jerked around. There was no one else in the room.

Blakely dropped to a bench. "Smith," he said weakly, "can you think of any earthly reason for butchering a long-buried corpse?"

"N-no," Smith stammered. "I don't get you."

Blakely repeated all that had taken place at the cemetery. In conclusion, he added, "I think I'm on the track of the solution. Wasn't Giles Riggs, the undertaker, one of the men suspected of committing the Vroon murder?"

The agent shook his head. "Nope. It was Art Riggs, Giles' and Tom's father. But they couldn't pin anything on him then, and he's dead now."

Blakely nodded. "Cecil Thrumb seemed to think there had been other cases of grave robbery around here lately.

"Yeah. Corpse butcherin', as you put it. Some of us fellows who are civic minded, as you might say, kept mum about it so as not to ruin the tourist trade. There's been grave robbing twice before in the past week. Once, the ghouls just uncovered a heap of bones. Again, it was a half rotten corpse—and when we found it somebody had worked on it with a knife!"

"We just covered the graves up again and kept our mouths shut. Then came this bat scare. Every mother who thinks anything of her children's been keepin' them in after dark, I can tell you!"

"If you had a map of the cemetery showing the various lots, could you show me just what graves had been opened?" Blakely asked.

For an answer, Smith went to his desk, searched the pigeon-holes, and drew out a piece of paper. "So happens," he explained as he flattened the paper on his desk, "that I'm chairman of the cemetery committee. I'll point them out to you. They were both in the same lot—Boothby's lot right here." He pawed his pencil from behind his ear and pointed with it.

Blakely snapped his fingers. "I'll lay ten to one that the butchered corpse I found tonight was in the same lot! Now, if I just knew when they died—"

"Takes a harder one than that," declared the station agent. "I was pallbearer to all the Boothbys exceptin' the old man. It was his skeleton that was dug up first. But his two sons were took by the flu about three years ago."

"Got it!" snapped Blakely.

"I ain't. What you got?"

"I know who murdered Simon Vroon. And I'm beginning to see daylight on the vampire business, too."

Smith stared at him. "You mean—you mean the Boothbys ain't dead—you mean they're *undead. . . ?"*

"I mean the man who killed Simon Vroon has been punished. He's in the grave right now—or he ought to be!" Blakely strode to the door.

"Where you goin'?" the station agent asked.

"Back to the cemetery and do a little digging on my own hook—if somebody hasn't beat me to it!" He hurried from the station.

But instead of heading directly for the church as he had done previously, Blakely headed along the route that led along the west side of the cemetery.

He quietly approached the spread-eagled corpse of Billings, working his way through the rain-soaked weeds until he was directly behind the body. There he crouched, peering from behind that gruesome shield. From the direction of the Boothby lot came a plumping sound as of someone digging in the moist earth with a spade. Occasionally, he could see the flash of white as an arm came up over the ever growing mound.

The digging stopped. A long sigh came from the newly-opened grave. A white figure, wraithlike in the gloom, appeared at the edge of the grave, stooped, picked up something, and went to work again. Now Blakely could hear the *chump* of an ax biting into rotting wood. Then came a grunt of satisfaction. Again, the white-clad creature came from the grave. This time it dragged with it a shapeless cadaver!

HOISTING the rotting thing upon its shoulders, the ghoul moved off towards the church.

Blakely crawled over the fence and followed as closely as he dared, ducking from one tomb to another. The ghoul stopped at the slanting trap door covering the church cellar-way, kicked back the door, and carried its grisly burden down the steps. Then the trap slapped back into place.

Crouching low, Blakely ran to the cellar door. A narrow string of yellow light passed up through the crack. Blakely knelt and looked through the opening.

The grave-robber dressed in mud-stained white duck trousers, was striding forward with his burden. But he stopped now at sight of a dark-haired, languid-eyed woman who was seated on a broken packing-case. The woman stared as if fascinated at the white-clad grave-robber. There was a black automatic in her right hand. The grave-robber laughed harshly.

"What kind of a game is this?" the woman asked. "What you got there?"

"This, dearie." The ghoul laughed. The cadaver slipped from his shoulders and clumped to the floor. The woman with the automatic screamed as she saw the ragged grave clothing, the bony hands, and the face with decaying flesh sloughing from the maxilary bones.

Pale-faced but stern, the woman said: "I've been following you. I've been watching you for the past two weeks. I know a whole lot about you, and I didn't drag out here into the sticks just for my health. Whatever your game, there's money in it—lots of it. I'm taking my cut and lamming out. I'll clam up if you pay well."

Again the husky laugh. "Blackmail, eh? Oh, you'll get your *cut.* And it'll keep your mouth shut, too!"

The woman's gun threatened. "No funny business!"

"It wont' be *funny,"* said the grave-robber. He picked up the corpse and threw it across a wooden bench. Then a long knife gleamed from his belt. "I'll just chop up this stiff and see what we shall see. Guess it must be Gabe Boothby we've got here. Gabe—" addressing the corpse—"meet Sally Laguartta, smartest little blackmailer I ever knew."

Blakely heard the knife rip rotting cloth and scrape across bone. A grunt of disgust from the grave-robber, followed by a shout of triumph. "It had to be this one! They were hidden in a Boothby, and damned if we hadn't tried them all but Gabe, here!"

A hand stained with moldering flesh and mud came away from the corpse, holding a long metal cylinder. Sally Laguartta became over-eager. She jumped from her box and seized at the metal case in the hand of the ghoul. The corpse butcher yanked it from her grasp.

"Maybe you didn't get what I meant about *your* cut." There was hideous menace in the corpse butcher's voice.

Sally paled, took a step backwards. "You hellcat!" she muttered. "You wouldn't dare!" Her gun came up.

Somewhere, a door creaked.

"Look behind you, Sally," said the corpse butcher. "A new boy-friend for you!"

Sally turned stiffly. A tight little cry of terror came through her lips. Her fingers forgot the gun, and it fell to the stone floor. Sally's hand went over her face to shut out the sight. Her knees weakened. She slumped to the floor in a dead faint.

Through the door, a grotesque black shape flopped. It had the appearance of a huge bat with finlike, folded wings. The face was a shapeless hairy thing, the mouth crimson and bristling with gleaming teeth. It moved, crouching, to the prostrate form of the woman. Its hideous mouth bent hungrily over the white throat.

"That's enough," rasped the corpse butcher. "She's out cold. Bleed her like you did the other."

Blakely saw a thin arm extend from the folds of the batlike wings. Its talon-like fingers were clenched over a curious forked glass tube.

Blakely waited for no more. He got to his feet, backed away from the slanting trapdoor, and leaped. He landed full weight upon the old door.

There was a splintering of wood. He felt himself falling, grasping involuntarily for support that was not there. The basement floor stopped him, sending an electric-like shock up his spine.

EVEN before he knew it, he was fighting for his life, grappling with a clumsy bat-winged thing, yet guarding himself from the flashing knife of the corpse butcher.

With a vicious shove, Blakely pushed the bat-creature away and ducked under the descending blade of the butcher. His eyes caught the dull gleam of Sally's automatic on the floor. He dived for it, felt its cold but friendly feel in his grasp. He pivoted, met a flying knife that lanced the fleshy part of his shoulder. He fired wildly. The corpse butcher weaved towards him, melting to the floor.

Blakely swung the gun on the clumsy bat. "Hold it, Mr. Vampire," he snapped, "or I'll let you have it!"

Eyes behind the furry mask goggled with terror.

Footsteps behind Blakely. He turned his head and saw yellow light creeping down the basement steps. "You down there, Blakely?" It was the cheerful voice of Jim Smith, the station agent. He came clattering down the steps followed by Tom Riggs.

"Good Lord! The bat!" Smith cried.

"Yeah," said Blakely. "Quite a get-up. Probably a blue-lens flashlight stuck down inside his clothes gives that hellish cast to his face. Take off your mask, Mr. Vampire."

A thin hand to which the tip of the batlike wings were attached, came up, jerking off the mask. Beneath was a heavy face, a face distorted by hate. It was the face of Cecil Thrumb!

"My brother-in-law!" Riggs gasped.

Blakely nodded. "That's why he was so anxious for me to get out of town. And Riggs, what did you know about your wife's life before you married her?"

"My wife—why er—she was a city girl," Tom Riggs stuttered.

"And what a girl!" Blakely laughed harshly. "Guess you forgot to look before you leaped. I don't want to rub it in, but just take a look at that 'man' in the white pants!"

Smith went over and turned the corpse butcher over, revealing the plump blonde face of Hattie Riggs. She was bleeding profusely from a wound in her shoulder. Her left hand was clutched tightly over a metal cylindrical box.

"What's this?" Smith extracted the box from Hattie's fingers. He unscrewed the cap. He spilled forth a handful of large, glittering diamonds! "Why—these must be the Vroon diamonds!"

"Right," said Blakely. "As I dope it out, the Riggs boys' father was the man who killed Simon Vroon. But because he didn't have the nerve to fence such well-known stones, he hid the diamonds in a corpse that he was embalming at the time. Somehow, Hattie learned of this—"

"She did," Tom Riggs interrupted. "My brother Giles and I were the only ones who knew about it for a while. Father confessed to the murder on his death-bed and wanted us to dig up the corpse of Gabe Boothby and return the jewels to the rightful owner. But Giles and I were too proud of the family name. We kept putting it off.

"Then it got to preying on my mind. I dreamed about digging up that old corpse. One night, I guess I talked in my sleep—because the next morning, Hattie knew something about it. She made me tell her the whole thing. Of course, I didn't suppose she'd do anything about it."

Blakely nodded. "And she and her brother doped out the vampire stunt to keep curious folk away from the graveyard at night when they were exhuming the corpses, trying to find the right one. Constable Billings caught them in the act. They murdered him, draining off his blood through a tube to heighten the vampire effect. They meant to do the same thing with this blackmailer, Sally Laguartta. Sally, I gather, had known Hattie in the city. She followed her out here, found that Hattie was up to something, and tried to get hush money out of her."

"Well, I'll be damned!" said Smith.

"Don't think so," said Blakely solemnly. "But there're two or three people in this room who will be!"

NEXT MONTH—

Tales of Terror and Dark Mystery by Hugh B. Cave, Ray Cumming, Nat Schachner, Robert C. Blackmon, and other Masters of Eerie Fiction

The February Issue Is Out December 26th!

THEY DARE NOT DIE!

By Nat Schachner

(Author of "Monsters of the Pit.")

What fiendish, evil lust drove on those drooling ancients? Why had the two lovers been lured to the house of horror on the hill? What vital, hidden treasure lay in their youthful bodies that would bring those wrinkled hags and toothless men fighting and clawing over them in blind, slobbering greed?

GRIMLY Lynn Hart pushed his roadster up the fast narrowing mountain road. The wilderness of tall hemlocks, black with approaching night, seemed to close in on him and the girl at his side with stealthy approach.

It feels as if—well—if I were a child I'd say ogres lived in these woods."

Hart patted her small fingers gently. The engine labored on the stiffening grade; the path grew more narrow, and the trees marched closer.

"I won't let the ogres get you, honey," he said with forced cheerfulness. He and Jane were soon to be married, and this was the third day of a tour in the back stretches of the Adirondacks. "But there's no room to turn the car around. We'll soon hit a house; there's always at least one to a road."

He wished he could be sure of that. There hadn't been a sign of house or human being for twenty miles. They went on in silence, the ominous hush of the mountain broken only by the panting

The girl shuddered. She pressed closer to his lean, athletic form. The waning light etched sharply the black masses of her hair, the lovely clean profile, the troubled depths of her eyes.

"We'd better go back, Lynn," she said. "This road isn't getting anywhere. We took the wrong turn into the valley." There was a little catch in Jane Porter's voice. "I know I'm foolish, but I'm scared.

wheeze of their motor. Little lines of strain began to show around Hart's mouth.

Then, from behind them, over the road they had just traveled, came a new sound. The deep-throated roar of an engine with the throttle wide, the slithering scream of tires whirling madly over gravel and rutted dirt. A high-powered car was coming along at insane speed over the tortuous, bumpy trail.

Damn fools! Lynn thought to himself. But the strained lines relaxed. He'd be able to get his bearings now, learn a way out of here..

He crowded the roadster against the overhang, pulled the emergency. Then he stood up in the seat, white slacks and open shirt a shining target against the dark green of the hemlocks.

The approaching car was still invisible. But the glare of its headlights preceded it, swept with breath-taking velocity over the sinister shadows, beat blindingly about his white-clad form, and raced up the mountainside. The long sleek nose of an Isotta-Fraschini swarmed around the lower bend and sprang like a great cat directly at them.

Lynn Hart waved his hand and shouted. Then he ground out an oath and jerked instinctively toward the girl on his right. Jane screamed.

The great car did not slacken its mad pace. The occupants of its open tonneau did not seem to have heard his hail, not even to have noticed the parked roadster. The chauffeur was a gigantic Negro. His ebony hands wrestled the wheel, the whites of his eyes rolled gruesomely. He ground the accelerator to the floorboard.

The Isotta shot forward to a mad eighty. It rocked and heaved in the ruts. It pounced on the mountain like a tiger clawing its prey.

Lynn shrank from the expected crash. His arm tugged protectively at the girl. There was the scream of rubber, the pounding of cylinders, the shriek of tortured, rending steel—and the Isotta flashed by, taking with it the rear fender of the roadster.

The back seat of the great car held a solitary man. He hunched forward, mouthing one word to the giant chauffeur.

"Faster!"

The yelling wind whipped it from his lips even as it tore the straggling white hair back from his brown, parchment-crinkled skull. He was frail and old, and his expensive clothes hung loosely on his flabby frame. But all the feeble remnants of his life were concentrated in his forward-urging eyes. They glittered with fiery pinpoints of flame, they clutched at some incredible Paradise directly ahead.

"Faster!" he mouthed, unseeing of the road, unhearing of aught but that luring vision. Then they were gone.

LYNN took a deep breath. Jane's face was waxen pale. Death had brushed heavily against them and fled by with whirring wings. Already the juggernaut of destruction was far up the winding path, its passage a rushing diminuendo.

Anger seized Lynn. He jumped out of the car, lifted the quivering girl after him. He shook his fist futilely up the long mountain.

"Damn the blasted fool!" he muttered feelingly.

Jane shuddered close to him. Her breath came in a long broken gasp. Her eyes widened on something they saw in the fast-darkening road.

Lynn stopped his tirade. His gaze followed hers. Just a moment ago there had been no one on the path. Now there were a man and a woman, standing in the middle of the trail, faces half turned from the damaged roadster, eyes fixed intently on the upward slope of the mountain. They did not seem to be aware of the young couple's existence. All their energies were strained to the flying echoes of the Isotta.

Jane whispered: "I—I want to get out of here. They're not human; they're . . ." Her voice trailed off and died.

"Still thinking of ogres and witches," Lynn whispered back. But he was startled, more than he cared to admit. He felt the slow prickling of his flesh; icy fingers wrested the mantling warmth from the twilight and left him naked to frigid, primeval fears.

Where had they come from, this strange odd pair? The mountain on either side was impenetrable with brambles and close-woven thickets. What were they doing here, in the depths of the wilderness?

The dim reflection of a dying sun made pallid blobs of their faces. Ancient, impossible faces! The musty odor of grave-clothes and moldering churchyards enveloped them in a miasma of rising mist. Male and female from their dress, but sexless alike in their ravaged decay. Leathery brown skins clung to wasted bones, pouched in hideous folds on pendulous chins and scrawny necks.

Mummies! Mummified man and woman standing there in the inscrutable wilderness, wearing modern clothes—Bond Street and Rue de la Paix unmistakably—clutching at a life that should already have passed them by.

So thought Lynn and shivered. For he had seen their eyes. Even as the eyes of the lone passenger in the Isotta, they blasted and seared. But with a strange difference. The ancient's in the car were avid with the lure of some unutterable quest; these were crawling with the red worms of hate. With screeching fear lest something within their grasp be swept away, with straining eagerness to catch some change in the rumbling progress of the Isotta.

Lynn tried to shake off his strange reluctance to accost them. Ogre and witch! Ridiculous nonsense! Just a very old man and a very old woman, who could tell them the way. They must live near by, might possibly put them up for the night.

Jane plucked at his sleeve. Her voice was small and imploring.

"Please don't ask them—anything!"

Lynn grinned tightly. He disregarded her.

"Hello there!" he called. His voice boomed hollowly in his ears.

They whirled on him with incredible swiftness, like cats disturbed from a mousehole. A snarl of rage strangled and died in the old man's withered throat. The ancient beldame's sere, berouged cheeks fell flabbily in, pulled back the corners of even redder lips to disclose the too-perfect whiteness of artificial teeth. Baffled fury and hate changed in the twinkling of an eye to leering, ogling smiles.

Lynn did not know which was the more horrible. Jane hung trembling to his arm. His senses crawled as at the sight of elongated, corpse-white slugs, slimed over with corruption. But he forced his voice to a semblance of casualness.

"We're lost," he said with a disarming grin. "We evidently took the wrong turn at the valley fork. Could you direct us to some shelter for the night?"

The old man and the old woman made no answer. They stood there and stared with strange red-rimmed eyes. The man at Lynn, the woman at Jane. Hot slithering eyes that pawed and defiled every part of their youthful bodies, that edged and wormed their way into every secret nook and cranny of their physical being.

A strange prickling sensation crawled over the girl. She shuddered under the impact of those eyes. She was being smothered in a bath of slimy putrescence.

Lynn shook off his mounting fear. He was strong and vigorous, and the ineffable pair were impotent for physical evil.

"A civil question demands a civil answer," he said angrily. "What's the matter with you? Didn't you hear me?"

THE ancients slowly withdrew their hot avid gaze, turned to each other. A long look of evil understanding passed between them. Simultaneously a hideous cackle burst from their scrawny throats. It bubbled and gurgled and choked them into a fit of retching. It sounded terrifying in the darkling shadows.

"Our hearing's still pretty good," mouthed the old man, still chuckling and retching. "Isn't it, Georgia?"

But the bedizened beldame paid no attention. She tottered closer to the shrinking girl. Her corpse-like head jutted startlingly from a gown of Poiret's creation—a low-cut swank that exposed a shrunken, bony chest. Withered, bony fingers reached out, pawed suddenly over the fresh firm flesh of Jane's cheek, swept downward in a furious strange greed over the lithe tingling body.

Jane gave a little cry of loathing. Her limbs refused to obey the shrieking protest of her brain. The old woman's eyes were balefully hypnotic. They turned her will to flowing water.

The old man, with an agility surprising for his years, literally sprang at Lynn, grasped his arms with feverish hold, and dug clawed hands into the flat muscular flesh.

Lynn jerked away in disgust.

"Now listen, you two." he said harshly. "What do you think we are? Keep your hands to yourselves, or else—"

The old man's face wore a hurt look.

"We mean no harm," he said. "We just love to see such an admirably youthful couple as yourselves. It in a way rejuvenates us, doesn't it, Georgia?"

The old woman smiled toothfully. Her little pointed tongue licked surreptitiously at her lips. Her sallow cheeks quivered with strange emotion.

"*Rejuvenates* is the word, Thomas," she quavered. "Very good!" And they both thrust back their heads and chuckled until they wheezed in gasping eructations.

"Now don't fret," Thomas spluttered finally. "There's a hotel farther on, at the end of the road. It's a very nice place; as a matter of fact we stay there. You just ask for Dr. Meldon Hunt and he'll be glad to put you up for the night."

A sudden memory struggled in Lynn's mind. He forgot his reluctant fears.

"Meldon Hunt!" he echoed. "Is that the surgeon who disappeared recently?"

The old man bobbed his head. "He did not disappear. He started a private retreat —a rest cure, so to speak. It has turned out to be a very lucrative undertaking."

"Very!" The woman's quaver was bitter, harsh. She thrust forward with sudden energy. "And you be sure and tell Hunt that you're our guests. That Georgia Palfrey claims the sweet young lady and Thomas A. Babbage the pretty young man. No one else is to have you; you are ours, *ours!*"

Her cracked voice rose to a tremulous shriek. The old man whimpered like a dog slavering over a treasured bone. He stepped closer.

"Remember!" he whispered fiercely. "No one else. You are *our* guests."

The ancient pair quivered alike with queer eagerness, their hands and jaws moving in trembling unison.

Jane shrank from their baleful, enfolding glare. The blanketing night disembodied them, showed only their wrinkled faces and glowing eyes.

"I don't want to go," she whispered to Lynn, pressing tight for comfort. "They're horrible; they're like evil old beasts. We *must* get away from them."

Lynn patted her hand absently.

Thomas A. Babbage! Georgia Palfrey! Names to conjure with.

Babbage was a millionaire, a retired automobile manufacturer of incredible age. Georgia Palfrey had been the arbitrix of the social destinies of a past generation. No wonder their diction and speech were impeccable; no wonder their clothes were what they were. But what were these two gargoyles, these ruins, doing in the remote depths of the Adirondacks?

Hunt's Sanitarium was evidently very secretive. The strange disappearance of the famous surgeon had bulked large in the newspapers. Lynn smiled tightly. There was money to be made from the private diseases of the very wealthy.

Then another memory struggled uneasily in his consciousness. There had been something else about Hunt. A strange tale that somehow eluded his grasp.

He gave it up. "In that case," he commenced, disregarding Jane's frantic pressure on his arm, "we'll be glad to avail ourselves—"

He was interrupted by a hideous splintering crash. Immediately on its heels came a piercing scream that choked off abruptly. A thin flicker of fire lifted its sinister finger through the upland forests; it swelled into a blasting sheet of flame and retracted to a red blaze that thrust the yelling darkness back on every side. The report of the explosion came howling through the night.

"Good God!" Lynn cried. "That's the car that just passed us. They've crashed and caught fire!"

All his former anger evaporated. Human beings were in that car.

He thrust the trembling girl into the roadster. He hopped into the driver's seat. He switched the ignition, ground with savage haste on the starter. The engine roared.

THEN for the first time he noted the weird antics of the ancient couple—the retired millionaire and the society leader.

They clawed on the running-board, they shoved incredibly withered faces into the tonneau. Gloating devils danced in their eyes, a mad flame seemed to flow from their shriveled bodies. Babbage drummed an insane tattoo on the running-board with spindly shanks.

"It worked!" he shrilled.

Georgia Palfrey glowered at him. "One less for you, Thomas."

Lynn shouted impatiently: "Now what the devil—"

"Get on with you!" Babbage screamed. "Take us up there, as fast as you can. Hurry!"

"All right," Lynn growled. "Hold on tight."

He shifted into gear, and the roadster leaped up the winding path with headlights lunging before it. Not until later was the conduct of the ancient couple to occur as odd to Lynn. Just now his senses were fiercely intent on the road, his scalp tight at the thought of the wreck. But Jane had noted—and felt the coils winding more and more tightly around them.

The car bounced and jarred in its mad flight, but Babbage and Georgia held on with the tenacity of age gripping life. Lynn swung the wheel hard. The roadster breasted a blind sharp curve that dipped suddenly around a ledge. Tongues of fire flickered off into space. Lynn jammed on his brakes, squealed to a halt not five feet from the holocaust.

He flung the side door open and his feet pounded on the dirt. But the ancient pair were ahead of him. They skipped and danced to the scene like suddenly rejuvenated old goats. Their shriveled forms made bloody blobs against the leaping flames. They seemed like demons—male and female—mocking the tortures of the damned.

Lynn felt the hackles of his skin rise and turn icy cold.

"Don't look!" he cried sharply to the girl in the car.

There was nothing he or any mortal man could do. The great Isotta was a twisted, flaming pyre. Its front was battered in as with a giant blow; it lay on its side gasping out life and upholstery in puffs of red fire.

The two men had been thrown clear. They lay in the sodden dirt of the road like broken worms. The grisly flare of hellish light etched clearly their lolling heads, their maimed and mangled limbs.

The gigantic Negro chauffeur sprawled face forward against the retaining bole of a huge hemlock. His head was twisted at an insane angle. His right arm hung by a bloody thread of pale white tendon.

The furious-driving ancient, mouthing "Faster!" imbued with an apocalyptic vision of his own, had found not Paradise, but Hell! His age-withered head was rammed clear through the jagged center of the secondary windshield; its shapeless, blood-pulped features seemed encircled with a halo of vermilion-starred glass. The neck was sawed in half and the dark blood oozed thickly down a dead-white shirtfront. The thin smear of his lips drew back in a wolfish, soundless snarl.

Babbage quivered like a bird dog. His writhing countenance was aflame with lustful fury. He forgot the presence of the others.

"It's old Will Norcross, by thunder," he crowed. "*He* won't stand in my way, the damned sniveling devil." He thrust his face almost into that frightful oozing head. "For once I got the better of you, you and your lousy millions. You're dead, do you hear, Will Norcross? Hunt can't help you—not God Almighty himself."

Georgia minced into the flare of light.

"Now remember, Thomas," she mumbled. "I aided you this time; you do the same for me the next. You've more money than I."

Babbage shook his head cunningly. "Not as much as people think. I lost most of it in the crash."

Lynn Hart stood as if paralyzed at the scene of unutterable horror. Jane moaned through clenched teeth, hands pressing against hot eyeballs to shield them from the frenzied hell.

Now, however, for the first time, strange suspicion awoke in him. It whimpered in his throat, made queer tumbling sensations in the pit of his stomach, sweated his palms with the clammy drench of terror. Years later, he would awake to the sound of his own nightmare screams, reliving that moment.

William Norcross, international banker, man of untold millions, impaled on a halo of splintered glass. And the octagenarian manufacturer and the beldame who had once been society's leader, dancing fantastically like warlock and witch of another time in the flare of the leaping hellfires, gleefully mouthing curses on the poor dead bodies.

Then Lynn saw the stout tree trunk that barred the road, prone where it had fallen by deliberate axing, hidden from the plunging auto by the swift curve of the path. Against it the Isotta had crushed out its sleek speed and the lives of its occupants. An insanely cunning trap into which Norcross had gone to his death.

Red rage exploded in Lynn's brain. The creeping terrors fled from its hot fury. He took a step forward.

"You devils!" he ground out. "You've done this; it's murder, and I'm going to see to it that you pay the penalty."

CHAPTER TWO

The Room of Death

BABBAGE rose from his ghoulish position, stared at him with evil mocking eyes. He thrust back his head and laughed. Shrill, gasping laughter that racketed through the gloom-filled hills, reverberated in demoniac peals from the clustering hills.

Lynn moved quickly toward him; then froze in his tracks.

A man had stepped from behind the hemlock tree. The dying flames flicked weird shadows on his face, caught and held with glinting fervor on the blue steel that was clutched in a hairy fist.

"Stand where you are—or I'll let you have it."

The brutal raucous tones tore jaggedly across Lynn's consciousness. He opened his mouth to emit an amazed protest.

"Shut up," said the man with the gun as the first words came. The smoldering char of the automobile flared momentarily to reveal thick sloping shoulders, prognathous jaw, flaring nostrils and recessive, apelike brow. The gun shoved unpleasantly forward.

The man's piggish eyes flicked indifferently from the broken corpses to the youthful figure of the girl in the roadster. She had half risen from her seat, a choked gasp in her throat. The little eyes crawled and Lynn tensed desperately for exploding action.

"She's mine, Joe," Georgia shrilled. "You leave her alone!" She too had seen that look.

"Okay," Joe mumbled reluctantly. "Whatcha want done with 'em, Mr. Babbage?"

His tone was obsequious, but the muzzle of his gun was dead-centered on Lynn's heart.

"Heh! Heh!" cackled the old man. "Why, Joe, I'm surprised at you. The young man's my private guest, and Miss Palfrey—well—you know what she thinks of that young woman."

"Yeah!" said Joe. "I know."

"They're coming with us to Dr. Hunt. We'll make the necessary arrangements."

"Now look here," Lynn protested. "You can't do this. We're going back the way we came. We—"

"You're coming with *me*, brother," Joe growled. "Yuh shoulda looked before yuh got this far. The road's posted ten miles down: *Private*. Yuh're guilty of trespassin' an' it's up to th' doctor to handle yuhr case. Now get going. You too, lady."

Jane's legs felt wabbly; she could hear the trip-hammer beat of her heart. God! If only she were dreaming, if only this were a nightmare that sunshine and the cooling morning breeze could rid her of. But the fantastic figures ebbed and glowed in the dull sheen of the burning embers; over to one side lay what were now mercifully shadowed shapes; and Lynn, the man she loved, stood stiffly rigid in the last circle of illumination, his face white and strained, his pain-filled eyes warning her with steady gaze.

She tottered to the road and went to him. She linked her arm with his. She felt braver at that comforting touch.

"Good girl," Lynn whispered. "Buck up. We'll get out of this somehow."

Jane squeezed his arm. She dared not trust her voice. She was brimming with withheld hysteria.

Cold steel prodded Lynn rudely in the back.

"Get going," said Joe.

They shuddered past the gruesome relics of what had only minutes before been men, and toiled up the stiffening trail. Pitch darkness enveloped all their forms. A wind moaned in their ears, gravel crunched eerily underfoot. The cold snout of the revolver burned searing fires into Lynn's spine.

Whispering in back! Lynn got small drifts above the panting of the ancient couple, the pounding of feet on slithering stone.

". . . must clear the mess up." Babbage's wheezy tones.

Joe's louder grunt. "Mike'll do it. . . . We split. . . ."

Then the blackness lifted as an electric torch sprayed white radiance around them.

"Who's there?" Then the holder of the torch relaxed. "Oh, it's Joe, huh? And Mr. Babbage and Miss Palfrey. Shouldn't be out this late. Dr. Hunt don't like no—"

"Okay, Mike," said Joe. He motioned him to one side. They whispered warily together.

Lynn patted Jane's arm, gritting his teeth silently. But he knew, though he did not see, that the gun was still trained on him. If only Jane were out of it, he thought, feeling the uncontrollable shudders that coursed along her slender body. There was a gate in front of them, a huge, iron-barred gate set in a high wall of solid masonry. Beyond lay—what?

"Sure, I'll do it," Mike's voice rose startlingly. The flash bobbed down the path. Mike was going back to the wreck.

Joe herded his captives through the massive gate. It closed behind them with a hollow clang. In spite of himself, Lynn's muscles tightened, his throat clogged with choking dryness. The sound had an irrevocable quality to it, as if engraved on that gate's portals were the doomful words: *All hope abandon, ye who enter here!*

A DULL coppery moon scudded from above the torn wrack of black-massed clouds, glittered with weird half-lights over level parkland and a long low structure that thrust wings like radiating fingers into the all-embracing night. Then the moon was gone, swallowed up in the rolling murk. A single yellow beam broke the eyeless glare of blank walls.

They were pushed toward it. A door opened, lights dazzled eyes too long accustomed to the dark.

Lynn stared around in bewilderment. They were in a huge reception hall, and electric torches threw soft reflected light on a scene of incredible luxury. The walls were paneled Circassian walnut; the scattered divans, love-seats and arm-chairs in the gold and ivory of Louis Quinze. Underneath an enormous single Kermanshah rug glowed with the jeweled threads of Persia. Paintings of young and glorious bodies dotted the panels, exquisite nymphs of Fragonard, laughing children of Greuze and Boucher, the virile athletic nakedness of Greek gods, and the warm rosy pinks of Renoir's marvelous nudes. Youth, virility, pulsing young life—not a sign anywhere of age, of the possible decay of the body.

What a bitter contrast they held to the people in the room! These tottered to their feet at the sudden entrance of the newcomers—a full score of them. Men and women in equal proportions.

A cold breeze stirred the short hairs on Lynn's neck. Death, corruption, worms, spawning in the midst of pictured life and laughter! Obscene cartoons out of Felicien Rops, gargoyles from the Gothic, monstrosities from a lazar house, denizens of a Witches' Sabbath!

Age had not mellowed or dignified these creatures. Shrunken, shriveled limbs sagged under bony heads like death masks. They sucked on toothless gums and the spittle drooled unheeded from fleshless lips. Eyes were bleared with rheum and cataracts; baldness vied with stringy lackluster hair. Yet every one of them, visions of death in a setting of youthful elegance, held one thing in common. Greed! Ineradicable greed for life, for departed youth, ached like a festering tooth in each hideous countenance.

They raised futile shaking hands, they clawed at each other to thrust closer to the shrinking bodies of Lynn and Jane. They peered with red-rimmed eyes into their faces, they slithered grave-cold hands over arms and legs and bodies; they slipped and fell and tottered weakly to their feet again, they pushed and shoved and scrambled and screamed horrible epithets at their fellows who blocked their stealthy hands.

"New ones!" "I want *her!*" "Mine, all mine!" "I *won't* be outbid this time!"

A clamor of voices, lustful, avid, filled

with strange overpowering fear. They overwhelmed Joe, pushed Babbage and Georgia weeping and screaming out of their path, flowed in loathsome slimy contact over the youthful bodies of the pair. Men to Lynn, and withered creatures who had been women to Jane.

Lynn struggled against the press of ancient bodies. Disgust and loathing shuddered through his every vein at their feeble pawings, the croaking cackle of their voices, the creeping greed in their eyes. As fast as he thrust one away, others fumbled at him.

Babbage skipped around the edges. "Leave him alone," he screeched. "I brought him here. He's mine, I tell you!"

Lynn was suddenly afraid. What did these creatures of death want with him? Why did these ancient men, who should now be at peace with their Maker, assail him with avid eyes and pawing hands? What was it all about? Were they mad, or . . . ?

A horrible thought assailed him. Then he heard Jane's faint scream, her long gasp of repulsion. He lashed out with both fists. He must get to her.

They fell from him, glaring, panting, nursing hurts. Joe stood on the outskirts, making no move to interfere, his thick evil countenance grinning unpleasantly. His hand rested watchfully on the gun in his holster.

Lynn plunged into the press of crones who surrounded Jane, sent them flying and hobbling on all sides.

"Oh, Lynn!" the girl sobbed thankfully. "Take me out of here. What do these terrible creatures want?"

He stood in the center of the room, grim-eyed, holding her protectingly to him. His free hand clenched into a balled fist.

"This has gone far enough. These people are mad," he said. He looked at Joe. "We're going out, and you won't stop us, gun or no gun. Come on, Jane."

HE MOVED determinedly forward. Joe plucked at his revolver. Its muzzle was terrifyingly huge.

"Zat so?" he snarled. "One more step an' I'll—"

Lynn, face pale but determined, took the step.

Joe's finger compressed. Jane shrieked: "No! No!" Babbage stumbled against the man, clawing with frantic rage.

"Don't shoot, you fool!" he screeched.

Joe's eyes flickered; then he lowered the gun.

"Okay, Mr. Babbage," he growled, "but how in blazes d'yuh expect me—"

A dull toneless voice cut across the clamor of the ancients.

"What's the row about?"

Deathly silence fell like a thunderclap on bedlam. The gargoylish men and women scuttered back to their chairs, trembling. The veins on their paper thin hands were gorged with sluggish blood. Their eyes implored like beaten dogs.

A tall cadaverous man stood in the doorway. His long bony nose twitched from side to side, and white hollows accentuated the bones of his cheeks. Lank black hair hung in a mop over his forehead. The pupils of his eyes were narrowed to black pinpoints and the balls were filmed over with a blank yellowish glaze.

Joe pocketed his gun. He said carelessly, "It's this way, Dr. Hunt. I found this here pair snooping around the road, an' thought I'd bring 'em in."

Lynn stared incredulously. Dr. Hunt's picture had been in the papers, but he would never have recognized the smooth, rounded features, the quick intelligent look of the portrait, in this lackluster individual. Yet he felt curiously relieved. If Hunt were running a private madhouse, if his secret place were a sanitarium for even more horrible perversions of these incredible old people, it had nothing to do with him. A short explanation and the surgeon would let them go, unmolested.

"There's been some mistake, Dr. Hunt," he said. "We had no intention of snooping. We had simply lost our way. You surely realize better than your man does that you have no right to detain us."

Hunt turned to him slowly. His nose twitched perpetually. His eyes held no understanding.

"I—have no right to detain you?" he said in a thick, strained voice. He seemed puzzled, blank. He wrestled with what he had repeated.

"Never mind, Doc," Joe bellowed harshly. "I'm handlin' this. Just you—"

"Joe, I'm surprised at you. Is *that* the way to talk to the famous Dr. Meldon Hunt?"

It was a quiet, oily voice that nevertheless carried far. It came from a fat little man with a rounded stomach and a pink bald head. His eyes, innocently wide, radiated unctuous good humor. He had come softly in behind the surgeon.

Joe's arrogance collapsed. "I'm sorry, Mr. Sombart," he said humbly. "I didn't mean to—"

Sombart waved a pudgy hand. "Of course not, my dear boy. I know you didn't." He turned to Lynn. His eyes flicked approvingly over the slim contours of the girl. "Welcome, my charming young couple. I'm Dr. Hunt's secretary. He will discuss your problem in his private office. Won't you, Doctor?"

Hunt emerged from his daze to say, "Certainly," then relapsed into blankness.

Lynn, because he could not help himself, went with Jane into the luxuriously furnished office. Now that he had seen Dr. Hunt, he was chill with apprehension. The man was not normal, that was evident. Nor was his establishment normal.

Beside him Jane said softly, "He's as horrible in his way as the others. He'll never let us go alive."

Lynn started. She had given voice to the racing fear in his own brain, but he forced a laugh. "Don't be silly, honey," he whispered.

Hunt sank into a leather chair. Sombart stood alertly at his side. Joe guarded the door. The doctor took a small white pill from an ivory box on the desk, swallowed it. A flush mantled his cadaverous cheeks, his pupils widened, and he spoke with sudden animation.

"You have come at a most propitious time," he said jerkily. "We were running short of subjects and my clients are becoming a bit—impatient."

"What do you mean?" Lynn said sharply. Then suddenly, he did not want to know. The truth, he was certain, would be far too horrible. Jane, swaying on his arm, must not face what was about to be said.

BUT Hunt smiled secretively. It was a ghastly smile and his long nose twitched from side to side. It fascinated Lynn with its macabre dance. The doctor ignored the question, turned to the little fat man.

"I think," he said with a certain feverish intensity, "that it would be better to hold an auction." The pupils of his eyes had widened. They flamed over the man and the girl.

"They are splendid specimens," he went on with peculiar intonation. "My clients will pay handsomely. Yes, by all means, an auction."

Lynn clenched his fists. He breathed heavily.

"You're crazy, all of you," he shouted. "What are we, slaves, to be put on the block like cattle?"

Sombart clucked commiseratingly with his tongue. "I am sorry for you, young man. And for your charming companion. But the doctor has certain obligations. His clients are all very wealthy; they have come here for a definite purpose. It is very unfortunate, but good sound specimens have been hard to get. The clients are particular; they turn up their noses at most of those we have submitted. The doctor seems to think you both are perfect. It is very sad."

Jane's face was drained of blood. "Oh!" she gasped. "Specimens! Us!" She swung blindly to her lover; her voice was edged with hysteria. "Lynn, what *do* they mean?"

Lynn's heart hammered. He dared not think of what they meant. Jane in the hands of these monsters! Jane exposed to God knew what foul practices! He exploded suddenly into action.

He pivoted swiftly on the ball of his right foot and dove straight for the guard at the door. He caught the apelike Joe by surprise. They crashed heavily to the floor, Lynn's hand clawing for the gun in the holster. Joe cursed and gouged his thumb savagely at Lynn's eye. Lynn ducked, and the sharp nail tore a long bleeding track along his cheek. His short powerful jab rocked Joe's head back on his shoulders.

The guard went limp. Lynn snatched the gun, twisted around just as Jane screamed terrified warning.

Sombart stood directly over him, his soft pudgy hand wrapped around a small but efficient-looking automatic.

"It would be a pity to spoil such a virile body," he said with regretful intonation. "Don't make me do it."

Lynn dropped the gun from suddenly weary hands. He rose slowly to his feet. He had muffed their last chance to escape.

"The auction!" chanted Dr. Hunt. His eyes glittered, his voice was mechanical. "We must go on with the auction."

"In good time, Doctor," Sombart soothed. Then his voice cracked with whiplash scorn. "Joe! Get up, and next time you let anyone take your gun away . . ."

He left the threat hanging, but the guard paled as he came groggily to his feet. His undershot eyes burned fierce hatred at Lynn. He lumbered back to the door; he held the revolver on his captives as if nothing would have pleased him better than another break.

The fat man turned with a satisfied air to Hunt. "I think," he said respectfully, "that it would be advisable to show your clients the successful results of the last auction. It would very probably raise the final bids to quite substantial figures. Your work, your research, you know, require considerable money."

"A very excellent idea," the cadaverous surgeon nodded. His lank black hair glistened with sweat; beads of moisture showed around his nostrils. The yellowish glaze was creeping over his eyes again.

"Good!" Sombart bowed. "Your orders shall be obeyed."

He pressed a button under the desk. The door opened softly and a man entered. It was Mike, the guard who had eradicated the last traces of Norcross and his chauffeur. He was squat and stocky, with long dangling arms and the face of a rat.

"Mike, you will notify Mr. Clegg that Dr. Hunt will take care of his case at once. And prepare Number Thirty-One in the Life Chamber in the usual manner."

Mike's features quivered with sadistic cruelty.

"Okay, Mr. Sombart."

Dr. Hunt raised his head. "Has Clegg given his check yet?"

Sombart nodded. "In full. One hundred thousand dollars, to be exact. But these, I think, will command considerably more. . . ."

Lynn felt Jane's body go limp against his own. Cold shivered over him, followed by flushes of heat. What nightmare were they entangled in? What were the strange horrors these monsters were discussing so obliquely? What did he and Jane have that senile millionaires were willing to bid fortunes for its gruesome possession?

He whirled in sudden agony, to attempt a last insane dash for freedom. Jane's half fainting form dragged at his clutching arm, impeded his movements. Joe's revolver butt gashed across his forehead, sent him reeling against the desk. His eyes grew dim with pain and nausea; he felt himself being bound with a stout cord. He was too weak to resist. . . .

CHAPTER THREE

New Life for Old

BY THE time his reeling brain was able to distinguish between objects he found himself walking unsteadily down a long corridor, arms twisted and lashed cruelly together behind his back. Steel against his spine urged him on, sent him staggering along with sharp, jarring blows. Joe was enjoying the game.

Jane moved as in a dream at his side. Her slender white hands were also bound. Her jet-black hair was in disarray, her eyes filled with shrinking terror. Her cheeks were paper white. She smiled wanly at Lynn's quick worried look. She was trying to be brave, but the blood dripped slowly from the lovely curve of her lower lip where teeth had clenched to restrain shrieking hysteria.

The pallid procession came to a halt before a steel door. It was locked and barred with massive chains. Mike fumbled with his keys; there was a creaking, groaning sound and the steel portal swung slowly open.

Mike thrust head and gun cautiously inside.

"Number Thirty-One!" he called.

His voice made metallic clamor as if the interior were a gigantic steel cage.

A girl's low moan was his only answer.

Mike said harshly: "If yuh don't come out, Thirty-One, I'll twist yuhr damn head off."

"I'm coming." The voice was a man's and it trembled incontrollably.

There was the shuffling of naked feet and a young man, naked except for a pair of shorts, dragged slowly into the corridor. His face was a ghastly mask of terror; he could hardly stand on fainting feet.

"For God's sake," he chattered through blued lips. "What are you devils going to do with us?"

Mike grinned nastily at the wretch's fear. It seemed like incense to his pointed nose.

"Don't yuh worry, fellah. Yuh'll be surprised when yuh see who yuh're gonna turn out to be."

Naked feet rushed inside, beat a desperate tattoo into the hall. A girl flung herself before Mike with an imploring gesture. Her blond hair streamed wildly over tear-drenched features, her somewhat ample bosom heaved tumultuously. A thin slip barely covered her florid charms.

"Leave him be," she blubbered. "He's my man; don't hurt him." She swayed in frightful anguish. "We never did you no harm, mister. We just was looking for jobs. You promised us good ones out here. I swear to God, if you'll let us go—"

Mike licked his thin lips. His beady eyes glowed on her generous bosom.

"I'd like tuh oblige, sister, if yuh'd be good tuh me. But—"

The man spoke with sudden energy. "No!" he shouted. "Do your damndest to me, but let her alone. I'm a-going."

The girl rose and flung her arms violently around him.

"Alec! I won't let them; I won't. . . ."

Joe tore her clinging arms away, thrust her screaming and yelling into the steel chamber. He slammed the door with harsh, irrevocable sound, locked it.

"Get on, all of yuh!" he forced through thick lips. "What's the matter with you, Mike? Want the boss to step on yuh?"

Mike spread his hands placatingly. "Aw, Joe," he said. "We need a little fun."

"Yeah!" Joe answered grimly. "Yuh

won't think it's fun if the boss gets wise."

The weird procession, augmented by the dragging shuffle of Alec's feet, moved down the corridor. The young man's body was rather scrawny; his ribs showed clearly against the ridge of his spine. He looked undernourished. His legs, too, were a bit spindly and slightly varicosed. His head lolled from side to side as he staggered along.

A right angle turn and Lynn found himself in a huge white-tiled room. The blood surged madly through his veins, pounded with great thudding strokes in his head. He felt faint. He shot a quick side glance at Jane. Thank God she did not understand! She did not shriek or fall unconscious.

BUT Alec saw, and knew. He sank to his knees in an ecstacy of fear.

"Not that!" he screamed. "Anything but that!"

He groveled on the floor like a dog whose back had been broken; he beat with his fists insanely against the hard white tile.

Mike kicked him deliberately in the ribs.

"Get up," he growled. He bent down, snapped a pair of manacles on the gibbering man, dragged him to his feet, shoved him sprawling into a white-backed chair.

A long porcelain table, extraordinarily wide, stood sinisterly in the center of the room. Floodlights beat white glare from the ceiling on its impeccable surface. A cabinet towered over it, glass enclosed, filled with a shining array of instruments. Surgical instruments!

They were in a modern operating room, completely equipped. White runnels edged the sides of the operating table, spouted over smooth round buckets. Impeccable except for one dark stain over the rim, where fluid had slopped over.

Dried blood!

The next instant, even as Lynn twisted insanely at his bonds, he was seized from behind by long powerful arms and carried bodily to a high-backed chair. They chained him with clanking steel into immovability. Jane was flung into a similar chair.

"Just in case. . . ." Joe grinned nastily. "The doctor's hand might slip if yuh made a break while he wuz workin'!"

Where he had been thrown like a broken doll, Alec moaned. He slumped over and his body jittered convulsively in a terrible nerve-twitching dance.

Feet made sharp firm contact on the tiles. Dr. Hunt came in through a door at the farther end. His tall thin frame was swathed in gleaming white costume, white rubber gloves covered his hands, an aseptic white mask shrouded his face. He moved with sure swift movements. Once more he was the famous surgeon, the man whose skill had saved hundreds of lives.

Sombart trotted at his side like a dumpy tug alongside a lean ocean liner.

"Mike, get Mr. Clegg," he said.

Mike sidled out of the room. Hunt went to the cabinet, took out sharp gleaming instruments, dipped them into an antiseptic bath, laid them out with loving care on aseptic gauze on a little stand to the right of the operating table.

The sight of those steel-bright tools sent Lynn's heart thudding against his ribs. Wicked-toothed saws, forceps, long razor-edged knives, lancets, artery clamps, all the terrible paraphernalia of a major operation. Meldon Hunt's eyes gleamed through the holes in his mask; the overlaying film was gone.

Alec moaned in a low singsong. Terror had mercifully dulled his perceptions. Jane said faintly, "What is he going to do?"

"Nothing much," Lynn returned as carelessly as he could. "I suppose the poor devil needs an operation. Just you close your eyes. It may be a little nasty to watch."

Jane turned her gaze on him. Her pupils

were large with fear; her shapely head sagged as if its weight were intolerable.

"You are trying to shield me from something," she said very low.

Lynn dared not trust his voice. He was almost relieved at the diversion occasioned by Mike's return.

He wheeled into the room an old, old man in a rubber-tired chair. Sly mockery twisted his evil features.

The old man looked almost a hundred. One leg dangled uselessly into the well of the chair; it was paralyzed. His face was seamed with a thousand leathery wrinkles; he snuffled and coughed with asthmatic breathings. The brown clawed hand he laid on the arm of the chair was the hand of a mummy. There was no life in that pallid, wisp-blown body except for the eyes.

"Ready, Mr. Clegg?" Sombart bobbed his head until its pink baldness shone in the glare of the operating lights.

"He! He!" the ancient cackled. His laugh had the dry unpleasant sound of scraping sandpaper. "I've been ready all day. Haven't much time to spare. Another attack of asthma and it'll be too late." His weazened monkey face screwed up anxiously. "You're sure, Dr. Hunt, that it'll work all right? Because I don't want to die. I want to live, *live*, LIVE!"

HIS voice broke and choked on a half-scream. His hand plucked convulsively. He shrank from death, from oblivion, with all the feeble strength of his wasted body.

Lynn turned in shuddering disgust from the horrible imploring old man. What sweetness could there be in life for that age-racked body? Hadn't he seen enough, done enough, experienced enough in ninety-odd years of existence to have become reconciled to the approach of the comforter, Death? But what was going to be done to restore life to him?

In a red haze he heard Hunt's voice, booming, hearty. The typical surgeon's tone to a frightened patient.

"Don't you worry, Mr. Clegg. You'll never recognize yourself. The operation hasn't failed once. All right, Joe, bring Thirty-One to the table."

Joe moved with catlike tread to the slumped drooling figure. He stooped, unlocked the manacles. He brought a heavy hand down on the thin shoulder, jerked the man erect.

Alec glared wildly around, saw the swathed surgeon, the array of instruments, the hot devouring glare in Clegg's eyes as they fastened vampirishly on his young, starved body.

He shrieked once. Light froth discolored his pallid lips; his face twitched with awful fear.

"You can't do this to me," he babbled. "Oh, God, make them stop! I can't—stand—it!"

He pulled with sudden maniac strength, broke free. He started to run. His blue-veined legs churned futilely over the tile.

Joe ground out an oath and lunged after him. His long hairy arm darted out, wound stranglingly around Alec's wobbly neck, constricted.

Hunt stood coldly calm. "Bring him here," he said in flat tones.

Alec's bare feet shot from under him —they dragged slithering over the floor. His head lolled from side to side; broken phrases yammered through clenched teeth.

Lynn's heart threatened to rip through its ribbed enclosure, his lungs heaved and strangled for air. He remembered now what first had made him uncomfortable at the name of Meldon Hunt.

A certain paper the surgeon had read before the American Medical Association. It had created a furore—though it had been only a tentative report. The ethics of such an operation had been unanimously condemned. Three days later Hunt had disappeared.

Jane's head drooped to her breast. Her face was congested with dark blood, her eyes were closed. Thank God, she had fainted;

Alec was lifted limply to the operating table. The guards strapped him down with immaculate white straps to the farther end. He lay on his right side, exposing the base of his skull.

At a nod from Hunt, Mike took out of the porcelain cabinet brush, shaving cream, and long gleaming razor. He lathered the unfortunate man's nape, and applied the cold bright steel to the hair. Alec screamed once at the swift-flowing blade, but his head was clamped into immovability. The hair came away in thick clots, leaving the rear of the skull ghastly smooth.

"Now, Mr. Clegg," Hunt said.

Joe sprang to the trembling millionaire, lifted him as if he were a child.

Nameless fear eddied into Clegg's eyes. Foam flecked his lips. He cried out: "I've changed my mind; I won't go through with it. I'll die; I know I'll die!"

"It's too late now to back out," Hunt said in a terrible voice.

Joe disregarded the feeble struggles of the old man, thrust him on the table. His twitching body lay alongside that of Alec, back to back. In seconds he was strapped into position. Mike swiftly shaved the base of his skull to the brown wrinkled skin beneath.

"Okay, Dr. Hunt," he said.

A SUDDEN hush blanketed the room. Even Alec's moanings and Clegg's gibberings died on their lips. The floodlights beat with fierce white glow. The walls rocked to Lynn's fevered vision. There was no air; he was stifling.

Hunt daubed their bare skulls with a dark yellow solution. He took up a thin surgical instrument, shaped like a tiny center-bit.

"It won't hurt very much," he said. His eyes gleamed through the mask with the intensity of a fanatic. "The medieval doctors suspected the truth, but I am the first to prove that the pituitary gland is the seat of nutritional juices which restore youth and energy. Only the glandular secretions must be tapped from a living person and injected directly into the pituitary body of the subject. That has never been done before. Even seconds' delay in transfusing the fluid causes profound chemical changes which destroy their potency. I guarantee you, Mr. Clegg, undreamed of youth."

Lynn cried out, uncontrollably. "And what happens to Alec, the victim of your operation?"

Hunt turned slowly to him, as if he had forgotten his presence.

"Alec! Number Thirty-One?" he said vaguely. "I suppose he'll be all right."

He shrugged his shoulders and set to work. The bit dipped in Clegg's skull. Dry bone grated horribly underneath. It dipped again and again, making the points of a small circle. The millionaire shuddered convulsively; his bloodless lips twisted over each other. But he did not consciously feel the pain, for the yellow fluid was an opiate.

Hunt picked up a miniature saw and set to work again. He finished by breaking off the trepanned segment of skull, dropped it on the pad.

Then he turned his terrible instrument on Alec. It drove deep, and the victim screamed, and screamed again. The anodyne had not taken full effect. But the surgeon worked on remorselessly, swiftly. He was a cold, unhuman machine. The section of bone came neatly out.

Then he picked up a hypodermic syringe, jabbed it deep into Alec's open skull, plunged it through quivering grey matter directly into a small dark rounded structure. He squeezed, and withdrew the glass nozzle. A pale yellow fluid filled the syringe. Without hesitation he squirted it directly into the pituitary at the base of Clegg's brain. Then he picked up two small silver plates, sutured them into the open skulls. He moved back, suddenly. The operation was over.

But Lynn, fascinated in spite of his fear, had seen the swift, surreptitious movement of Sombart. That benign-seeming individual had bent solicitously over the twitching form of Clegg. A silver needle was hidden in his pudgy hand. It jabbed into the millionaire's wrist, and withdrew out of sight as if it had never been.

Clegg's body jerked against the straps. The guards untied him.

Lynn groaned and bit his lips. Great God in Heaven! Was he going mad? To his horror-swept gaze it seemed that the dried parchment skin of the wasted cheeks was plumping out, as if fresh new blood were coursing through ancient arteries, bringing immortal food to long-forgotten tissues. A vampirish glow emanated from mouth and eyes and scrawny neck. They grew rosy. . . .

The elderly millionaire moved suddenly to a sitting position on the table, thrust a formerly paralyzed foot lithely to the floor, sprang alertly down. His face twisted and writhed into a triumphant gargoyle; he skipped and hopped like a goatish Pan.

"Look at me," he cried in a cracked voice, "I'm—"

Mike thrust him back with a growl. Hunt said sharply: "You'll have to rest an hour."

"Of course," said Sombart. "Now we can proceed with the auction."

The guards moved toward Lynn. In a haze he felt the leg chains slipping. He came unsteadily to his feet.

Alec, sprawled on the porcelain, turned his head feebly around. Lynn looked into his eyes and cried out. He could not help it. They were the eyes of a mindless idiot, twin portals to a blank hell within. Alec was no longer a man; he was a body without a soul, without a guiding intelligence. The operation had done that to him.

Jane was lifted in Mike's huge arms. She opened her eyes. They fastened on the idiot thing on the table. She moaned and collapsed into a faint again.

Lynn felt himself pushed forward by the cruel steel of a gun. He stumbled out into the corridor. His legs were wobbly but a cold burning rage seared away the last spasms of nausea.

His fists ached with straining against the metal chains. Beasts, monsters, devils! They had defiled nature with foul experiments; they meant to do the same with Jane and himself.

Jane! The thought forced reason, sanity back on him. He must not give way to rage, to blind terror. Otherwise she was doomed—the girl he loved—given over to a horrible life compared to which death itself was a shining glory. He must be cunning, he must plan—there *must* be some way out. His brain whirled round and round like a squirrel in a revolving cage. There *must* be some way. . . .

HE FOUND himself back in the great reception room. It was filled with the cackling horde who had clawed at their bodies only a short while before. They swept upon the two, tearing half the clothes from their bodies in their mad desire.

On the outskirts of the whimpering, greed-lusty mob, were Babbage and Gloria Palfrey. They tried vainly to force their way through the panting crowd. They shouted things to Hunt and Sombart, but the noise was too great for them to be heard.

"Put them in the cage," said Sombart.

Lynn was prodded to one side, past the clutching fingers of the ancients. Jane was still unconscious in Mike's arms. Lynn stumbled on, the bitterness of utter futility flooding his soul.

A great steel cage, heavily barred, stood in the farther corner of the room. The barred door swung open. Joe unlocked his manacles, sent Lynn sprawling inside. Jane was dumped with a thud. Then the steel clanged into position again.

The shock of the fall jarred Jane back to life. She opened her eyes in bewilderment.

"Where am I?" she asked feebly.

Lynn had her in his arms, straining her to his breast. It might be the last time. There was nothing he could say.

She stared wildly around, saw the thick steel bars, the panting, avid mob outside.

"Oh!" she said faintly, went silent. Her lips met Lynn's fiercly.

Sombart rubbed his hands.

"Now, ladies and gentlemen," he commenced genially, "we shall follow the same procedure as in former cases. Dr. Hunt believes that it is the fairest method."

"It is not," Babbage quavered from the outskirts. "It's a damned money-making scheme. That youngster is mine; I brought him here; I want him!"

"And I brought the girl," Georgia Palfrey shrilled.

"We can not deviate from established methods," Sombart said severely. "Everyone must get an equal chance."

"Yes, yes!" Eager approval from the few whose millions were staggering. Uneasy growls from the others, as if they saw another lost chance of cheating death.

"These are splendid specimens of young men and young women," Sombart went on. "As fine as we have been able to provide thus far. The lucky bidders will indeed be fortunate. Think of it—restored to the youthful twenties, endowed with marvelously smooth and life-drenched limbs, able to eat, drink, love and be merry, in ways that your own elderly frames have long forgotten. A veritable immortality, my friends. Vistas open before you. What is to prevent you from living forever?"

He knew how to whip up the passions, the innermost lusts of these decayed old bodies. Conscience, the dictates of reason and civilization, fled before his smooth periods. They yammered from their seats, they shook feeble fists in the air; their foul breaths seemed to poison the very atmosphere. Each octogenarian pictured himself an athlete, each withered crone the reigning toast of the season.

"Oh God!" Jane moaned, shrinking from those eyes that stripped her to the very bones.

An old man's voice penetrated the uproar, edged with suspicion.

"How do we know Dr. Hunt can make good on his promises? It sounds incredible. In fact I hesitated about coming here."

Sombart smiled. His smile seemed the epitome of good nature.

"You are a newcomer, Mr. Fellowes. You have not had an opportunity as yet to witness the proofs with your own eyes. Fortunately Dr. Hunt is in a position to oblige you. You knew Mr. Clegg?"

"Of course. I saw him this morning. He's an old friend of mine."

"Good. Mr. Clegg was the fortunate bidder in the last auction; he has undergone his operation only an hour ago."

A murmur rustled over the audience. Scraggly necks stretched like rubber.

Fellowes, a multi-millionaire, whose heart was a leaky pump, whose stomach was engorged with cancerous growths, whose bones were twisted with fierce aches, forgot his skepticism.

"What happened to him?" he cried.

"Behold!" Sombart said dramatically.

Two men were walking in through a door behind the platform. One was Dr. Hunt, more cadaverous than ever. Bright red spots made a hectic glow on his cheeks;

his eyes were yellow and lifeless. . . .
The second man was William Clegg!

CHAPTER FOUR

Blood-Mad Ancients

THE ancient paralytic of the wheelchair walked with a youthful springiness; his cheeks were dyed with the red flush of vigor. His eyes were bright and sparkling. His very wrinkles seemed smoothed away.

"Good God!" Fellowes screeched. "Will! It can't be you. You're younger, your face. . . . It *is* your face; you've regained your youth! Will, speak to me!"

"Hello, George," the apparition grinned. "I feel a hundred years younger. Look!" He executed a pirouette, jumped lithely into the air, came down clicking his heels.

"So long, everybody," he shouted exultantly. "I'm going back to New York. I'm going to live, to enjoy, to live all over again. I am young, *young, YOUNG!*" He flung out his arms and rushed swiftly through the door behind the platform.

If there had been pandemonium before, there was frantic madness now. They had seen with their own eyes—these life-avid ancients. Clegg had been even as they—and now he was reborn.

Their eyes glared; spittle and slime dripped unheeded down their slavering toothless jaws; every last vestige of humanity was stripped from them. They flung themselves forward; they screamed and yelled and prayed; they cursed and ranted; they clung to the bars of the cage, clawing vainly at the bodies they desired with such insane lust.

"Hurry the auction," Fellowes screeched. "I can't wait; the doctors gave me a week to live. I have cancer. Hurry!"

Their poisonous breaths enfolded the couple, their glaring eyeballs grew into a single writhing nightmare.

"Steady, Jane!" Lynn backed her to the remotest corner. God! There *must* be a way out. It wasn't possible this could happen to them. . . .

"Shall we start, Dr. Hunt?" Sombart asked respectfully.

The surgeon nodded mechanically.

"Very well, then," the fat man said. "Gentlemen, first. Let us have your bids for this splendidly virile young man."

"Thirty thousand," Babbage yelled.

"Forty thousand," someone answered.

"Fifty thousand!" Babbage screamed defiance.

"One hundred thousand." That was Fellowes.

Babbage tottered. "It's an outrage. I brought him here; you *must* give him to me. All I have in the world is seventy-five thousand. Take it, take every penny of it. I've been here a month, and every time I'm outbid. I want to live too; I don't want to die. *I don't want to die!*"

"One hundred and fifty thousand," someone shouted from the side.

Fellowes glared insanely at the bidder. "Half a million!"

A deathly despair gripped the room. Half a million! Even if they matched it, bid more, up to their entire fortunes, Fellowes could double, triple their bids. They knew it. Another chance at life gone. Perhaps—perhaps the next time. . . !

"Sold to Mr. George Fellowes!" The inexorable finality of Sombart's voice. "Now we put the young lady up. Look at her lovely form, that smooth soft skin. Ladies, your bids!"

Babbage gave a great cry, tottered and fell flat on his face. No one noticed him.

Georgia Palfrey quavered: "Thirty thousand. All I have!"

Hardly had she spoken when a gross fat woman, a bag of flabby putrescence, shouted: "Fifty thousand!"

Lynn heard no more. He crouched in his corner, panting, holding Jane with a deathlike grip. He felt himself going mad.

Jane Porter went to the swollen greasy woman for one hundred and fifty thousand dollars!

Sombart rubbed his hands. The financial returns had been beyond expectations. Hunt stood rigid, without expression. A twitching nose was his only sign of life.

The steel door clanged open. Joe entered the cage. Mike stood outside, gun in hand.

"Okay." Joe grinned brutally. "We're going places."

Lynn rose dully from his crouch. Now if ever he must act. He moved slowly toward the door. He seemed dazed. Jane, her hands pressed tightly against her body, went with him. She had drained the last lees of shame and terror.

But as he pressed close to the guard, Lynn galvanized suddenly into a bolt of lightning. His fist crashed out to Joe's jaw. Every ounce of accumulated hatred and red rage went into that blow.

There was the sound of crunching bone. Joe's face smeared into shapelessness. He went down with a crash, blood spurting from pulped flesh. He lay still.

LYNN pivoted in a single flowing motion. He leaped for Mike. The rat-faced guard jerked his gun around. Lynn's fist exploded in his face just as he pulled trigger.

A sear of flame furrowed along Lynn's side. Mike goggled foolishly. He fell slowly, like a tree to whose root the axe has been laid. Lynn snatched the gun out of palsied fingers.

"Jane! This way!" he called.

The girl darted after him. They turned and ran for the door in back of the platform. It was open.

The place was a bedlam of shrieks. Hunt moved quickly toward them. Sombart plucked at his hip pocket. His round good-natured face was transformed. The mask had fallen, and a snarling vicious demon emerged. His gun was out; he fired. The room rocked with the concussion of sound. The doorjamb splintered into a rain of wood.

But Lynn and Jane were already through. The stout oak door slammed behind them.

Their feet raced down a long corridor. Behind them was the noise of pursuit. Shouts. Shots. They whined unpleasantly past their heads, crashed into wood.

Then Lynn saw the door to one side. He skidded in, half-carrying Jane. It was the operating room. He whirled, gun thrusting. His face was grim behind its mask of blood. The last bullet was for Jane.

Someone was coming down the corridor. He was coming very fast and his shoes made a clattering sound. Lynn poked his head out quickly.

It was Dr. Meldon Hunt and he was running. His eyes blazed feverishly; his cheekbones were aflame with hectic red. A gun was in his hand. It jerked once. The bullet slammed wildly down the hall.

"You fool!" Lynn cried desperately. "Don't you see—"

The gun made roaring sound again. The steel slug missed Lynn by a hair's breadth. Hunt came on quickly; his eyes were the eyes of a killer.

Lynn groaned and let him have it. Just above the heart. A red splotch oozed through his shirt. He spun once, and went down in a heap.

"Too bad!" Lynn muttered. There was no exultation in him. He had not wanted to kill Hunt. The corridor was clear now. The frightful screaming of the milling mob came faintly through.

"Look out, Lynn!" Jane shrieked behind him.

He whirled, too late.

Sombart stood propped against the wall

to one side. His face was contorted with fierce triumph. His right hand held a gun. It was dead-centered on Lynn's belly. Over his shoulder, through an open door, leered the smeared fury of Mike. His lips were puffed abnormally, his nose was a pulped mass.

"Drop it," Sombart snarled.

Lynn went suddenly cold all over. He dropped his gun.

Sombart said: "You didn't know of this passage, eh? You thought you were getting away with it. Well, nobody ever got the best of Julius Sombart. You've busted up things for me, but I'm going to kill you."

LYNN said steadily: "Okay. But before I die, I'm going to tell you something. I've found out what your racket is."

The pudgy little man laughed.

"It won't do you any good. It's a sweet racket. I've got a cool million out of it so far—enough to retire on. But there's millions more in it. I figured everything in advance after I saw that article by Hunt. I fixed this place up. Then I kidnaped the doctor and fed him dope. Made him crazy for the stuff. He'll do anything I want."

"A stroke of genius," Lynn murmured. His muscles were tense, waiting his opportunity. But Sombart's hand was steady, and Mike, the dropped gun trained on them, stood between them and the outer door.

"Yeah," said Sombart. "I contacted every doddering old geezer with dough who had one foot in the grave. You'd be surprised how they fell for the scheme, especially with Hunt's signature to the come-on literature. They lapped it up, secret stuff and all. You'll be dead a long time, and the racket will still be working. It's air-tight."

"I wouldn't be too sure of that," Lynn said softly. His hand brushed Jane's quivering body, his brain raced in vain attempt to overcome the menace of those guns.

"What do you mean?" Sombart queried sharply.

"Just this. The whole scheme depends on Hunt."

"Well?"

"Dr. Meldon Hunt is dead, out there in the corridor, with a bullet in his heart."

The pudgy man's triumphant grin masked to a sickly yellow; his rounded cheeks sagged into hollow folds.

"Dead?" he whispered incredulously. Then his eyes slitted into hard agate lines.

"Mike!" he barked. "See if it's true."

The guard clumped out behind them. In seconds he was back, his face pasty.

"Boss," he gasped, "it ain't nothin' else but."

Never had Lynn seen such insane fury in a human face before. Sombart's features were a twisted mask of unglutted hate.

Lynn awaited with shrinking flesh the tearing torture of a bullet; Jane screamed.

"Don't kill them that easy, boss," Mike cried. "Let me get to work on 'em first." His gory rat face quivered with lusting cruelty.

Sombart released the pressure of his finger. He smiled suddenly. That smile made Lynn's blood chill, sent prickling knives over his body.

"You gave me an idea," Sombart said softly. "Tie them up."

Lynn jerked forward. He'd rather take death now than later, under shrieking torture.

But Mike was too fast for him. He leapt forward, gun upraised. The roof seemed to collapse on Lynn's head.

When he came to, dizzy and retching, he was manacled in the tall-backed chair; and Jane, breasts heaving tumultuously, was in the next one. Mike was gone.

"You devil!" Lynn raged frantically. "Kill us, get it over with!"

Sombart beamed on him. "Not so fast, my dear sir. Do you know where I have sent Mike?"

Lynn groaned. The ache in his head was unbearable.

"I have sent him," Sombart said carefully, "to bring our entire clientele into this room."

For the moment the fiendish deviltry of the scheme did not penetrate Lynn's consciousness. Then it burst in his brain like a Very shell.

"No! No! Anything but that," he said wildly. "Not Jane, not the girl! She was not to blame. Do what you want with me, but leave her out of it!"

Sombart grinned evilly. "I'm afraid they won't be able to make nice distinctions," he asserted.

Already Lynn heard a confused shuffle of feet down the corridor, heard quavering voices shrilling suddenly into hideous lamentations.

"Mike has shown them the dead body of poor Dr. Hunt," Sombart said with gloating satisfaction.

THEY poured into the room, scarecrows clothed in human garments. They came with shrieks and moans and cries of anguished self-pity. Dr. Meldon Hunt was dead, and with him, shattered in the dust, lay life, the universe itself.

Death, rotting death stared at them with slimy eyes. They were no longer human; they were mad with the agony of hope dashed from their greedy mouths.

The leaders paused an instant in the doorway, blinking. They were Babbage and Fellowes and Georgia Palfrey. The tide of thrusting bodies piled up behind them, pushed them irresistibly into the operating chamber.

Sombart raised his hand. "My dear sirs and ladies," he said, "I grieve for you. Dr. Meldon Hunt, the man who could have made you live your youth again, is dead." There was a quiver to his voice, the quiver of genuine grief.

A long lamentation burst from a score of scrawny throats. Georgia Palfrey thrust back her head and howled, while the tears made long hideous channels down her rouged cheeks.

Fellowes lifted his voice. "Who did it?" he shrieked.

Lynn knew what was coming. He saw the whole damnable scheme in its entirety. Only the arch-devil himself could have conceived it. He jerked at his manacles until the iron seared into his wrists.

"Listen to me, friends!" he shouted desperately. "Sombart is—"

Mike dived for him. His balled fist crashed across Lynn's mouth, sent his already wounded head smashing against the hard back of the chair.

In a daze he heard Sombart's voice go on smoothly, convincingly.

"It was these two who did Dr. Hunt to death, who snatched from you all chance for immortal youth. It is for you to decide their fate."

A savage roaring was his answer. Lynn forced his swollen eyelids open. If the rabble of old people had been unhuman before, they were now ravening beasts of prey, glaring at their kill. Hate made bottomless pits of their eyes; toothless mouths snarled awry and dripped with the drool of spittle; vulture necks stretched in the direction of the chained man and girl.

Jane slumped against her manacles. Lynn yelled, knowing in the depths of his despair that his words were hopeless: "Sombart is deceiving you! He is a criminal. The operation was a fake! He—"

Fellowes led the screaming, bloodthirsting horde. They came forward in a stumbling, clawing rout, more terrible than a pack of wolves, more hideous than devils streaming out of Hell. Weird ululations split the air, hands like skeleton talons groped before them. On they swept, straight for the helpless, fear-chilled pair.

Lynn set his teeth hard, and jerked madly away from the chair. If only he could rip it from its bolted bed, it might smash; the manacles might shatter. The skin tore away into raw flesh from his wrists, agonized pains wracked his arms; but the chair held firm.

Sombart and Mike stood to one side, grinning at his futile struggles. There was no mercy in their eyes. Mike dangled the key to the chains tauntingly.

The next second the horrible ancients were on top of them. Lynn barely heard Jane's cry of repulsion, of quick shrieking agony—then he felt himself overwhelmed under a mass of swarming squirming bodies.

Insane eyeballs glared into his, fetid saliva slobbered over his face, long taloned nails gouged down his cheeks, ripping flesh to the bone, seeking for his eyes. He heaved and twisted his head vainly from side to side, seeking to avoid those terrible hands, trying hopelessly to save his eyes from gouging blindness. He felt his arms and legs twist into unbearable agony; his body was a straining quivering mass of rips and slashes and torn flesh.

LYNN felt himself going down in a red haze of pain. Fellowes, the man with cancer in his stomach and not a week to live, pressed closer and closer. He was like a gigantic crab; his red-dripping nails stabbed again and again for Lynn's shrinking eyes. They dug into his cheek; the next would pierce into soft, fear-struck eyeballs. He arched himself like a monstrous cat for that last downward slash. His sere features writhed with horrible anticipation.

Lynn, his head a leaden immovable weight, could not duck. He forced swollen lids down, shuddering against that last supreme blaze of pain.

A shrill cracked voice seared through the gabbling tumult. In the far-off darkness in which Lynn weltered and sank it sounded somehow familiar. Then, incredibly, the smothering bodies that crawled and swarmed over his, went away. His pain-flogged limbs lightened. The awaited blow did not fall.

He opened his eyes, blinking. The hate-ridden mob, blood-smeared, panting, craned toward the door. Lynn's first fearful glance was for Jane. She sagged in her chair, moaning feebly. Her half-nude body was a gridiron of gouged flesh, but her face, pale and taut, was hardly marked. Thank God, she was still alive!

Then his eyes swerved to the doorway. Two men, if they could still be termed men, were coming slowly into the room. Alec, made into a mindless idiot by Hunt's operation, his face a grinning horrible blank, supported with his naked shoulder the dragging feet of William Clegg. Clegg, who but a while before had danced and pirouetted with new-found youth before the avid eyes of his fellow ancients, was now a thing of horror, a loathsome creature that still gripped life with incredible tenacity.

His withered leg dangled with dreadful uselessness. The other barely held the floor. His face was corpse-white and the bones jutted startlingly through the paper thinness of dried skin. Live coals burned deep in creaking sockets. The seal of death was manifest upon him.

He raised a bloodless arm. A hush fell on the nightmare throng.

"We've been cheated!" he shrilled, while his companion swayed and nodded with vacant foolishness. "We asked for life and they gave us death! Look at me, what I am. Hours to live, who wanted youth, who paid—" Sobs ripped his throat apart. The silence grew dreadful. Even Sombart crouched, glaring.

Suddenly Clegg screamed: "Vengeance!"

A sullen roar answered him. Georgia Palfrey, scraggly locks flying, like a Fury incarnate, shrieked back: "Vengeance!"

Too late, Sombart realized what was going to happen. He whipped his gun up and fired. Clegg sagged against the idiot, Alec, and collapsed like a pricked balloon.

Something must have penetrated the tortured dimness of the sense-bereft man. With a hideous yell, he threw himself forward, straight for the pudgy body of the fiend who was responsible for his condition. Sombart, staring white, jerked the lever of his gun again and again. The bullets found their mark, but could not stop the dreadful rush.

Hands, steeled with the super-strength of madness, fastened themselves around his throat. They constricted with awful pressure. Something snapped. Sombart's face, livid with strange surprise, seemed to spread. He crashed to the floor, with Alec on top of him.

Mike cried out in terror as the old men and women, hunched like animals, went for him. His automatic jerked with spurts of blue flame. Babbage reeled screaming; then the others clawed over him.

Lynn watched with dull horror. Sombart was dead, but he and Jane were still manacled, helpless before the renewed onslaught of these ravening beasts, inflamed with the odor of blood.

Mike went down with a long burbling scream. The human ghouls swarmed over him, plucking, ripping. Lynn turned his face away with a shudder; Jane's eyes were closed.

Something made metallic clattering sound. The chained man's head went down. Hope flared suddenly through his weary, tortured body. He turned cautiously to the snarling mob, but they were busy with their hideous task.

Lynn pushed his foot out as far as it would go. It just barely touched the shiny key. The instrument of salvation, the key to their manacles—if only he could bring it up to his immovable hands!

HE SCRAPED it nearer, strained downward. Impossible to reach it. The sweat beaded on his brow. So near to a fighting chance for life, and yet so inconceivably far. Then a plan came to him.

He brought both bare feet together, with the key between. He lifted. Up it came for six inches and fell down again, with a noise that resounded in his ears like thunder.

The blood-howling throng had not heard, but soon they would be glutted with the dead, would come for the living.

He caught it again, pressing hard with the ridged surfaces of his feet. Up and up, as he bent his knees outward, until it hung, tantalizingly, a few bare inches from the tip of his reaching fingers. Strain and heave as he might, until the blood dripped from his open wounds, it would go no farther.

Lynn gritted his teeth and took the last desperate insane chance. If it failed, he was doomed; the key would be beyond possible recovery. A wild prayer issued from clenched lips.

He jerked his knees as hard as he could. The key left the tenacious embrace of his feet, sailed up into the air. It dropped again in a shining arc, hit the flat of his quivering thigh, rolled uneasily while Lynn held his breath. If it dropped off, it would bounce far out of reach.

The precious metal teetered, rocked, and lay still! Hardly daring to move, Lynn extended his stiffened finger. It touched, worked the key back to where he could grip it.

Feverishly, racing desperately with

time, Lynn twisted his hand, stabbed again and again for the tiny keyhole. Already blood-streaming creatures were rising from their gory vengeance, looking as through a red film for more victims.

The key connected. The lock clicked! Lynn, forgetful of pain and wounds, staggered to his feet. He tottered toward Jane. The pallor of her face deepened; she murmured weakly: "Save me!"

His hand trembled as the key went in the orifice. Fellowes, satanic, no longer human, saw him. His shrill cry of warning brought the pack to their feet, growling in their throats like dogs withheld from a toothsome bone.

Lynn worked desperately. He pulled the half-fainting girl up just as Fellowes sprang upon him. Cold, deadly rage surged through Lynn at the sight of those arching talons, that had once tried remorselessly to gouge out his eyes. Holding the trembling girl close to him, he lashed out with his free hand. All his strength went into the blow. There was a sickening crunching sound and Fellowes' face seemed to disappear in a blur of splintering bone and flesh.

Lynn did not wait. He flung Jane over his shoulder and flogged his leaden limbs toward the door. The pack pounded after him, screaming filthy curses, clawing at his naked body with barely-touching hands.

Luckily, they were old and winded from their previous hideous exertions, or the fleeing man, staggering under the weight of the girl, would have been dragged down and torn to pieces. But gradually he pulled away, thudding down the corridor. The avid cries and blood-thirsty yells fell farther and farther to the rear.

Out into the reception room, where the grisly cage still stood, crashing through the door into the cold but blessed dawn, out through the huge portal that had closed with such an ominous clang upon them earlier in this night of terror. Moments later, panting, they reached the spot, down the rutted road, where their roadster stood quietly like a guardian angel.

Lynn shoved Jane inside, followed swiftly. He kicked the starter into thundering action, and slithered the car dangerously around.

At that instant, the wild rabble burst into view at the head of the hill. Like a spew of fiends from the seventh circle of Dante's Hell, he thought. Their weird cries and shaking fists still echoed in his ears as he drove recklessly down the mountain, toward peace and civilization, and the safety of their own kind.

Jane shivered against him. A steamer rug enfolded their bodies. Her eyes still held shadows from the valley of death.

"Tell me, Lynn," she said, "that operation on Clegg—was it—could it possibly be. . .?"

Lynn shook his head. "I saw Sombart squirt a hypo into Clegg right after the transfusion. Any one of a dozen powerful stimulants could have accounted for his sudden access of energy. Nitroglycerine, for instance. It was purely temporary in effect, of course; just long enough to fool the victim and the others into bidding heavily for the privilege of being next. Within another hour, Clegg would have been dead; his heart would not have stood the strain. I suppose Sombart intended ultimately to place all the blame on Hunt."

A turn in the road and the valley lay shining below, like a rainbow at the end of the trail. Jane said nothing more. only clung more closely to him.

THE END

THE BLACK CHAPEL

WHAT was it, in that gripping, spine-chilling tale of Arthur Leo Zagat's, *When Love Went Mad!*, that froze the blood in the veins of Emma Wayne, that stiffened the very muscles of her young body and left her gelid, incapable of movement? What was it that drove her to the brink of gibbering madness? Was it the sight of the hideous grey Things as they attacked the man she loved more than life itself? Was it the feel of that unhuman foulness as it oozed over her and stifled her?

No, it was more than that. Fearful as those happenings were, they were not what inspired shrieking terror in the breast of Emma Wayne. Rather it was such things as the waiting, every sense alert, while her husband's car crawled slowly down the mountain, for what fearful tragedy she could not know. It was the wondering at what hideous fate would be in store for her, once the grey Things had seized upon her—the dreadful doubt as to what these ghastly beings were.... It was the thought of what was to come! . . .

That, then, is the thing that brings on true terror—the thinking on what unknown horror lies ahead. And so it is that only the imaginative can truly feel terror. Only the man whose nimble brain can see beyond the menace which faces him, can picture vividly the fate in store for him, is capable of the greatest fear of all.

Hence we do not publish TERROR TALES for the dull ones, for the unimaginative clod who can see only what is before him. To such these stories would have no spark of life. TERROR TALES is for the hardy and imaginative, and for them alone!

Our writers know this well, and shape their tales accordingly. For the next great issue we have gathered a bevy of blood-chilling yarns by masters of the terror story—by men who know how best to give sustenance to the imagination. There will be weird yarns of creeping horror by Arthur Leo Zagat and Robert C. Blackmon, a tale of black gods by Ray Cummings, a spine-tingling story of the dark unknown by Wyatt Blassingame. These and many other chilling masterpieces will be found in the next issue of TERROR TALES—the magazine for those who think!

Help Kidneys

Don't Take Drastic Drugs

You have nine million tiny tubes or filters in your Kidneys which may be endangered by using drastic, irritating drugs. Be careful. If poorly functioning Kidneys or Bladder make you suffer from Getting Up Nights, Leg Pains, Nervousness, Stiffness, Burning, Smarting, Acidity, Neuralgia or Rheumatic Pains, Lumbago or Loss of Vitality, don't waste a minute. Try the Doctor's prescription called Cystex (pronounced Siss-tex). Formula in every package. Starts work in 15 minutes. Soothes and tones raw, irritated tissues. It is helping millions of sufferers and is guaranteed to fix you up to your satisfaction or money back on return of empty package. Cystex is only 75c at all druggists.

LONESOME?

Let me arrange a romantic correspondence for you. Find yourself a sweetheart thru America's foremost select social correspondence club. A friendship letter society for lonely ladies and gentlemen. Members everywhere; CONFIDENTIAL introductions by letter; efficient, dignified and continuous service. I have made thousands of lonely people happy—why not you? Write for FREE sealed particulars.

EVAN MOORE P. O. BOX 988 JACKSONVILLE, FLORIDA

BECOME A SUCCESSFUL DETECTIVE

Trained Men and Women In Demand. Write for Free Particulars and Detective Paper. NATIONAL DETECTIVE SYSTEM, Dept. M, 340 Electric Bldg., Omaha, Nebraska.

PILES DON'T BE CUT

Until You Try This Wonderful Treatment

for pile suffering. If you have piles in any form write for a FREE sample of Page's Pile Tablets and you will bless the day that you read this. Write today. E. R. Page Co., 2346-G Page Bldg., Marshall, Mich.

START

$1260 to $2100 Year

Work for "Uncle Sam"
Many Winter examinations expected.
Common Education Usually Sufficient
Men-Women, 18 to 50
Mail Coupon today sure.

COUPON

Franklin Institute, Dept. K-175, Rochester, N. Y.

Sirs: Rush to me without charge, (1) 32-page book with list of U. S. Government jobs. (2) Tell me how to get one of these jobs.

Name..............................

Address..............................

TIRE USERS by the thousands all over the U. S. A. vouch for the LONG, HARD SERVICE, under severest road conditions of our standard brand Tires reconstructed by the ORIGINAL SECRET YORK PROCESS. OUR 18 YEARS IN BUSINESS makes it possible to offer tires at LOWEST PRICES in history with 12 month guarantee.

Don't Delay—Order Today

BALLOON Tires

Size Rim	Tires	Tubes
29x4.40-21	$2.15	$0.85
29x4.50-20	2.35	0.85
30x4.50-21	2.40	0.85
28x4.75-19	2.45	0.95
29x4.75-20	2.50	0.95
29x5.00-19	2.85	1.05
30x5.00-20	2.85	1.05
28x5.25-18	2.90	1.15
29x5.25-19	2.95	1.15
30x5.25-20	2.95	1.15
31x5.25-21	3.25	1.15
28x5.50-18	3.35	1.15
29x5.50-19	3.35	1.15
30x6.00-18	3.40	1.15
31x6.00-19	3.40	1.15
32x6.00-20	3.45	1.25
33x6.00-21	3.65	1.25
32x6.50-20	3.75	1.35

CORD Tires

Size	Tires	Tubes	Size	Tires	Tubes
30x3	$2.25	$0.65	32x4½	3.35	1.15
30x3½	2.35	0.75	33x4½	3.45	1.15
31x4	2.95	0.85	34x4½	3.45	1.15
32x4	2.95	0.85	30x5	3.65	1.35
33x4	2.95	0.85	33x5	3.75	1.45
34x4	3.25	0.85	35x5	3.95	1.55

HEAVY DUTY TRUCK TIRES

Size	Tires	Tubes	Size	Tires	Tubes
30x5	$4.25	$1.95	36x6	9.95	3.95
34x5	4.25	2.00	34x7	10.95	3.95
32x6 (8)	7.95	2.75	36x8	12.45	4.25
32x6 (10)	8.95	2.75	40x8	15.95	4.95

ALL OTHER SIZES

DEALERS WANTED

SEND ONLY $1.00 DEPOSIT with each tire ordered. ($4.00 deposit on each Truck Tire.) We ship balance C.O.D. Deduct **5 per cent** if cash is sent in full with order. **ALL TUBES BRAND NEW — GUARANTEED.** Tires failing to give 12 months' service replaced at half price. ORDER NOW!

YORK TIRE & RUBBER CO., Dept. 970-A
3855-59 Cottage Grove Ave. Chicago, Ill.

Home Study

Accountancy Training

Accountants who know their work command responsible positions and good incomes. And the need for trained accountants is growing. About 12,000 Certified Public Accountants in U. S. and many thousands more executive accountants. Many earn $3,000 to $20,000. We train you thoroughly at home in your spare time for C. P. A. examinations or executive accounting positions. Previous bookkeeping knowledge unnecessary—we prepare you from ground up. Our training is supervised by Wm. B. Castenholz, A. M., C. P. A., assisted by staff of C. P. A.s. Low cost—easy terms. Write for valuable free 64-page book describing opportunities in accounting field and telling how you may enter it successfully.

This Book **FREE!**

LA SALLE EXTENSION UNIVERSITY
Dept. 1334-H Chicago

Be Your Own MUSIC Teacher

LEARN AT HOME

to play by note, Piano, Violin, Ukulele, Tenor Banjo, Hawaiian Guitar, Piano Accordion, Saxophone or any other instrument—or to sing. Wonderful new method teaches in half the time. Simple as A B C. No "numbers" or trick music. Cost averages only a few cents a day. Over 700,000 students.

FREE BOOK Write today for Free Booklet and Free Demonstration Lesson explaining this method in detail. Tell what your favorite instrument is and write name and address plainly.

U. S. SCHOOL OF MUSIC 3671 Brunswick Bldg., New York City

www.ingramcontent.com/pod-product-compliance
Lightning Source LLC
LaVergne TN
LVHW061224100826
845148LV00004B/847

* 9 7 8 1 6 1 8 2 7 7 2 9 9 *